Praise for

THE WHOLE WORLD AT ONCE

"Erin Pringle's stories leave you no choice. They sing so gorgeously, break your heart so perfectly, that you're forced to revise your understanding of loss, luck, and love."

—Tom Noyes, author of *Come by Here: A Novella* and *Stories*

"Pringle (*The Floating Order*, 2009) works nine variations on the theme of grief in the wrenching stories of her second collection. The characters dream intensely, waking in terror, and the stories themselves have a dreamlike intensity heightened by Pringle's lyrical voice. Readers willing to immerse themselves in sorrow, and sometimes in narratives that twist and shimmer before taking definite shape, will find reflected in these stories the unsteady path of coming back to life—or not—after loss."

—*Kirkus Reviews*

"In these restless and relentless fictions, the unstoppable storyteller Erin Pringle is at it again. 'It' being the most American of dramas— the endless conflict between mobility and stability. In these patently patient, transparently transparent, overly understated stories, the characters constantly fidget and fret in low frequency worries; all the while their vital signs are sighing and simmering. These are pristine and persistent visions of hobble-hearted people going nowhere fast. Her writing, word after word, will stop you in your tracks, will ease you over the edgiest of edges. Don't blink!"

—Michael Martone, author of *Michael Martone*
and *Four for a Quarter*

"There's no writer working today who excites me more than Erin Pringle. Her stories stretch like planks off a cliff, past solid ground, offering breath-stealing views of grief, love, and mystery. I love this collection."

—Owen Egerton, author of *The Book of Harold* and writer
and director of the thriller *Follow*

THE WHOLE WORLD AT ONCE

—

STORIES

—

ERIN PRINGLE

VANDALIA PRESS

MORGANTOWN 2017

First edition published 2017 by Vandalia Press,

an imprint of West Virginia University Press.

ISBN:

Paper: 978-1-943665-57-0

EPUB: 978-1-943665-58-7

PDF: 978-1-943665-59-4

Library of Congress Cataloging-in-Publication Data

is available from the Library of Congress.

Book and cover design by Than Saffel.

Cover photograph by Annette Shaff.

For Jennifer

CONTENTS

HOW THE SUN BURNS
AMONG HILLS OF ROCK AND PEBBLE

———

But aside from the black crepe ribbons that flap on the white poles of the fair-entrance archway, anyone who didn't live in the town last summer or close enough to hear the nightly news or who didn't ask about the luminaries running up the fair's dirt midway last night wouldn't know that a young woman named Helen Greene disappeared from last summer's Agricultural Fair.

Under the fair-entrance archway linger the men who served pancakes at the church last month and sell fabric poppies at the one lighted intersection on Memorial Day weekend. They wear neon yellow vests over their T-shirts and bellies. Just before dark, the traffic into the fairgrounds will become steady, and when dark falls, they'll swing their flashlights and raise their hands in greeting to the people they recognize, and they recognize most everyone.

Tonight, the carnies will speak in tongues and the town will drop screams from the rides, buy tickets, carry whorls of cotton candy back to their trailers and leaning homes—until somewhere in the middle night the sound of the fair will become one constant chord, like the interstate in the distance or the light rushing through glass bulbs.

This afternoon, most of the game booths are as empty as the stores in town or the houses out in the country or the eyes of the divorcées whose children, after the fair each night, will drag themselves back to a garage and sit in lawn chairs and pick seeds from dry leaves before filling the pipe and passing it on. They want to talk about the fair but say nothing because it's the same goddamned thing as last year, which they do say.

In one stall, a carnie sets a box down. He takes off the lid and plucks out tiny, mechanical birds and lines them up on the narrow counter. He turns each knob, and when the line reaches the wooden maze, he lifts the small sliding door, and the birds waddle in. Tonight, he and all the game carnies on down the row will prop a boot on the counter, throw open their arms to the dawdling fairgoers, and tell whoever hears that it's yer lucky night, just a dollah, ownee a dollah and win yerself a purdy animal. They wink. Their eyes crinkle in the lights. The birds wobble and wheeze up the wooden avenues, like the clusters of teenage girls who drag their flip-flops up the fair's dirt avenue.

The girls' new hips pull at the seams of their cutoffs. They walk in the most middle of summer, which, after the fair packs up and disappears down the interstate, will tip toward autumn and school doors and Friday night football fields. The girls carry bottles of water and soda cans like boredom. They roll the bits of string from their cutoff shorts against their thighs, balls of lint under their fingernails. Now and then one of their prepaid cell phones rings, but if it's not *that* boy, they don't answer since their mothers won't buy another refill card from the dollar store until next month.

Past the lemon and orange shake-up stands, the band shell where tonight the revival band will sing in glittering sequined jackets. Past the old wooden stadium where pigeons question the rafters and a few kids roam the splintering bleachers, pinging popcorn kernels at each other. The horses will race here every afternoon, the cars on Friday, and the fair queen will crawl out from under the bleachers on Sunday morning, mascara smeared, underwear in her fist.

The girls are too young for driver's licenses and jobs, outside of washing their mothers' boyfriends' trucks while the men across the street watch between baseball caps and beers. In a couple-three years, the teenagers will abandon the sidewalks to drive back and forth across the town, from the fairgrounds to the gas station up by the interstate. At town curfew, they'll leave the town for the country roads that go everywhere but return to nowhere—every night, they will drive, until they forget about ever wanting to leave the town for fortunes as bright as the running lights on the semitrucks that breeze by in the dark.

The fair's dirt avenue runs past the rides and game booths and twirling taffy and into the animal stalls filled with farmer kids and their hogs and cows and lambs raised for ribbons, then slaughter. But most the fairgoers don't venture that far, and those who do go late, drunk, stumbling, heads down.

In the afternoons, most the carnies sit at the picnic tables, strange men with growing beards and tight red shirts and jeans stained down their thighs from wiping the grease after taking a wrench to this or that ride. They're shuffling cards and watching the next murder of girls walk by, until the one who can't bear it any longer bangs his fists against the rotting table and cries, Everybody's a winnah!

The girls giggle, and their women's masks fall into their hands, but they can't see how young they are, poised between childhood and womanhood, blush-ripe on the plucking branch. As with every week before the fair arrives, the girls have been warned not to talk to the carnies, to stay away from the dark shadows behind rides, under old oak trees. And at the end of every fair night, each girl comes home and lies in her bed, staring out the window where her imagined self hurries up the dark street to where a handsome carnie waits, the one whose knuckles brushed her midriff as he buckled her into the Tilt-A-Whirl, The Octopus. The one who winked at her from the balloon dart game. The one who gave her an extra turn at the milk-bottle toss. Then she's in his car, her feet on the dash, and he's driving to the stone quarry where the town boys take the town girls, who pretend not to know what happens among the hills of rock and pebble, or he's merging onto the interstate, headed to the next motel with a vacancy or to a courthouse that opens early.

As the toads sing about the night from their dark ditches, the girls fall into sleep like a deep pond and so they don't see the handsome carnie driving back in an empty car, or with a marriage certificate in the glove box and the rest of his and his bride's lives glittering like the fish that people win at night and find dead in the morning.

When the toads stop singing, they pull themselves onto the country roads to cool their bellies as they wait for the night to sing back to them. By morning, most will have returned to their moist homes, but a few will not feel, until too late, how hot the sun is, how hot the asphalt is beneath the sun, under their bodies, beginning to boil their insides. By noon, they'll be dead, by the next night, as flat as the beer cans thrown from cars.

* * *

A girl is out walking the country roads with her wagon. Last night, after the fair, she pulled the wagon up the dirt avenue, filling it with the paper-bag luminaries that had been set out in memoriam to her sister. By the end of the night, many of the paper bags were missing, smashed, or knocked over. She saw several people reach into the bags for a candle to light their cigarettes and then seem irritated to find not a candle but a small glowing puck with a plastic flame. A guy in a black leather coat asked what it was all about. A woman in tight jeans shrugged, saying, Some dead girl went missing at last year's fair. The man chuckled, Probably she wasn't dead when she went missing. The woman slapped him playfully, You a teacher or something?

The girl bends past her dust-covered legs to pick up another beer can. She tosses it into the wagon behind her, then moves back to the middle of the road, the wagon rattling behind her. She has worn the same, faded plaid dress every day all summer. It no longer has, as her mother would say, room to grow in, which is what her mother said about all her sister's hand-me-downs. Now it's so tight that, even without a bra, the fabric between the buttons gapes like the mouths of small fish.

The oil-and-asphalt road vibrates through the wagon handle and up her arm. The wagon's rusty corners flake down when a wheel hits a large stone or puddle hole. Before her sister got too old for kid stuff, she used to pull her in the wagon, up and down all the country roads, out to Riggin's Pond, Troll Bridge, the Slave Cabins, down to the creek where she dug up a mussel and took it home in an ice-cream tub, watching until its shell opened and its body slid out like a liquid eye.

After Helen disappeared, she began going on long walks. At first she did it thinking that she might run into Helen out here, on her way home from wherever she'd been all these days, then months. Where you been? she would ask her. Oh, you know—just around, Helen would say. You worried Mom and Dad real bad, she'd say. Well, everything's okay now, Helen would say and maybe wrap her arm around her neck and tug on her earlobes like she did when she wanted to rile her up.

But the days kept coming and Helen didn't, and so the girl kept walking. When her mother asked her if she thought it was healthy to be alone for so long, she started taking the wagon with her, and eventually started picking up the beer and cola cans littering the roads and weedy ditches and bringing them home.

Though her sister has been found, she still startles at every bird that flashes out of a windbreak or out of the fields, thinking, Helen's home. When she'd brought home enough cans to fill about ten trash bags, her father told her to haul them down to the salvage yard, that they'd pay her. So she did, and ever since then, she's been walking farther and farther from home to find the cans she pulls back to town, week after week, now for nearly a year.

She used some of the money for the orange bracelet on her right wrist. She bought it yesterday, the first day of the fair, and so for the rest of the week she can ride as many rides as many times as she wants—her body jerked this way and that, her mind taken away from itself, her thoughts like a million fish nipping at a pond instead of her sister who was pulled out of one, a million droplets of water rolling down her limp arms and the yellow all-you-can-ride bracelet on her dead wrist.

She had thought she might not want to go to the fair, that it would be too much for her. After all, that's why her mom took this week off of work, and kept trying to convince her to go with her to visit her grandparents. She even went as far as to promise to take her to the museum one of the days. Your grandmother would love to see you, and you don't have a bad time when you go, do you? No, she didn't. So why do you want to hang around here, how can you even think about going to that fair?

She didn't really think about it. She just has a feeling that she ought to stay. Also, she just needs to walk around the fair, to see it as Helen saw it, even though she herself has seen the fair so many times she can walk through it in her mind, and she has in her dreams many nights since the disappearance. Often in the dreams the game booths are empty but still lit up, scattering shadows across the dirt avenue, and she's walking past them, and all the rides are shut down but blinking except for the octopus ride in the distance, its mechanical tentacles whirling around and around, and then she sees a flash of Helen's hair, and at first she thinks it's a bird scared up, but no, it's Helen's hair, Helen in one of the spinning seats, and so she starts hurrying to it, thinking Helen was here all along, they just hadn't looked hard enough when she disappeared, why hadn't anyone thought to look here— that somehow the fair had packed up the ride with Helen in it and taken Helen from town to town, and she was always in this ride but no one knew to look for her, no one would have asked why the same girl never left the ride because, after all, she was wearing the ride-all-you-can bracelet, which was yellow that year.

When she finally gets to the ride, Helen's screaming and screaming because she wants off, she's scared, and each time the twirling seat swirls down from the sky before returning to it, her sister's face is more pale, her lips trembling, her eyes large and black, and then she suddenly stops screaming and sits still in the spinning booth, pale and upright.

Every time she tries to rescue Helen, there's no lever to pull beside the carnie's empty lawn chair. No lever, no box of electrical wires, no red shut-down button—no buttons at all, just a chair with a miniature fan clipped to it and spinning, and on the ground a bucket of torn tickets.

Every time she finds the ride and still can't stop it, panic fills her stomach and then an ache because she has to tell Helen she'll have to save herself. Somehow. As she calls up to Helen, the ride's metal arms go faster, rising and lowering, and large splashes of water start falling, and when Helen's seat comes close, she sees pond water inside it, lapping up her sister's plaid dress, spilling over the side.

Today's only the second day of the fair, and after last night, she sort of wishes she had gone with her mother to visit her grandparents. But she also wants to go to the fair again, to ride, to shove her heels firmly into the aluminum footboard, to clutch the safety bar that reminds her of her mother's arm thrown out against her chest in the car, trying to keep her from jumping out of the funeral procession, her feet stuttering against the pavement as the men outside the barbershop watch.

The dress strap slips off her shoulder. She pushes it back up. Her face is covered in freckles like her bare shoulders. She tosses her head back and forth. She wishes she felt as light as her newly cut hair rather than like she's looking through a smeary storm door.

Last night after the fair, after she came home in the light rain that made the paper luminaries sag, she cut her hair to her ears then walked around the backyard, snapping the kitchen scissors and imagining she was beheading the flowers in her mother's garden like she and her sister did years ago, upon her sister's insistence that a fairy queen had come to her in a dream and demanded a sacrifice or she'd unleash armies of fairies on the house and terrible things would happen.

When she went back inside, she poured herself a glass of milk while the town's AM radio station gave away tickets to Friday's demolition derby. She sat at the kitchen table and smoked the pile of cigarette butts she'd collected that day. Outside, the streetlights buzzed and she shook her head and pieces of hair fell around her like rusty bits from her wagon.

Her mother doesn't understand about the cigarette butts. Why you want to go and do that for? What will people think if they knew? Take one of mine if you have to, which you shouldn't, but it's filthy smoking the ends of strangers' cigarettes.

She thinks it's sort of funny to smoke strangers' leftover cigarettes, and that's what she tells her mother. What's funny about it? her mother wants to know. It just is, she says. Just like she thinks it's sort of funny to wear pants too big for her or try to hypnotize her mother's parakeet with the cross she got at church camp last summer.

You're a weird kid, her mother will say, and that pleases her. Or her mother will say, I don't get you girl. But she thinks her mother does get her. Gets her more than anybody has, because she gets her mother.

She gets exactly why her mother stays waitressing at the town diner instead of looking for the better job she's always swearing she'll find one day and then she'll show them—whoever them is: at one time the town, but since Helen's disappearance then funeral, the whole world, which has grown larger in order to hold Helen's murderer.

She pauses a moment to run her bare foot up the inside of her leg, and a piece of gravel spins out onto the road. Then she's walking again, and the wagon bangs against her calves and ankles, and the few cans she has bothered to pick up slide back and forth. She doesn't need any more cans, but her hair's cut, she's out of cigarette butts, the library's closed, the pool doesn't open until one, and at the fair, only the kiddie rides run in the afternoon.

A man stumbles out of the windbreak, and trips into the ditch.

She wonders if it's a trick. Even a year since Helen, she still sometimes expects her sister to walk out of the field, into the house, into their bedroom. Helen throws up her arms and laughs, shoulders shaking like they would. Surprise! Did you believe I was the girl in the closed casket? You did! I can tell by your face. I really got you good, kid. Then Helen's ruffling her hair, pinching her nose.

The man's on his knees and hands. His hair is sweaty or oily.

She imagines a television crew inside the woods, a group of comedians hiding behind tree trunks and covering their mouths to muffle their hilarity. Cameramen crouch on an abandoned deer stand, aiming lenses out at her while people on couches at home yell at the microwave popcorn to hurry up because this is going to be really, really funny and shocking because when the girl goes to help this man, he'll tell her he's the one who killed her sister.

Last night, she realized she had gone to the fair to find him. But after walking up and down the fair's midway, after riding every ride twice and watching every carnie very closely, none seemed more likely than another to have killed Helen—since none and all seemed likely to talk to her. Besides that, she told herself, whoever it was probably would have found another job or, at least, another fair circuit. Unless he was just a stupid idiot, but she didn't like the idea of her sister's murderer being stupid. No, he had to be smart, a genius.

She scans the fields and roads again. Quiet as daylight.

The man stands up in the ditch. The bottoms of his pants are dark with last night's rain, and his arms are speckled with muddy water. She keeps forgetting it rained hard last night until she sees a puddle, then she remembers waking to the rain clattering against the roof.

He wears a red polo shirt like the rest of the carnies and her dead sister, found by a boy out collecting trash to earn a scout's badge, who mistook Helen's skirt for a plastic bag. After being under the pond and exposed to the sun for so many months, the back of the shirt had faded to pink.

The boy told his parents he thought the woman was a mermaid at first because of the color of her legs. Her ankles were tied. His parents said to leave that out when you explain how you found her, the part about the mermaid.

The man hasn't noticed her. If she stays still, he might never. He turns, facing the road that leads away from the fair. If she says nothing, if she takes her wagon and walks on, he'll walk for several hours before reaching the next town, a village of four standing houses and a post office. Nothing about him suggests he'll make it.

Hey! the girl calls. He turns. His shirt is a darker red around the left shoulder blade. Their eyes meet. Weed lashes crisscross his arms, like he has tripped several times, falling in brambles, thorns, against trees in ways that the bark scraped.

Before she can tell whether he's dangerous, he's walking to

her, and then his knees are collapsing, and they're both reaching out, dropping down, unbalanced, the road tearing at their knees.

A bird sings.

They kneel, where they fell in the road. One of her dress straps has ripped. The dark spot on his shoulder spreads out farther. The soles of her feet are gravel white and speckled with the man's blood. The man's arm hangs over her shoulders. His bloody shirt presses wetly against her arm, and he leans in a way that she knows he could be heavier, is heavier, that death would keep everyone on the ground if nobody tried to stand.

She looks into the field behind him, searching for the blood trail that follows a wounded deer, but there's hardly one and whoever began the hunt has let him go. Which makes her the lazy hunter who tags someone else's kill. Buzzard hunter, her father would say. The worst kind, she knows. If the man were a deer or a coyote.

The man arches his neck, his head lolls. By their legs lies a beer can. She lets go of him and stands. She kicks the can, which rolls, then rocks, sloshing. She picks it up and holds it out. A little beer's better than none, as her father now says—if he says anything.

Here, she says, shaking her arm a little.

He looks at her.

Beer, she says.

He keeps looking at her. She shrugs, then dumps the beer in her mouth. It's warm and tastes of rainwater. She thinks to herself, You won't understand this, which is what she tells herself when her mind's gone panicky from thinking of Helen in the pond—what was her sister even doing in a pond? Ponds were for swimming, fishing, for cows and frogs.

* * *

That poor boy who found her sister. That's what everybody in town said, she could tell by the way they looked at the boy when his parents brought him to the memorial service. Seeing something like that, well, it's hard to forget a thing like that, she heard them thinking. She had thought the same way when she watched TV programs about murdered people.

At times she was jealous of the little scout for finding her sister, since, really, hadn't that been why she pulled a wagon up and down the country roads? Nobody deserved to see that but her. Her sister's body was the last thing that belonged to her sister, and so she felt it had to belong to her, too. Not some boy scout her mother invited to dinner after the memorial service because she didn't know what else to say, and his parents wished the woman hadn't asked but said of course, and the next week everybody but Helen sat down at the dinner table.

All of them sitting around the table.

Her father looked at the boy scout, and said, That's where Helen sat.

The boy looked at his parents. His mother looked at her husband.

Her mother looked at her father who was staring at his empty plate, gone back into the silence he lived in now. He didn't mind the silence. He felt closer to Helen that way, like he understood a little if he could be as quiet as her. For him to hear nothing just as she had heard nothing all these days of months. His wife said he was punishing himself.

Just wait, he had told his wife. She's just fine. Didn't we teach her well? She has a good head on her shoulders, doesn't she? Just you wait, tomorrow or the next day she'll be making pancakes when we wake up. And his wife pressed her lips into his shoulder as they remembered little Helen by their bed in her mother's apron, covered in flour and syrup. I made beckfast! she hollered, smiling big.

But when the police knocked, they learned that Helen's body had been close by—as close as she used to bicycle when she went down the road looking for tadpoles to bring home in her water bottle. Close enough so that when he or her mother stood in the lawn and called her name through the neighborhood trees, she turned her bike for home.

His wife said grace. That's good, he thought. Good for her to say grace.

The same cow pond where he had taken Helen when she was five or six with long hair and dimples. She'd wanted her hair cut once she started kindergarten, and the other girls came to school with bobs.

And hadn't she gotten tangled in the fishing line when it wouldn't reel in? Or was that his younger daughter? He looked across the table at her, trying to remember. She felt him turning her into her sister.

* * *

The man reaches out toward the wagon. I need to sit down, he says.

She brings the wagon up. Helen's wagon. *Helen's Wagon* was burned into the side where her father had written it in his loopy cursive with a wood-burning kit he got one Christmas. Helen was to be an only child, and so everything had her name on it. Above their bedroom door: *Helen's Bedroom*. At the back of the closet, old backpacks embroidered with HELEN GREENE on their front pockets. *Helen G.* on the tags of T-shirts, jeans; in gold letters on fifty green and blue pencils; in flowery letters across a sleeping bag; in magic marker on the bottoms of pink slippers; boxes of toe shoes whose frayed ribbons were named *Helen, Helen, Helen*. And now *Helen* on the three wooden crosses that fit into the cross carved in the lid of Helen's casket which was now in a grave named after her.

Then her mother came home one day with a bandage on her upper arm. You won't believe what I did, she said.

What?

Her mother smiled in the forcing way, and peeled off the white tape holding the gauze to her strong arm—the arm she balanced the diner trays on. Tattooed around her bicep was a rippling banner with *Helen* in the middle, a heart on either side.

Her mother looked at the tattoo then up at her. What do you think? Pretty good, huh?

Are you serious? she said to her mother.

Don't you think Helen would think it was funny? begged her mother.

You asked what I thought.

* * *

The man drags his hands from his sides and pushes off of the road with his palms. His left arm trembles, its elbow threatening not to take the weight.

She pushes the few cans to the front of the wagon then removes the small gate from the back. Then the man's standing and, as he sits, the wagon tips, and she has to push down on the other end to keep it from tipping over as he sits all the way down. His thighs press against the wagon sides, forcing him to cross one leg over the other. She sets the gate in his lap.

Our father made it, she says.

What?

The wagon, she says. Dad made it for my sister.

Oh, yeah. Good wagon, he says.

A damn fine wagon, she says and wonders if there's enough beery rainwater to get drunk. She has heard drinking helps somehow, but her mother never buys alcohol and her father drinks all he buys.

You need to go to the hospital, she says.

Not that bad, he says.

You're shot.

He looks at his shoulder. Yeah, he says. I don't think it's . . .
what's the word? Mortal?

Fatal?

Yeah, I don't think it's that.

You're in shock.

Maybe. Probably I'm alright. Heart's in my chest, bullet's in
my shoulder. Might not even be in there anymore.

She should run all the way back home, but her mother has the
car, and she doesn't have a license anyway, and even if the car
were there, her mother always takes the keys, ever since she ran
away after Helen was found. She didn't think she'd run away, and
was planning to return home, but then her sister's car ran out of
gas and she had to call her parents to come get her.

As her mother drove her home, their father driving Helen's car
behind them, her mother said, You're out of control.

She patted her mother's leg, brightened her voice like a joke
and said, What *will* you do with me?

Her mother leaned her elbow against the windowsill and
rubbed her forehead. Jesus, kid. I can't take much more. And I
didn't think I could take what I already have.

* * *

The man's left arm dangles uselessly off the side of the wagon,
and he uses the other to hold the rim. He says, If you could jess
take me back to the fair. You know the way?

It's a small town, she says.

He nods.

It's a long road back and she feels suddenly tired, like when she
begins climbing the tilting stairs to the apartment her father
moved into last month. I just need some time, her father said about
it. Sort of ironic, don't you think? she said to her father, pointing
at the revolving bank sign that flashes on and off outside his

apartment window all night and day. She used to look at the bank clock from the school bus, and think her father was tall enough to touch it if he stood beneath it and raised his arm. But since Helen, her father has seemed shorter, or the world further away.

She says to the man, It isn't safe for a girl to be alone with a carnie, you know.

Yeah, he says, but he seems to be talking to the sun he's looking up at, squinting.

Maybe you're in trouble with the cops or something.

Maybe, but I'm not.

You wouldn't tell me if you were.

Sounds like you watch a lot of TV.

Not much else to do in a small town, she says.

Only trouble is in my arm, he says. But you can go get somebody if it makes you feel better.

Doesn't bother me any, she says and begins to pull him on the same road Helen might have walked alone or with a carnie or even with some boy she'd fallen in love with, though she hadn't said anything about a boy, and when the police questioned all the boys around her age, nothing came up.

They'll pass silver silos, the collies that run barking from under the tall wheels of silent combines, past sun-struck cows. Above the farthest tree line shows the top of the Ferris wheel, its empty seats probably rocking back and forth. From here, she can't tell.

The heels of the man's boots drag against the road, making pulling him increasingly difficult. She read in the autopsy report that her sister was wearing brown sandals and that her feet were frostbitten, postmortem. When she read it, opening the envelope then resealing it before her mother got home from work, she thought, At least she didn't feel the frostbite. There's that.

There's that and *At least* had become the refrain to the family theme song.

At least the winters don't get cold enough anymore to have frozen the pond—the idea of Helen trapped beneath ice came to them and they thought that somehow that would have been worse.

At least it wasn't years before she was found.

At least the weather was sunny every day of last year's fair. *At least* that's how I'm going to imagine it, her mother said. But her father imagined it as gray, gray sky every day since he had taught both his daughters how to tell direction by the sun. No, her mother said, there was sun.

There's the sun, that bright sun that makes summer what it is and winter seem a bit ridiculous when it shows, makes the snow graying in the ditches seem overmorose, ludicrous. Helen was always looking into the sun as a child, and we were always warning her not to because the sun burns dark holes into sight, burns holes through it, dark holes that cover the world like you're seeing it from above, the patches of forest and mountains under the ocean, a world that—if you go blind—you'll suddenly want to see.

But I like the sun, Helen would say. It's not *that* bad, she would say.

There was sun that day. There's that. There's the sun, there she is slumping down in the field, her spine a dandelion stem blown down by a passing coyote.

Can't you hold your legs up or something? the girl says.

The man lifts his boots, groaning.

Fine, let 'em drag, she says, and suddenly feels the now-familiar rage at her sister for disappearing and then turning up the way she did. *Pissed*, as her sister would say, and her mother would say, Can't you think of another word? She could, but that's all there was. She was just *pissed*. *Pissed* that her sister didn't know what would happen the night that she buckled her brown sandals and walked into the fairgrounds, waving hello to her father's friends who wore yellow vests and directed the parking cars. *Pissed* that her sister walked down the country road, followed some carnie into the field. And if her sister wasn't dead, she wouldn't be out here pulling a gunshot carnie back to the fair in a wagon with her sister's goddamned name on it.

* * *

The town is its usual vacant. A few cars are parked down at the gas station and a few cars in front of the diner. If it weren't the Midwest, there'd be tumbleweeds blowing up the streets. The buildings that aren't falling down and condemned are still outlined with the white Christmas lights that will begin blinking the night after Thanksgiving. Except for a movie-rental store, thrift store, the diner, and the sewing store that is sometimes open but usually isn't, the store windows are dark, tracked with dirty tape and a few fair fliers from last year and this year and for the farmer's market held each month in one of the surrounding towns.

But all the fliers of her sister's senior picture are gone. The photographer's proofs had come in earlier that summer. Their mom had been hassling Helen to pick out the ones she liked most. I will, I will, Helen kept saying, but the envelope of proofs was still on the kitchen counter the morning Helen wasn't in her bed or with any of her friends.

The girl pulls the man in the wagon along the gutter. Crisp gum wrappers stand against the curb. Like grief, his weight isn't as hard to pull once she's already moving.

She had to stop once when it felt different pulling him, turned, and saw the heel of his socked foot stuttering against the bumpy road. Bits of sock and skin had torn off and filled with blood. One of his boots lay sideways in the distance. She ran back for it. It was heavy, misshapen from being both cheaply made and worn often. One of the shoelaces had slipped out of the brass eyelets, and it was frayed enough to make it hard to thread back through.

As she crouched with it before him, trying to figure out how to fit the boot back on, he said, You think I might be dying?

I don't know, she said.

Lotta blood, he said, and he began to reach to touch his shoulder.

She slapped his hand away. Don't touch it. Your hands are dirty.

They ain't dirty.

Too dirty for touching anyhow, she said and set the boot in his lap. He held the boot gently, resting the pads of his fingers on the toe.

She pulls him through the parking lot where, according to her mother, an ice-cream parlor stood when she and their father were kids, where all the neighborhood's kids met on the hottest days, on the picnic bench or inside on the hard, cold booths, eating hot-fudge sundaes and blowing straw wrappers at each other.

She grips the wagon handle tighter. The new blisters on the heels of her hands shift liquidly. She pulls him past the parking lot of the extinct car dealership, their shadows moving across the huge windows covered in hearts and initials. Her sister's are there, or were. She hasn't looked since the funeral when she left the house crowded with food and confusion and her father's eyelashes like a clock's stuck second-hand.

She doesn't know if it's her sister or the fair's return that makes the town seem even emptier, the cracks in the asphalt deeper, the sun hot enough to melt her into one of the heat waves rippling off the pavement.

She pushes her dress strap back up her shoulder before passing by the diner, even though her mother isn't there and her father is probably in his apartment above the street, but she has never seen him look out the windows. One of his windows has snowflakes on it from the fake snow that comes in aluminum cans, sprayed up long enough ago the snowflakes are gray. She tried to wash them off. He told her to leave them be. I sort of like them, he said.

You wanna a ginger ale or something? she says over her shoulder to the man.

Why?

I don't know. Because maybe it's really hot or maybe because when you're shot or dying or whatever it is you are, you get a craving for coke, like that's all you can think of. Like my friend's dad, right? He said that in the war, all he wanted was a fat juicy burger and fries so greasy they drip when you squeeze them. He'd lay awake over there in the desert eating imaginary burgers on white oval platters, dragging fries through ketchup. How am I to know? My mom craves burgers on her period. Maybe when you lose blood, you crave blood, she says. You're shot, it's hot, so maybe you want a ginger ale or something.

Don't have any money.

I got some.

I'll pay you back, he says.

Whatever, she says and starts for the diner, then stops to say, If you go anywhere, leave the wagon. Then she feels stupid for saying it and opens the diner's screen door.

The diner walls are covered with fair memorabilia from the past fifty, sixty years: purple, pink, and red ribbons for best pies, best canned beans, best-of-show sheep; wooden paddles strung to pink rubber balls; unicorn-shaped balloons; tightly stuffed teddy bears, toucans, rabbits; manicure sets with foil mirrors; 10 x 10 glass pictures of boy bands and NASCAR drivers, dull with dust. Like a temple to a plastic god that visits once a year to accept the fair queen as sacrifice.

The owner's cleaning the grill, which is thick with grease after a busy morning. He's shaking his head. His best waitress took off fair week, the busiest week of the year, for her vacation, and he can't blame her because of the circumstances, but he also can't afford any of the waitresses and the few waitresses who apply are teenagers who never have time to work or women knocked up or knocked out, coming to work with bruises thick as their mumbled sorries, but mostly the problem is none of them give a hell, and probably he can't expect them to, after all, here they are serving burgers, chicken fried steak, refilling coffee for the elementary schoolteachers who had promised they could be anything they wanted.

Hey, kid, one of the waitresses calls out from a booth in the back. She's rolling silverware in paper napkins.

Hey yerself, the girl says and walks behind the counter and takes one of the styrofoam cups, throwing back the ice lid and scooping it up.

Your mom having a good vacation?

Probably.

She said she was gonna help her mother in her garden. Said she was taking her some seeds to plant.

Sounds right.

I'm always meaning to start a garden, but you know how it is. My grandmother had a really great garden.

Yeah.

Silverware rattles in the plastic tub. Fork, fork, spoon, knife, the girl thinks, because she's sat at the same booth with her sister, helping her mother roll silverware so her mother could get off her shift sooner.

Whatchya up to? Going to the fair?

She looks out the corner of her eye at the man outside.

Thinking about it, she says, pressing the cup against the plastic lever. The coke shoots out, perfectly, dark, sweet, just like soda does whether or not your sister's dead and a man sits in a wagon on the other side of the window, staring up at the sun.

I meant to make it out last night, the waitress says. Heard it sure was pretty, all those candles lit up for your sister. She would've thought it was real pretty.

Guess so.

When the girl comes out of the diner, and hands the man the styrofoam cup, he nods at her. I'll pay you back when we get to the fair.

If you're not dead by then, she says.

Yeah, he says.

She takes up the wagon arm again, leaning against his weight, pulling him out of inertia. So why were you out there, anyway? You in trouble with drugs or something?

Naw. It was stupid. A bunch of us were drinking after work. Some town kids were there, too. Told us about that missing girl— the one all the fuss was about, how she'd been found out aways, so we went out there. Something about a ghost. Kidstuff, you know. It was stupid.

Yeah, she says, trying not to look back at him. And then her ghost shot you?

He chuckles. One of the kids had a gun, and got to shooting it off and hollering. You know how kids are when they're drinking. Wrong place, wrong time. Probably could have been worse.

There's that, she says.

What about you?

What about me?

Just aren't many girls who go collecting cans in wagons.

Guess there probably aren't.

Thanks for the coke, anyway.

She nods, and waits for him to talk again, but he doesn't. She feels alone. So alone.

* * *

A coven of little girls is standing by the corner fire hydrant as she pulls the man across the street from the fair, just past the hive of mobile homes, to the third house with fake brick siding peeling away in chunks. The girls' lips are smeared with lipstick from tiny Avon samples. They wear jelly sandals and dirty band-aids, and a few wear their brothers' plastic machine guns on their backs, strung on rainbow shoelaces and kite string. Before the brothers or fathers went to the war, they told the little girls to watch over the place—take care of Mom, be good to yer sister, yer baby brother. And don't let anybody but yer mother give you lip, hear?

They clutch baby dolls whose naked bottoms show beneath cotton dresses. One thumps hers against her shoulder. Another cradles hers beneath her shirt. The little girls like the wagon girl because she gives them the pop tabs off the cans she collects. Sometimes, if they're awake when she comes by and she has room, she'll take the beer cans they sneaked out of the trash, and she'll come back with enough quarters for a container of gummy worms from the gas station, where all the food has expired, and it smells like a basement. The candy, though, is excellent.

When they see her, they turn. Can you can take us to the fair, pretty please. Pretty pretty pretty pah-leez, they beg, clasping their hands, sucking the inside of their cheeks, leaning forward onto their toes and ready to fall on their faces if she says no. Our mothers won't care. They thumb over their shoulders at the dark windows of the houses behind them. Really, one of the girl squeals, they won't care—cross my heart and hope to die! Another little girl elbows her, Shut up about dying.

It's okay, the girl says, knowing they've all been told to avoid saying anything about Helen. But don't hope for that, she says and pulls the wagon up the alley to the back screen door of the house. The little girls follow her. Who's that there? Never seen him before. That yer boyfriend?

Sundust settles in the kitchen window. Gingham towels shroud the pillars of dishes lining the counters and table. The brass ashtray has been emptied, and her mother's black sequin cigarette case isn't beside it. A glass with milk in its bottom is beside the sink. When her mom was a little girl, she was in a local commercial for Opalman's Dairy Farm. In it, she wears a blue gingham dress and matching pigtail ribbons as she sits atop an upside-down milk pail, holding an oversized glass of milk. The commercial ran for so long on the public TV station that when Helen and then she were about that age, they were mistaken for her mother as a little girl, and told how good it is to know the youth of today are making healthy choices. More than once she has heard men at the diner counter ask her mother how much for a milking. Her mother turns away, and the men mistake her smile for a good sense of humor.

For a second the sounds of a small rollercoaster cross the road, the happy screams of children surely dressed in bright colors.

Watch him, she says to the girls.

Who *is* he?

That's a carnie man, says one little girl.

Greg, he says.

Hiya, Greg, the little girls say, their voices suddenly shy.

She goes inside, crossing the living room where her mother sleeps at night, the blue TV light flashing off her glasses. Then she's in her bedroom, grabbing a pillow and the top sheet. When she comes out, the little girls have formed a tight circle around the wagon. The man is having a hard time keeping his eyes open. They're swelling shut, the skin under his left eye has turned black.

When they see her, one says, Greg needs a doctor.

Greg? she says, then remembers he said his name to them before she went inside. He doesn't want a doctor.

What happened?

Somebody shot him.

With a gun? You see it?

She shakes her head.

Who shot him? You?

No, she says.

I never seen anybody shot before.

My daddy killed a five-point buck two years ago. He hung it by my tire swing and all its insides fell out, and when my daddy cut it open there was a balloon inside and my mother said drugs and daddy said never mind.

For a second the other girls look at the little girl, then back at the man. One girl switches her baby doll to her other nipple.

Maybe, says another little girl, Maybe Greg's the carnie man that drownded her sister.

Hush!

The man's eyes open more and he turns to look up at his rescuer, who's unwinding a sheet above him. She tucks the sheet up under the T-shirt that sucks wetly away from his skin. Then she wraps it around his shoulder and brings it over his chest. Blood rushes up through the fabric.

He says, You the sister of the missing girl? The girl all those candles were about?

She shrugs.

That's her, Greg. But her sister ain't missing anymore.

Lean forward, the girl tells him. He does. She tucks the pillow behind him then takes up the handle again.

He curses under his breath, and she wonders if it's because it hurts him to move or because he's thinking about telling her how it really came to be that he got shot out where her sister was fished out of a cow pond.

Like everybody else in town once Helen was found, the little girls' parents had probably driven out past the pond, slowing down, driving past once, then twice, maybe three times before going back home and standing outside in the road with the neighbors and talking in hushed whispers about how they just didn't know what to think about it, as though there were some kind of answer, and it seemed like they thought there must be, and so they went to the visitation and funeral, standing in the same tight circles, shaking their heads, sharing details heard from someone else or the newspaper.

But there wasn't any answer, and when the newspaper stopped talking, they started having breakfast or lunch at the diner, watching the dead daughter's mother refill coffee—trying to catch the mother's eye so they could give her the look that meant if she ever felt like talking, she could trust them. As though they would have any kind of advice about what to do with a dead daughter's clothes.

Sorry about your sister, the man says.

Never mind about it, she says. She wants to run back inside the house, lock the doors, not come out again ever. The little girls can pull him across the road. Hell, he can walk across the road himself or shout until one of the men across the street hears and comes over to find out what's going on. Or he could just die here and in a few days her mom will come home to find him, then find the girl in her bedroom and pull the blanket off her face and say, Jesus, kid, why's there a dead man by the back door? I've already taken more than I could.

She starts pulling him toward the road.

Weird coincidence, he says.

Small town, she says.

But still . . .

Never mind about it, she says. Please, she says.

The little mothers follow for a few steps, but when the girl doesn't give them any more attention, they drag their babies back up the sidewalk to the fire hydrant where they'll nurse them and guard their houses until their mothers come out and tell them to get inside already.

* * *

She pulls the wagon through the fair parking lot. If it weren't midday and early in the week, more people would be milling about. The men in the yellow vests aren't at the entrance anymore. Probably on lunch break inside the fair, eating corndogs at one of the picnic tables. Blood saturates the sheet wrapping the man. She tries to wave the flies from the wagon without having to stop and draw attention.

You can just leave me there by the tent, he says, gesturing at the blue first-aid tent used primarily by lost children and children with scraped knees or bee stings. Nobody's inside it. A few first-aid kits sit on a long folding table. The town ambulance is parked behind it, and a couple EMTs sit on its tailgate, swinging their legs and looking at their cell phones.

Alright, she says and turns around, pulling the handle with both hands and walking backward. The ground is bumpy and scattered with acorns from the oak trees.

Thanks for helping me, he says.

I'll just come back for the wagon, she says. You don't have to pay me back for the coke. It was free anyway because my mom works there.

She can see that he's trying to think of more to say, but she doesn't want to stay around to hear it. She's heard all that he could say from everybody else.

Inside the ticket booth sits the same woman who yesterday sold her the all-you-can-ride bracelet. The woman's red polo shirt is unbuttoned. Her breasts meet on a long, thick wrinkle. The girl waits for the woman to recognize her from yesterday.

The woman says, How many?

She raises her hand so the woman can see her bracelet.

The woman sees it and says, Don't need to show me that, just show whoever's working the ride you want to ride.

She starts to turn toward the avenue that leads to all the rides, but then she turns back to the woman. Don't you recognize me?

Excuse me?

From yesterday, I bought the bracelet from you yesterday.

Sure, kid. I remember you like I remember everybody.

The woman idly spins the ticket wheel like a fortune-teller without fortunes.

Then she's thinking of her sister in the vivid way that makes her eyes water and means she needs to go be alone as fast as she can. The vivid way that hurts her chest when she wakes out of the nightmares or wants to tell someone about her sister but doesn't because she knows they're tired of hearing about it or won't understand anyway since they can't remember with her.

Please recognize me, she says.

The woman rolls her eyes then laughs, Aren't you the girl who bought an orange bracelet from me yesterday?

She knows the woman's making fun, but she keeps going, wildly, feeling like when she and her sister took turns running down the quarry hills and the rocks would start sliding under her. Yes, and you saw my sister, too. You sold her a yellow bracelet last year.

I sell a lot of bracelets, kid, in a lot of towns.

Waves of heat are rippling up her legs, flushing her chest, her face. As the ticket booth bulbs flash on and off around her peripheral vision, she sees herself walking back to the first-aid tent, helping the man out of the wagon, and he's saying thanks again as the EMTs load him into the ambulance, and she's pulling the wagon home. She's smoking cigarette stubs and calls up her father who says c'mon over. But she can still hear her voice talking to the ticket woman, insisting in the desperate way that always gets more desperate the more she tries to control it.

But this was last year, the girl says. This town. She bought two yellow bracelets. One for me, one for her. She didn't let me go with her that night. I'll remember you, if you could just say you remember.

This about that missing girl?

She was wearing a white skirt. Like a plastic bag if you saw her in the distance. You don't even have to say you saw her later that night or that you saw her leave alone or with the carnie who gave her a red shirt. But if you could please just say you did it.

The woman leans forward. You accusing me of something, girly?

I mean, say that you saw her.

I don't like calling security on mouthy girls.

Even if you didn't. Just say you saw, I won't tell. Someone had to have seen. You don't even have to say you saw her leave alone or with someone. She wore a white skirt, her hair was the color of mine except a little lighter and went down her back to about here. I just need to know how. No one saw her. It was sunny. You saw her staring up at the sun. So you looked up, too. And maybe when you looked back, the black sun was where she had been. Right? That's what you did. And around your vision, everything else was exactly as it still is. See?

THE BOY WHO WALKS

———

The boy wakes on a winter morning with the urge to go on a walk. And so he decides to, feeling the good feeling that decisions often have. He pulls socks over the ones he slept in, mainly because he doesn't feel like taking off the others. He zips on his snowsuit and wraps his face in a scarf, knotting it in the back like his mother does.

The snow in front of the house is mussed with boot tracks filled with gray water, but the snow around back still follows its own created planes, on and on, into the field that turns into the backyards of houses edging the nearby subdivision.

The white quiet of the backyard decides it.

He steps out of the warm house where his parents sleep. The snow is bright in his eyes, dazzling his brain. His boots crunch in the snow, and the air is cold. Crisp, his mother would say.

A few blackbirds cross the sky like a meaningless thought. As he nears the weeping willow, he imagines the yellow ghost of his dog trotting beside him.

Come with me, the boy says.

He waits. The dog was older than the boy. His mother cried. His father says another dog would be nice. A little pup chewing on your fingers and rolling over. His mother says when you find a pet that lives forever, sign me up. The boy looked it up on the computer. Parrots live a long time. Longer than most grandparents.

Parrots bite, his mother said. And make fun of everybody.

Where do you get this stuff? the boy's father said.

The boy walks on. Now and then he stops to see if the ghost of the dog is following. It doesn't seem to, but perhaps the snow makes it difficult to see ghosts. He doesn't know what to think about ghosts.

How glad he feels to be out here in the crisp air and the snow going on and on. Like a new self, like a man but not a man. If not for the black trees in the distance, he'd walk into the sky without realizing it. How good to do as he fully wishes!

He walks along the edge of the neighbor's backyard. Smoke rises from the chimney. The old couple that lives there mainly stay inside in the winter. The wealthier older folks spend winter in Florida. Snowbirds, they're called. He doesn't know why. Snowbirds should be made of snow.

The old man repairs lawn mowers now that he's retired. He used to work down at the blacksmith's shop, and still wears his long-sleeved work shirts with his name embroidered on the pocket, even on hot days.

On the roof of the shed a black iron bird waits to turn in the wind. The bird used to scare him, but today he waves at it.

How nice to stop and look, he thinks. Usually he'd run right by. He can't quite see where the large garden is. The stakes that mark it in summer, tied with foil pie pans that flash in the sun, must be put up for the winter.

Last summer, he helped the old woman dig up potatoes from the large garden. When the old woman and man were in town, the boy dug up more potatoes, with a gusto that the old woman didn't share when they arrived home. She said he should go home. It hurt his feelings.

I'm sorry, he thinks at the back of the house where the old woman taught him to snap beans. The air is cold through the zipper of his snowsuit.

As he trudges farther out, the row of black trees slowly approach. He used to call the trees a forest until his father said a forest was larger. These trees once were part of a forest, his father said, but when the town sprung up with the oil boom about a hundred years ago, the forest was mainly torn down.

For what?

For houses, buildings, lumberyard, things like that.

Beyond the trees on the left, the land drops into a sort of ravine. His father and he found it one day when they were out playing Frisbee.

Well, I'm not going there today, the boy thinks.

That's good, he imagines his mother replying, though she probably doesn't know about the ravine. It's beautiful at the bottom, closed off by the boughs of trees that don't look tall until you're right beneath them. The floor spread with sun-speckled autumn leaves, the deep quiet marked now and then by birds calling one to another.

It was easier running into the ravine than climbing out of it, and his father and he kept slipping. The boy must have looked scared because his father said that,worst case, they could still find their way home the long way, out the other side of the ravine and over the creek near where the boy's girlfriend lived. You smell the creek? his father said.

He could. She's not my girlfriend, he said.

Okay. But you understand where we are? That you don't have to worry.

The boy nodded. They had to take running starts, leaning far forward and digging their fingers into the ground like there were stairs built into it. They finally reached the top on their knees.

Today, he wouldn't be able to get out. Not in this snow.

He pans the distance. He's farther from the house than he has ever been by himself. Summers, he rides his bike around the subdivision, sure, but his mother knows where he is, and everyone's awake, lawn mowers puttering.

He's far enough out that by the time he reaches home, his parents will be awake. His mother might make him a grilled cheese for breakfast, after he explains how responsible he was on his morning adventure.

You didn't wear your thermal underwear, she might point out.

I should have, he'll agree.

And he should have. His thighs already feel bright red.

Sure would be nice to discover something, though. Since he's come all this way.

Near the tree line is the burn pile that the old man lights up once or twice a year. The boy's father drags branches out too, and once the mildewing camping pads. But today it's a thin pile of nothing.

That, he thinks, is not the way explorers think. So he heads toward it.

There's a metal fifty-gallon drum rusting through. He looks into it. Ash and a few soda cans. He kicks the drum.

On past it stands the small shed where the old man keeps his good lawn mower.

The other day his mother was reading about a woman who had been locked away in someone's backyard for years. Only a fence away, his mother said. She shook her head. Can you imagine?

The boy tried. Wouldn't people have heard her scream?

After enough time, people stop screaming, his mother said.

Jesus, his father said.

It's true, she said.

Maybe there's a woman in this shed, he thinks.

You'd never think it, he thinks.

But if she were there, surely the old man would have found her by now, since she would have been sitting on his good lawn mower, maybe sleeping beside it.

Unless she was put there after summer. By someone who knew the old man would lock the shed for winter.

Or the old man put her there. Or the old woman. Maybe the old man hasn't lost his hearing. Maybe those aren't even the old man's work shirts. He just bought them somewhere, or his wife embroidered the name on them but isn't his name.

Whose name is it?

Maybe the old woman was mad about the boy digging up the potatoes, not because she had to replant them all, but because he was alone in the garden, close enough to hear the woman in the shed.

All those times the old man dragged things out to the burn pile, he was taking food out to the woman. And this morning, sometime before sunrise, the woman died in the shed, and her ghost, finally free, crossed the snowy field and into his house, up to his ear as he slept, and she whispered, Have a walk.

Why me? the boy thinks.

That's what people in the bible ask, the boy thinks.

Well, she'd seen you, watched through the shed's lock as you flew kites or hit the ball over your father's head or jumped, trying to catch the Frisbee on your fingertips.

Find me, he imagines the ghost of the woman call out.

He tries to run. But the snow is deeper out here, like in a dream, sinking him to the knees. Then he steps into a drainage ditch obscured by the snow.

Icy water quickly rises up, grabbing his snow boots and legs, and pulls him down. He falls forward. Onto his face. His chin knocks the ground. Bloody snow enters his mouth, turning pink and sliding up his teeth.

Violent rainbows curve behind his eyes. He feels dizzy. He screams. He reaches out. His gloves slip. He kicks. His boots fill with water and snow. He can't feel bottom.

The great white distance between him and his house.

His parents are asleep under the electric blanket. The small dials glowing on the floor on either side of their bed.

He's dying and they don't know.

It's a shocking thought.

He throws off his gloves and claws at the snow. Mud. Green grass.

He lunges forward, trying to rock his chest onto the edge like when he pushes himself out of the park swimming pool.

Then he is out.

And scrambling.

On his hands and knees. Away from the ditch, the toes of his boots dragging through the snow behind him.

He rolls onto his back in the cold snow. His chest burns. His eyes sting. The snow is a mess.

Blackbirds cross over him, laughing.

The houses in the subdivision are still standing, red and blue and brown. Smoke rises from their roofs and wrecks with the air. Summer furniture and barbeques wait on back patios under drop cloths draped with snow. Curtains are shut over back patio doors.

Exactly as before he fell into the ditch.

He pulls himself to his knees, and then into crouching. He walks to the shed and places his face against the wall. The wood is cold. He looks between the slats. The old man's lawn mower is covered under a tarp. Gardening rakes in the corner.

When he finally gets home, the house is quiet and warm. His parents are still asleep.

The boy peels off his winter clothes and sits at the bottom of the stairway.

His thighs are red with cold.

* * *

After that day, the boy's different. Like his own ghost thinks he died, though he didn't, but now tags him everywhere he goes. He sees through the ghost's eyes, feels with the ghost's hands, moves through air muted by the ghost's cool skin. The ghost knows people can't hear it, so doesn't bother talking. The ghost knows there's no point in cracking jokes because everybody's going to die anyway. The ghost likes the warmth of the boy's body.

Everyone seems to notice the ghost except the boy. The little girl who lives near the creek notices the boy's faraway look when his mother brings him over.

It's your turn again, she says.

What?

Your turn.

He picks a card from the stack and discards it without looking at it.

What are you thinking? she says.

Nothing, he says.

Like what nothing?

Stuff, he says. Your turn.

It would be nice to hold hands with him, she thinks.

When the snow melts, he again walks out behind the house, searching for where he'd nearly died. It takes him two different times before he finds it: an innocent grassy incline, hardly dipping enough to be called an incline. More like a slow slant. The heel of his hand rolls into his palm at a sharper angle than this. Dandelions grow stupidly around the gaping drainpipe.

He feels embarrassed.

His schoolteacher notices the change in him, but says nothing since his new behavior benefits her. No longer does he suddenly slam his desk shut to get a laugh during silent-reading time. No longer does he tug the ear of the boy beside him, eliciting a yelp that causes the teacher to drop her chalk and the class to whirlwind into laughter. Broken chalk, she says to them. You think that's funny? They do. Absolutely they do.

Now the boy sits quietly, drawing, or finishing his homework. Day after day, month after month, until the teacher begins to regret suggesting medication or holding him back this year.

The other children notice, too, but mistake the difference as strangeness. They stop inviting him to play kickball or a hot game of tag football. No matter. He and his ghost hardly notice as they sit against the wall of the school, watching ants putter about the white gravel.

Why had the birds laughed at him when he was dying?

It bothers him.

He crouches down close to the ground, close to the ants, to see their small faces.

An ant struggles to climb a piece of white gravel.

You'll die someday, the boy whispers. The ant's feelers flicker in the air.

The little girl watches from the blacktop where she skips rope with the other girls. She has started doodling his name in her mind, in notebooks, on the inside wall of her bedroom closet where her mom used to track her height. She's in a different classroom than the boy, so when her class passes by his, she walks on tipsy-toes, trying to see into the room, his head bowed over his desk.

At the school's open house, the teachers pull back the dividers between the classrooms, and the little girl keeps scanning faces for the boy and his family. Then he's there. His father's hand on his shoulder. His mother nodding. The boy's teacher smiles and points vaguely at a wall of paintings.

The girl's mother waves at the boy's mother. The girl slips away as her own parents bend over the new classroom computer bought with cereal boxes.

When she locates the drawing with the boy's name beneath it, her stomach flips. The paper is covered with snow and black trees. The snow is made of waves of silver glitter. A green bird lies in the snow.

A green bird!

Her heart flips. If she had a little green feather, she could stick it behind her ear as a sign to him.

Hey.

She turns. It's him.

Hi, she says. She nods at his picture. I like it, she says.

You can't, he says, frowning.

Of course I can.

That boy is dying, he says, pointing at the green bird.

Why's he have wings then, if he's a boy?

He sighs, then walks out of the classroom. There's singing coming from the library. When she sees him next, he's leaving through the heavy doors with his parents. The dull orange carpet leads out to the sidewalk.

A bit high-strung that one, the girl's father says. Her mother raises her eyebrows and purses her lips.

There's nothing wrong with him, the girl says.

Of course not, her mother says.

There *isn't*, the girl says.

Once home, the girl lies in bed. She stares into the lightbulb under her lampshade. Then up at the ceiling. Green spots fly across her room when she blinks. Green! Green! Green!

* * *

Of course, the boy's mother notices the change. He talks less, jokes less, and doesn't mark off the calendar days until summer. She sits at the computer. She types growth spurt. She types *listlessness*.

Do your bones ache? she says.

He shrugs as he lies facedown on the couch.

Just then as you shrugged, did your bones ache? she says.

He shrugs again in slow motion. No, he says into the couch pillow. No ache.

No ache?

No ache, he says, turning onto his cheek long enough for her to hear.

What about listless? she says. Do you feel listless?

He doesn't answer, even into the pillow.

Maybe you're in love, she says, trying to get a rise out of him.

He flops over, staring at the ceiling like his father.

Love, she says, is natural.

What? he says.

That girl, she says.

He rolls his eyes. She wonders if his father did that as a boy. She wants to say, That's no way to behave toward your mother, but her own mother would say that. And she feels slightly superstitious about repeating her mother's wisdoms.

What do you think of her? his mother says.

Who?

She's friends with the girl's mother. They'd grown up together, different houses, a few grades between them, and now there's only a hill and creek between their houses. Of course the girl and boy didn't have to fall in love and get married. It would be convenient if they did, though. The two women exercise together, walking out to the yield sign and back, or to the cows and back, every other morning, pregnant one season, pushing strollers another, and in hardly any time at all, with the kids pedaling tricycles beside them, helmets tipping over their eyes.

The women have little in common, outside of upbringing, each with habits that slightly annoy the other, but they're good at sharing details similar enough that it sounds like they're talking to themselves—how they have to help the kids decorate their bikes for the homecoming parades, or this weekend's another game to lug folding chairs to, or will you be going to craft sale in the high-school gym? Yes, while their husbands would be helping the kids work on science projects. Just like their own mothers. Like all the good women who get married, drive through town with cans and shoes jumping from the bumper, then move into houses once owned by an earlier generation of good women.

But this. His mother didn't expect this.

The boy glances at the window.

His mother follows his eyes.

Birds cross the sky, over the tree line toward the park.

When her husband comes home from the oil fields, she follows him into the bathroom. He sits on the edge of the tub and unlaces his heavy boots. Bits of dirt fall out of his hair and off his shirt.

Something's wrong, she says.

He says he hasn't noticed a difference.

Watch him, she says.

He agrees to.

Think of some wise things to say, she says.

Like what?

I don't know. I've been trying, but can't think of any.

He pulls her to him, pressing his face against her belly. She rests her hands on his shoulders.

Okay?

Okay.

* * *

All through dinner, the man feels his wife watching him watch the boy.

When they're in bed that night, the man says, The boy's fine.

You sure?

You want something to be wrong with him?

Of course not.

Then let him be, he says. He turns over.

She doesn't want him to think she's picking a fight, so she counts to thirty. Then to sixty. She reaches across the dark and lets her hand slide down his back.

Maybe you could ask him, she says.

Gonna give the kid a complex, he says.

You could take him out to look at birds.

Birds?

He likes birds now.

Since when?

This week, last week. Recently. Remember the picture at the open house?

Bird face down in the snow.

Sort of strange, she says.

You said you liked it.

I did. I do. I just. No, I didn't like it, she says. Is that bad, not to like it?

I'll talk to him, he says.

You can bring it up real casual while you're showing him how to look through the binoculars.

He knows how to look through binoculars, the man says.

Oh.

If you want me to talk to him, I will. There's nothing wrong with him, but I'll talk to him. But you gotta let me do it my way.

That sounds familiar, she says. Is that a song? She starts with the letter A and moves through the alphabet, trying to think of the names of the singer that might have sung that familiar lyric. Crooners. That's what they were called. But who sang it? What's the song?

* * *

After dinner, next day, the man takes a cigarette outside. He presses his bare feet into the grass and breathes slowly. The boy's inside, his bedroom window dark except for a lamp. But the days are getting longer, so it's not as dark as it could be. Funny how that happens. Days growing and shrinking, year after year.

The boy is hunched over his desk, drawing.

Your mom's worried, the man says.

The boy looks up.

The man sits down on his bed.

Yeah. She looked me up on the computer.

What did the computer think? the man says.

The boy shrugs, chooses a red colored pencil and returns to drawing.

Should she be worried?

Mom?

Yes, Mom.

About what? the boy says.

I don't know. Something about birds and bones.

The boy sits still. The man reaches out and turns the boy's chair to face him.

Don't tell Mom, the boy says.

Pretty young for love.

I almost died, the boy says.

When?

Last winter. Out in the snow. It was stupid. I fell in a ditch.

The man waits.

The boy imagines his father telling his mother, his mother asking, Where were we? Where was I?

The boy shrugs. No big deal, I guess.

The man watches him.

That's a tough one, the man says.

The boy looks up without raising his head. When he was a toddler, he'd eat all his crackers, or a movie would end, or it'd be time to leave the park, and the boy did the same thing, look up without raising his head, eyes real serious. Then he'd hold up his index finger and say, One. One more, he'd say, slow and nodding a little, as though trying to get his mother or father to nod in agreement.

Same sort of look.

And the man has the same feeling that he wouldn't survive it if the boy died. It would just be over. Done.

The man leans back. He feels his chin. Out in the snow, you say, the man says.

The boy nods, watching him fully.

But you're alive, the man says, as though taking notes. He tries to remember his father and he having this talk. What his father would have said.

Yeah.

His wife's right. The boy does talk like him. He doesn't like it so much. Because then there's other things, surely, that they share.

Hard to be alive sometimes, the man says.

The boy's eyes water up just as he looks down at his drawing.

The man wants to do right. Keep his wife from fluttering, keep the boy fine.

Am I in trouble? the boy says.

Why would you be in trouble?

I shouldn't have wanted to go on a walk. Not by myself, too young.

The man never thought of his boy wanting to walk. He feels struck by it. He has the same thought, often. He'll be out in the oil field, the sun a certain way in the sky, or the trees at a certain distance, and he'll imagine walking and walking and walking until he doesn't recognize where he is.

You wanted to walk? the man says. He tries to keep his voice casual. Like he and the boy are on break at work, just shooting the shit over cold cokes. Though he hopes the boy doesn't wind up at a place like that.

The boy nods.

You left while your mother and I were asleep, the man says.

I wanted to think, the boy says.

Out back of the house?

The boy waits for his father to ask why the boy didn't wake him, why the boy didn't prevent what clearly would happen.

Must be that drainage ditch, the man says. Would have been a violent way to die.

Relief surges through the boy.

I'm glad you're alive, the man says.

Thanks, the boy says, feeling embarrassed.

The man keeps sitting there.

When your grandfather was dying, the man says, he started making birds.

I know, the boy says, glancing at his window where one of the wooden birds hangs from a string.

You don't know what I'm going to say, though, the man says.

Sorry.

The man knows he said it too quickly, sharply. He's hurt his son's feelings more than once because of this.

Understand, the man says, that my father's life was spent working, eating, and sleeping. Now and then he watched TV. But mainly he spent his days slitting hogs' throats. You remember his own father came down from Chicago, from the slaughterhouses up there. To leave them.

The boy remembers but doesn't remember. It's hard to keep track of when he wasn't alive. It all seems like one jumbled time, war, cars invented, his parents are children, then he's born.

I don't remember much about growing up, the man says, but what I remember most about my father, when I was a kid, is how he smelled. He'd come home with it on him, real thick, and leave the next morning with it, still there. All us kids could smell it. He could smell it. Mom could. Shit, blood.

The boy straightens.

Shit and blood, the man says, on a tired man has a particular scent. It's a creeping one. Gets into the walls of the house like smoke. Deep in the wallpaper so that it's there even when you scrape up the wallpaper. We all smelled it, and we all said nothing. Mom, me, all of us. Soon as he'd come home, no matter how much hell we'd given Mom that day, she never had to tell us. We kept out of his way. Out from underfoot is what they called it.

He never got a vacation long enough to drive out of the state, and never enough money to fly out of it. But every summer, he took one week off work, and probably he would have spent it alone whittling animals if he'd known back then that he had a knack for it, but he didn't have time or energy to know it. But for that one summer week, he'd pack us into the car and drive us down to the southern part of the state, where it's all hills and green, and we'd stay in this cabin by the lake.

The one you talk about, the boy says.

That's the one, the man says.

But that smell. It would start to fade as soon as we were out of town. About midway through the week at the cabin, it'd finally be gone. We'd all notice. Even Mom would hang around him more, rubbing his back, chasing him into the water, sneaking off on walks with him. This one time, I'll never forget, he's making burgers on the porch, singing to the radio, and he announces that he feels alive again. Kids, I'm alive. Can you tell? He says to us. We nod. Then he says to us, I smell like a real man again. Like he's half-joking. And we laugh, right? But it embarrassed him. I remember my little brother begging him not to make us go back home, just bawling, grabbing onto his belt loops and hanging there, so that Dad had to hitch his pants up with his other hand.

Of course we had to go back home. And next day, he'd go to work, and come back with that goddamned smell all over him, and we'd pretend we couldn't smell it.

Until my dad said that, though, about smelling like a man, I thought he couldn't smell it. But maybe we were pretending so he didn't have to think about it.

The boy nods.

The days would have grown and shrunk either way, the man says.

Like an accordion, the boy says.

I guess, the man says. Yeah, like that.

All those years he worked down at that slaughterhouse. Thirty, forty years? Jesus. Then, when he's dying, my mom, your grandmother, tells me she thinks death was like the permission Dad needed, finally. And that's when he starts whittling all those little birds and animals in the shed.

The boy looks at him.

The man shakes his head, wipes at his chin again.

These strange, little wooden creatures you never would have thought were from his imagination. He'd put one or two in his pocket and go to the diner downtown and have coffee, and give them away to some old farmer or a waitress for her kids. Why do you think he did that?

The boy shakes his head.

The man shrugs. Me neither.

The boy has never liked the wooden bird, though he's always known he should. He hardly remembers his grandfather. He tries to remember him, remember him whittling, but imagines only the old man next door.

The man stands up and touches the boy's arm. I'm glad you didn't die out there. I would have saved you if I could have.

The boy watches his father leave the room.

The man walks into his bedroom. It's dark and his wife's on

her side like she's asleep. Maybe she is. Sometimes, she'll be quiet for a long time before she starts to snore. He feels his way to his side of the bed. He takes off his clothes. In the darkness, he can't know whether he's him or his father. Strange how the mind works.

He lies down and looks up into the darkness.

She creeps over to him, sliding her arm across his chest.

You were in there a long time, she says.

Yeah, he says.

The hallway light clicks on as the boy leaves his room. The man hears the hollow clunk of the toilet lid hitting against the base. The stream of pee. The flush of the toilet. The boy's footsteps back down the hall. The light switches off. The house goes still again, quiet. He tries to listen to the boy pulling up his covers. The man feels that hard twist in his chest that will become a sob if he lets it.

THE BOY IN THE RED SHIRT

———

It's night, snowing. No one's outside except the girl on the porch. She sits in the old swing as the snowflakes come down big as plates, shattering against the ground.

She holds her ears like it's loud.

She chuckles at her joke.

Not so funny, she thinks.

She tugs at her nightgown. The swing's cold under her legs.

Her mother's somewhere in the city, in a factory feeding fabric to a sewing machine.

Her mother wouldn't like her out here. Stay in the house when I'm at work.

Nobody can see me in the dark, the girl says.

Someone's always watching, her mother says. Windows look like mirrors by streetlamps, but they aren't.

The girl can't sleep. She pushes her toes against the railing, swinging like a boat on the ocean. The boy was in a boat. So was his mother. Until now, she never thought of him having a mother. Of course a mother. Of course.

She pulls her legs to her chest.

No one's out. Not even the neighbors who run out of the

apartments screaming love and goddamn you while teenagers smoke cigarettes and push strollers to anywhere but here.

Beyond the yard, the street's thick with old snow and ice. The neighborhoods on the rich hill of town were cleared weeks ago. This sidewalk's littered with milk cartons and cardboard boats curdled with ketchup, from the high schoolers that flock here all day, talking loud, trading cigarettes like dreams.

They don't scare me, she thinks.

But they do.

Inside the house, the computer screen stares in the dark room where she left it holding the pictures of the boy in the red shirt.

The boy first appeared this morning, in the newspaper dispenser outside the diner where her mom washes dishes on weekends. The people brought him inside to look at him over breakfast. After they left, the girl cleared him from tables, booths—circles of coffee and dots of syrup on the beach where he lay, belly down in his red shirt, small black shoes, his face blurred out, his palms like two cups to hold the sky.

Her mother looked, then away.

Why's his face blurred out? the girl said.

Are his eyes open or shut? the girl said.

Her mother pressed her fist to her mouth, her red raw knuckles.

When her mother left for the factory, the girl found the boy on the computer, easily. Boy. Red shirt. Dead. Ocean. Beach. Picture after picture of him tiled across the screen.

The ocean moves, but the boy doesn't. His cheek against the shoreline. His eyes shut. In another picture, a man carries him like a son but not like a son. The man not his father but the man who picks up dead children from beaches now that the war has turned the ocean into a bridge. Just like that. Abracadabra. Magic.

The snow comes down like a bridal veil or shroud. She just learned the word shroud. From a book. A romantic word, she thinks.

It's cold. She holds her legs. The chains on the swing clink.

When the violin starts playing, she thinks she's dreaming.

She's not. She holds her breath, listening like when she listens at the bottom of the public pool in summer.

Maybe it's not a violin, but a broken-hearted someone. The music teacher says the violin is the instrument closest to the human voice. The music teacher gives them pictures of instruments, then plays a song. Raise the card when you hear yours. The girl loves the game. Loves listening for herself among the others.

Yes, that's a violin. She stands up. Opens the front door, takes her coat, steps into her mother's boots. The coat's striped blue and green, like rain down a window until you sit at a window and watch rain. This winter, the coat's tight in the shoulders, short in the sleeves.

But that's good, right? her mother says. Means you're growing. Means you're alive.

The violin plays.

The girl crosses the yard. Unlatches the gate. Then she's making her way up the whitening sidewalk, the snow like shampoo in her ears.

She walks fast, curling her toes to keep the boots from slipping.

She walks fast, looking at her feet and just ahead.

She walks like her mother walks when there's another new bill—another round of layoffs—another status-pending from unemployment—another time her debit card's rejected at the grocery store, and the cashier rolls her eyes, and the manager voids the bill, and her mother offers to put the groceries back, but the bag boy says, No worries, and the people in line shift weight, and her mother says, I'm sorry, and the girl wishes they didn't have faces, and they walk home fast, staring at their feet and just ahead. Until they're too tired to think—until it's okay—has to be okay for life to be like this.

The sound of the violin carries her past houses, past porches weighed down by old couches, storefronts with plywood windows. Another store for sale. Another corner like a grave surrounded by dirty footprints.

Her boots thud against the sidewalk. Like a boat in waves, maybe. She has never been in a boat.

Into the park, over the long, wide bridge where people sit for summer fireworks or throw themselves from like rocks lonely for the rocks below.

The river is loud, like god if god made sounds.

She passes the corral where the pony stands in hot summers, wishing to be made of wood like the horses in the carousel across the way.

Music, her teacher said, can make a person understand what it is to be alive.

The other kids giggled.

What's so funny? the teacher said.

How can you *not* know? one kid said.

Just wait, the teacher said.

Maybe the violinist has seen what she has seen.

Maybe that's why he's up late, too.

The girl has seen the violinist before, in his old top hat and ragged coat.

In the morning, when her mother comes home, she'll see the boy's face on the girl's.

You looked, she'll say.

The girl will murmur sorry, but will say nothing of the other pictures, bodies scattered across beaches like strange seashells with arms and legs. The beach like the beach they visited last summer, off-season. Empty except for them and a bird that stood still.

Is it okay? she asked her mother.

Leave it be, her mother said.

The girl shivered in the swimsuit she'd packed because she thought oceans were warm.

The bird wasn't there next day.

On the drive home, they stopped at an empty gas station. Music piped through speakers. No one there. The pump turned on with the swipe of her mother's card. A phone booth with a directory but no phone. The interstate roared in the dark.

What if the downtown's the same? The violin coming through speakers, out of time.

She crosses the intersection. The traffic light clicks from green to red, and the red glows over her. The snow falls.

There's the violinist, right there, near the end of the next sidewalk. A couple stands listening, wrapped in each other like scarves. How strange that the world happens in places where you aren't.

She imagines the notes floating up, past the snowflakes, over the ocean until they reach the faraway boy in the red shirt. So he doesn't have to hear the roaring water anymore. The song fills him like a beautiful red seashell, unlike any seashell ever seen. Until someone does see it and carries it to the king and queen who set it on a soft cushion. And we all travel to see the shell that's so beautiful that to behold it is to finally understand god or the world, and any wish for war vanishes as quickly as a boy dies expecting his mother's hands to catch him beneath the water.

The violinist lowers his bow.

The couple walks away.

The violinist takes up a rag, and wipes the strings, the backs of his hands. Then he crouches to set the violin in its case.

One more, the girl says.

He looks up, startled.

What's that? he says

Another, she says.

What song? he says.

I've never heard it.

Well, that's a funny joke. Go on back home. It's not safe out here for little girls.

Please, she says.

He shuts the case, the clasps jangling.

Let me show you, she says. She holds up her palms, walking backward. He picks up the case.

It's the only song that can come after *this*, she says. She lays down on the slab of sidewalk like the boy.

She rests her arms at her sides.

Her cheek against the concrete.

She turns her palms up like two cups.

The snow twirls like tiny cyclones in her breath.

Like this but not this, she says.

He has a hard time hearing her, the snow like a veil made from a billion stars over a dark ocean, obscuring her face.

She closes her eyes.

She holds her breath.

Is this love? she thinks. And begins waiting to feel alive.

WHEN THE FROST COMES

———

The girl and her mother sit at the small kitchen table, eating their cereal. On TV, the weatherman stands in front of his colorful map. He has gray hair and a red bow tie and is the same weatherman who visited the girl's class and explained about Ls and Hs. Ls mean lousy weather and Hs mean happy weather—For the most part, he said. She and the rest of the class were impressed since he was from the larger city where the shopping mall, movie theatre, and hospitals are, besides they saw him every night on TV, and there he was shaking hands with Mrs. Lindsey in front of their chalkboard. It was almost as good as the shopping-mall Santa visiting, but since none of them could believe in Santa anymore, the weatherman would do.

The weatherman moves his hands like a sorcerer swirling the stars. He's actually standing in front of a green wall, no map behind him, even though she sees it and her mother sees it. Like magic, he told the class. One of the kids said, If it's like magic then why are you always wrong so much? Their teacher and the weatherman laughed.

The girl thinks about the map, the green wall, how the weatherman looks at them in their nightgowns and trailer but can't see them in the camera he's actually looking at.

The weatherman smiles and says, This is why the frost will come earlier than it has in years.

The map's clouds churn then stop then churn again.

See the pattern of low pressure moving this way? the weatherman says to the girl and her mother who he is but is not imagining. This means—

Lousy weather, the girl says—trying not to see whether her mother is proud of her for knowing the right answer.

—possibly even a frost tonight, the weatherman says.

We should cover the flowers then, her mother says. You'll have to remind me.

Okay, the girl says.

Promise?

Promise, the girl says, smiling.

Her mother smiles.

The weatherman drops his hands and smiles.

Now it's the woman behind the news desk. She smiles and says at least the frost can't stop all the regional festivals going on this weekend. He chuckles in agreement. The woman turns in her chair so that she's facing the girl and her mother. She'll talk more about this weekend in the Wabash Valley right after the break. Very quick footage scrolls across the screen—of a Ferris wheel turning, horses racing around a track, and a machine turning taffy.

That's us, the girl says, thinking of tomorrow's demolition derby. She has never been to one, but her father won four tickets on the radio or somebody gave them to him. He and his wife Sharon are already up at the festival. All summer his wife Sharon travels to festivals and sells silver jewelry at the flea markets.

The girl hurries to eat the last of her frosted wheat before they taste like hay bales after a rain.

When she looks up, her mother is sitting still, her hands on either side of the placemat. The small bones strain against the skin, and crescents of pressure blossom inside her fingernails.

She is trying to press her headache down her arms, out her fingers, and down the table's metal legs into the dark linoleum patterned with gold flowers.

How bad? the girl says.

I'll just lie down for a little bit, her mother says. Then we can go.

Promise? the girl says but wishes she hadn't.

Her mother stands, pushing down on the table to help herself up. The girl holds down her side, too, so the table doesn't tip. Their spoons clink lightly against the bowls. Her mother moves slowly down the hallway toward her dark bedroom made darker by the towels hung over the curtains.

The girl takes their bowls to the sink and runs them under the water before the frosted wheat can dry to the porcelain. She turns off the TV and goes outside to play while her mother's headache passes, or lightens.

* * *

The girl stands in her tire swing, hugging the rope close to her chest and cheek. The cornfields and soybean fields seem to surround the trailer, the whole village, the whole ten miles between the village and town, the whole fifteen miles between where she lives with her mother and where she visits her father on the weekends, the forty miles between the village and the hospitals, the village and the university where her mom once took a night class that she later dropped when her work schedule changed. Oil derricks swing over distant fires that are hard to see by daylight.

The country roads are more like paved rows that cross through the fields and are walked as often. The oil-and-gravel road runs past the trailer and crosses the old state highway that was once the main way to travel between the farm and oil towns, after it replaced the train—its tracks long dug up or sunk beneath the soil, soil that her mother says is more clay than anything. None of the farmers who farm the fields around the trailer live on this road, and the only other house, about a quarter mile down the way, is only foundation and the shape of a house made by the trees that remain.

The girl lies chest down in her tire swing. She pushes off and watches the patch of dirt blur beneath her. She stops herself with her hand and digs at an acorn in the dirt. She pulls herself over to the tree trunk where the roots begin and twigs collect from storms. She finds one of the thicker sticks and stabs it into the dirt under her, using it like a canoe pole, pushing herself back, then pulling herself forward. She imagines herself at the bottom of the sky, suspended from the swing's rope tied so high above her that she has forgotten the names of the people who sit in the boat above, waiting for her to tug on the rope so they know to pull her up.

The highway is just a bare silver strip unraveling into both sides of nowhere, like the dead snake on the road that she and her mother found on a walk. Its blood baked black in the sun. Ants hurrying over and around it, as though drawing flowers. For several walks, the girl would see the stain its body had left. Then one day she couldn't.

A tractor turns off the highway and onto the road. The line of cars and trucks behind it speed up, the spaces between the vehicles expanding as they go. The tractor's huge sharp teeth bounce as it bumps over the large ruts in the road made by past seasons of tractors and combines and school buses. The two big dogs that live in the house on the other side of the highway run out of the shade, and chase after the tractor. When it enters the field, the dogs stand at the edge, barking. Even from here, the girl can see the muscles in their chests.

* * *

The light has changed, and her mother hasn't opened the door yet. The girl's still in her nightgown, but sitting in her swing now, drawing in the grass with her bare toes. She has already pulled all the locust shells from the trees, from the skirting around the trailer, and from under the hanging flower pots where she thought not many people would think to look.

Once her mother feels better, and comes out of the trailer to go to town, her big blue purse over her shoulder and her tortoise-shell sunglasses over her eyes, they'll drive to get the flour and caramel to make the muffins with the apples that the girl's father bought during their visit last weekend. Her mom has been promising they could make them, but then she'll have one of her headaches, or what seems like one long headache interrupted only now and then. The apples are softer now, but her mother says this won't matter for baking.

While the muffins are baking, they'll lick the batter off the beaters and spatula, and her mom will turn on the radio and they'll twirl in their socks on the linoleum, and her mother will shake her hips like she's a contestant on TV, and the girl will laugh and laugh. Maybe they'll even get sheets from the closet and unfold them in the living room and watch a movie or play their favorite board game.

They haven't played in a long time. The last time was probably on her mother's birthday. As a surprise, her father and she had picked out a cake from the grocery store during a weekend visit not long after the divorce. They also bought a plastic tablecloth that said HAPPY BIRTHDAY!! with matching plates and cups, and a roll of tape. They set it all up in one of the park picnic shelters and waited for her mother to come pick the girl up.

Do you love it? the girl asked her mother as they all stood

under the shelter in the park. The girl watched her father watch her mother. Her mother crossed her arms.

I do, her mother said.

Do you? her father said.

It's very thoughtful.

Thoughtful, he said.

Thoughtful, she said.

Christ, he said.

I want this piece, the girl said, pointing at the corner cluster of icing flowers.

I'm not trying to be difficult, her mother said.

Then don't try any harder, he said.

Her mother closed her eyes. I have a headache, her mother said.

You always have a headache.

Her mother glared at him.

The girl felt her chest ache, and so knew she was supposed to walk away, to go play until one of them drove away furiously or they called her back to them and tried to explain love. Love, her mother would say. Love, her father would say. Well.

Wanna watch me do a cartwheel? the girl said.

Sure, baby, her father said. Her mother nodded. The girl walked just far enough to seem like she couldn't hear them. She wanted to know about the headaches, too. She knew her mother pretended to feel well a lot, which made it hard to know when she was pretending and when she wasn't. So it felt like her mother was never quite right.

Just go back to the doctor, her father said.

They're working fine, her mother said. It's just stress.

Because you're a doctor now.

That's what he said, she said.

Family doctor.

You're an expert on doctors now? she said, smiling up at him.

Dark as a tomb in that trailer, he said.

It's dark, she said. But just on those days. There aren't so many.

He tipped the bill of his baseball hat like he does when he's frustrated.

It's just headaches, she said.

Brain's nothing to dick around about, he said.

So they find something, she said. I can't afford to take off the work.

He tipped his hat back farther then pulled it down until the bill touched his nose. He tilted his head back to look at her. I told you we can make this work, we can work this out, he said.

Her mother glanced over at the girl.

Ta-da! the girl called, as though she'd turned another cartwheel, though she hadn't.

That was a pretty one, her father said, turning to look at her.

Sure was, her mother said. You ready to eat the cake?

She nodded, running toward them. They sat under the park shelter and ate the birthday cake. The wind kept blowing back the tablecloth to show the old faded and rotting picnic bench beneath it. There was no one else in the park.

* * *

The girl slips out of the tire swing and pulls the tire back until it's above her head. Then she lets go with a push, so it swings like a pendulum. She runs across the yard to the trailer and up the steps. When she tries to open the door, something blocks it from the other side. She tries again, but it opens only a few inches. She tries to peek through the crack but sees only the dark linoleum floor in the kitchen, its pattern of repeating gold flowers.

She calls out for her mom. She looks over her shoulder. The tire swing swings on its own. She turns back to the door, calling through it, Mom, the door's stuck!

She backs up, and the snapdragons in the planter beside the door graze the back of her leg. She runs around the side of the house, to the back door. It's open. She steps into the trailer. Water dribbles distantly in the sink. She looks to the right, into her mother's bedroom where the hallway ends. The door's open, and even though it's dark, as her eyes adjust, she can see the bed is empty, the comforter and sheets pulled back. She starts down the hallway, passing her own bedroom, the bathroom, the linen closet, and walks into the kitchen.

Her mother's there, lying on her stomach on the kitchen floor in front of the front door, in the place just before the linoleum meets the living room carpet. She's dressed to go to town. One of her arms is above her head, as though reaching to open the front door but instead her hand covers a gold flower on the linoleum.

The girl is a hammering heart dropping at her mother's side, wedging herself between the door and her mother.

Mom?

Her cheek by her mother's face.

Mom?

Looking into eyes slightly open.

A light sheen of dust crosses under the light on the linoleum.

The girl's shouting her mother's name then pressing her ear to her mother's back, her face between her mother's shoulder blades. There's no sound. She presses her fingers in the space under her mother's jaw where there's always a heartbeat. Where it's strongest, her mother taught her.

The girl's all adrenaline and scoops her hands under her mother's side and rolls her over. Her mother's arm slides against her chest, her hand resting on her stomach. Her shirt raises a little, above her belly button. The girl pulls it down.

She watches her mother's shoulders, her chest, for movement.

She picks up her mother's hand and pulls at her, no differently than the mornings she wakes up before her mother and goes to get her out of bed. But her mother doesn't open her eyes, doesn't squint up and ask what time it is.

It's four o'clock on the clock hanging in the living room, but it's always four o'clock in the trailer because her mother keeps forgetting to buy batteries for it.

She stands up, straddling her mother's waist as she grabs her mother's arms and shakes her, shakes her. Her mother's head hardly moves. The girl stands up. There's dust on the heels of her hands, and she wipes them on her shorts.

The girl looks around. Her mother's phone is on the kitchen counter and plugged into the outlet. She goes to pick it up, but the screen is white and says *Charging*. She tries to turn it on, but it won't turn on. She dials 911 anyway, but the screen stays white and *Charging—Charging—Charging*. It's an old phone, the cheapest pay-per-minute phone even when she'd bought it. Her father kids her mother about it. Waste not want not, her mother says.

The car keys aren't on the hook by the door. Her mother's purse is on the couch. She steps over her mother and goes into the living room. She turns the purse upside down and shakes it. Her mother's wallet, a pack of gum, pads, receipts, car keys. She grabs the keys.

She has to move her mother's arm to open the front door. Down the stone stairs, careful not to trip on the planters that suddenly seem very fragile, very there and outlined by the day. Everything seems sharper. The tire is still swinging from the tree in large sweeps.

* * *

It's hot in her mother's car. She pulls the belt across her chest. The seatbelt burns her leg. She jerks down the window. The car squeals like it always does just before she puts the lever into drive. Her father hasn't taught her to reverse yet, so she drives slowly forward, turning the steering wheel hard so that the car turns through the yard and back onto the gravel driveway.

But where is she going?

Her father's already up at the festival with his wife Sharon. Probably they're sitting under the hot tarp watching people walk by, maybe talking to the man in the space beside them who's selling hand-tooled leather crafts or sunglasses or tie-dyed dresses, or maybe her father's gone off into the crowd in search of lemon shake-ups.

Meanwhile, her grandparents are mowing their lawns in other towns, other neighborhoods on streets she doesn't know how to get to. This is what her father must have meant by being too far out when her mother began renting the trailer after the divorce, and why, near spring, he decided that the girl's legs were finally long enough to reach the pedals in his truck.

He'd begun letting her drive in the country even though her mother wouldn't like it. If there's an emergency, you need to know how to drive. And so each time he picked her up from her mother's, and they were out of sight of the trailer, he would pull over to the side of the road and they'd change seats. Driving terrified her. Easy does it, he'd say. You're doing real good.

Her mother had almost let her drive home when they were driving into the sun and a headache sharpened. Her mother pulled to the side of the road. They sat there with the radio off. I can drive, the girl said. Since when? her mother said. But she didn't answer because she didn't want to get her father in trouble. When they got home, her mother made the doctor's appointment that led to the doctor saying the headaches were likely from stress, that he saw it a lot with single mothers. He wrote a prescription and let her know that it was hard for him, too, after his wife died, but that he had started dating recently. If you ever need someone to talk to, and not as a doctor, my cell phone's on there, too, he said, gesturing at the prescription he had handed her.

The girl brakes at the end of the driveway. The car jerks forward as it stops. There's nowhere.

Across the road, birds sit on the phone line, quivering as they dig mites from their feathers.

There's the hollow rush of a lone truck going down the highway.

She can't see the tractor anymore.

A breeze rustles through the corn.

You will not cry, the girl thinks. You will not cry.

* * *

It's still four o'clock.

The tire swing isn't swinging anymore.

Her mother still isn't breathing.

The light in the trailer has changed, turning the gold flowers on the linoleum even golder but unevenly.

Everything else is as it was a hundred years ago when her mother went to lie down, and the girl went outside to swing.

The apples are in their bag on the counter by the refrigerator, softer but still good for baking.

The refrigerator hums.

The kitchen faucet is dribbling. The girl turns the knob until it returns to its slower, steady drip. She presses her palm against the spout. The water slips in small streams over her palm. The new faucet her father keeps meaning to replace it with is under the sink.

There are kernels of corn in the drain from last night's dinner, but the plates have been washed and put away. Once the girl's mother stopped working third shift at the factory, they started having regular meals again. The cereal bowls are still in the drainer where the girl left them this morning.

On the kitchen table is an open bag of bread, beside it a

peanut-butter-and-jelly sandwich. It's cut in four squares and its crusts are cut off. There's a knife with jelly on it on the floor. The girl throws the crusts into the trash and puts the knife in the sink. When she goes to wipe the jelly off the floor, a fat housefly is on the bread. She waves at it. Finally, it flies up beneath the curtain in the window, buzzing off the glass.

The girl stands there, barefoot, her hair still not combed. She picks up a square of the sandwich, staring off as she chews.

The trailer is quiet and still. Even more than when she stays up past bedtime but pretends to be asleep, her back to the door when her mother comes in to check on her, leaning over her, sometimes lightly brushing the girl's hair from her forehead before kissing her as the girl watches her mother through her eyelashes, shadow against the wall. After the bedroom door shuts, her mother goes to bed or, sometimes, slips out of the trailer. The girl will prop herself on her pillow, press her cheek against the screen until she can just see her mother sitting on the stone steps or moving around the yard watering the flowers. Once, her mother got in the tire swing, but she was too heavy and the tire touched the ground. Her mother laughed softly, shaking her head, but sat there a while more. Or her mother crosses into the road and stands there looking up and down it. She used to bicycle up one side of the road and then back, but never far enough that she couldn't see the trailer, the tire swing, the yellow and pink snapdragons, the daughter pretending to sleep, but one time the dogs at the end of the road chased her so hard they knocked her over. It had hurt the girl's feelings to see the red scrapes on her mother's knees and forearms, the scrape on her cheek.

* * *

When it's nearly dark, the girl opens the linen closet. She likes the way it smells and stands there a little bit before reaching for the sheets. A few tablecloths fall on her. She stuffs them on another shelf even though there's not much room. Then she remembers her mother can't do it, so she drags a chair from the kitchen table to the closet so she can climb up and put the tablecloths back up where they belong. The girl doesn't know how funerals work, but if strangers come over, her mother will be embarrassed if there are clean tablecloths all over the floor. When she and her mother live in a bigger house, they'll have a bigger table and invite people over for dinner and set the table with the thick tablecloth and beautiful crystal glasses her parents got on their wedding and that her mother sets out special for the girl's birthday.

She takes the sheets outside, but uses the back door instead of the front and walks around the trailer to the front steps that lead into the trailer and to her mother's body. She's just taking a nap. That's it. Maybe it's a coma or something, like on the soap operas she watches when her mother's at work. People are always dying but not dying in the soap operas. Let this be a soap opera. If they wore nicer clothes and lived in a nicer house, it would be.

The front steps are cold under the girl's bare feet and she shifts from one to another as she unfolds the sheets and covers the planters, tucking them in so the frost can't creep through so easily. The snapdragons, the pansies, and the two house plants that they'll bring inside for the winter when it's closer to Halloween. But her mother says that the snapdragons and pansies likely won't live through winter since they're annuals. It's almost not worth it to bring them inside.

* * *

In the backyard, clinging to one of the fence posts, is a locust shell, hole blown out of its back. It's the yellow of the cornhusks that scuttle across the road in autumn after the fields are plowed and the whole world seems so much vaster than it did over the summer. Maybe the shell has been there since the middle of summer—maybe even last summer when they didn't live here yet. Maybe it has been here for years, as long as the girl has been alive, longer than her parents' marriage, longer than even they have been alive.

Her father taught her about counting a turtle's age by its shell. Probably it's not the same with locusts, but she leans forward anyway, because maybe the shell can tell her something. Its tiny crusty legs, the tiny sheer bulbs of its eyes. She can see through the shell eyes and into the rest of its body. Her mother said the shell isn't a dead thing, just what remains. It's just their overcoats, her mother said. They hang up their overcoats so they can fly. They're beautiful once they can fly, sort of like turquoise beetles with veiny wings. The girl hasn't seen one of those. Her mother said she's only seen a few in her life.

So those don't die? the girl said.

No, those die, her mother said. The shell is just part of its life like changing clothes is part of our lives. Or maybe sleeping is a better example. We need to sleep, but sleep doesn't stop us from dying one day.

If the locust opens its eyes inside the shell, does it know it's a body inside a shell looking out at the world? When it peels its eyes from the shell eyes and again sees the world, does it think it's the same world or a different one? Surely the world looks somewhat different, even though the world itself has not changed, like when the girl puts on her mother's glasses to be silly. Can it know the world is the same if it now has wings? Or does having wings change the world slightly?

Had the girl found the locust before she found her mother, she would not stand here this long, would not think of her mother as she looks at it, would not wonder if it's bad luck to leave it here now that she has seen it while thinking of her mother. Maybe she should keep it. Maybe if she keeps it and goes into the trailer, her mother will be breathing again. Or maybe if she leaves it here, her mother will be breathing again.

She watches it, lost in worry. Her breath rattles inside the shell.

* * *

Her mother doesn't come around the corner of the hallway, wearing her glasses and one of the oversized T-shirts she wears to bed, saying it's time for bed.

The sound of nothing hurts the girl's throat.

I covered the plants, the girl says.

Her mother doesn't answer.

She unplugs the phone and takes it with her down the hallway to the bathroom. She plugs it into the outlet over the sink and sets it next to her toothpaste.

She runs a bath. She unscrews the bubble bath and measures it into the cap, but the container is heavy and she spills some. When she can bear the temperature, she sits down and runs her fingernails down the grooves of the orange and green fish her mother stuck to the bottom of the tub when the girl learned how to take showers.

She takes the hippo from the basket of tub toys. Only her best friend knows she still plays with them, but it's okay because her best friend still plays with her bath toys, too, and her best friend thinks a lot of kids in their class act like they don't to be cool or whatever.

She fills her pink plastic hippo then tips it so the water comes out of its ears and mouth. She watches the water reenter the water. She holds the hippo up to her face and stares into its eyes. It smiles shyly at her, like it's happy to know her. She drops it and sets her foot on its side and slides it around the bottom of the tub. It makes underwater scratching sounds, hollow and screechy. She covers her ears like she can't stop the noise and keeps pushing it with her foot around the bottom of the tub. Bubbles rise to the surface from the hole in its back.

When she rescues it, she kisses its painted nose and empties it of the water it took on. I love you, she says to it.

It smiles shyly at her.

I think she's dead, she says.

Don't think like that, she says in the hippo's voice.

I don't want her to be dead, she says.

Maybe she isn't dead.

Maybe not.

She loves you, the hippo says.

She doesn't like the echo of her voice against the tile walls. The girl worries that while talking to the hippo she didn't hear her mother start breathing. She listens for her mother moving about the house, locking the doors for the night, picking up any toys from the carpet and dropping them in the hamper by the couch, turning on the nightlight by the sink.

But there are no sounds like that.

The pads of her fingers are wrinkling.

She washes under her armpits and the back of her neck.

When she gets out, she combs her hair back with the big-toothed comb she and her mother share. But she doesn't brush her teeth because she doesn't like to brush her teeth. She heads to her bedroom, watching the water dripping off her and into the carpet as she goes. She doesn't want to wear the nightgown she has worn for most of the day. She looks for her other one in her closet, in the box of clothes her mother's taking to the thrift store. She finds her winter pajamas. Penguins in scarves waddle or ski down the pants. The bottom is worn down from scooting around on the carpet like she's not supposed to. She pulls the pants on. The legs end above her ankles. She leaves the top off because it's too hot to wear full flannel in the summer, even if it's late summer and the windows can be left mostly open at night because of the breeze.

She takes her pillow and blanket off her bed and all the pillows off her mother's bed and carries them into the kitchen, almost tripping on the blanket a few times. She drops them beside her mother.

Her mother's head is heavy, but she manages to slip the pillow under her. The skin across her mother's throat has turned patchy, bluish purple. She lifts her mother's arm and slides the other pillow under it like her mother will do when she sleeps.

Then the girl lies down beside her, pulling the blanket up over them and arranging it over their feet. She can see over her mother into the living room where the TV sits, screen black and blank. It seems to be reflecting them, but they are so tiny it is hard to tell if it's them or something else. The girl raises her arm and waves. Her reflection waves back at her in the screen. Yes, that's them reflecting darkly.

* * *

Later in the girl's life people will ask her what it was like to lose a mother so early. When they learn she's the one who found her, that it was a brain aneurysm, that nothing could have been done, they will say they can't imagine it, they just can't imagine. She will shrug, say it's hard to describe, and try to change the subject. But when she thinks of what it was like, she thinks of the story her mother would tell her:

When you were a toddler you liked climbing into the kitchen cabinet where I kept the flour and sugar. You'd shut the doors, and take the lids off and often pour the flour everywhere. I'd go around the house calling your name like I didn't know where you were. Up and down the hallway, into the bedrooms, opening and shutting the closets and drawers, knocking on the walls like they contained secret passageways.

The girl heard the story enough times that she could see through the crack in the door where the light changed as her mother crouched on the other side, the floorboards squeaking beneath her. Her mother keeps quiet, saying nothing. Even though the girl can hear her breathing, the longer her mother keeps quiet the less the girl believes it's her mother she hears. She's too young to think to hold her breath and listen. She wonders if her mother really is there, and she starts to worry that her mother has left, that her mother is rushing across the yard and up the road searching for her, maybe running into the cornfields. What if her mother gets lost and she can't find her? The girl begins to panic, her little fists sweaty and curdling the flour.

But her mother always opened the cabinet door, and the girl's face broke into a huge smile, drool on her lips. That squeal, so high, and her little body backing up but also reaching forward, toward her mother.

Were you hiding from me, little ghost? her mother said, looking into her eyes, noting the happy flush in her cheeks, the clutch of her little hands on her arms, the flour smeared across her forehead, dusting her hair, sticking in balls on her legs.

I missed you, her mother said. Did you miss me?

Boo, the girl said.

Boo? That's right, what a smart girl you are! I called you a ghost. And what do ghosts say, little ghost?

Boooooooooo! Oo! The girl smiled and her mother helped her out of the cabinet, and the girl stood up on her mother's legs, bouncing as she leaned back and clapped.

And that's when the girl's father took the picture on the refrigerator that the girl stared at when she fell asleep that night on the floor beside her dead mother.

* * *

The girl wakes up pressed against the pillow and her mother's arm. Outside, car doors are shutting. She has pulled most of the blanket over herself, and there is a speck of blood on her own pillow, from her nose. If she dreamed, she doesn't remember. The low light from the light over the kitchen sink. Her mother's colder, and her fingers seem to have pulled back in the night.

Wake up, the girl says.

There's dust on her mother's eyelashes.

She goes to the window.

The moon is up. There's a police car in the driveway and two men are walking toward the house, shining their flashlights over the grass as they go. One shines the light into the window where she is. She hops back, heart thudding.

Footsteps climb the stone steps.

The girl thinks of the box of winter clothes in the closet, of climbing into it and staying quiet. She hurries over to her mother and is covering her with the blanket when the knock comes, rattling the door. She crawls back under the blanket, pulling it over her head and lying flat as a pancake. She doesn't want to go to jail because that's what happens to the murderer, her mother says when they're playing their favorite board game and look in the little manila envelope and find out who killed Mr. Body in the conservatory.

Sarah Tully? Officer Jake Bailey and Officer Philip Jones here. Can you please open the door?

The girl clutches the hem of her mother's shirt and watches the door where the knock comes from.

There's the sound of their walkie-talkies. Nobody seems to be home, the officer says.

There's the sound of the footsteps coming off the stairs and then the light through the window and against the wooden paneling of the wall. There's another voice, coming from the walkie-talkies, but she can't understand what it says.

Maydith Tully, are you there? My name is Officer Jake Bailey, and I work at the police department. We got a call from your father. He's worried. We just want to know if you're okay and your mom's okay.

She goes to the door, trying to think of what to do, what her mother would tell her to do. She's not supposed to answer the door if she's home alone. If anyone comes to school and says her mother or father sent them to pick her up, no matter who they are, they must say the secret password.

What's his name? she says.

Gordon Tully.

Did he tell you the secret password?

Is your mother okay?

I need to know the password or I'm not supposed to open the door.

Okay, Maydith, just a second. There's the walkie-talkies again. Another hundred years pass before they crackle again. And then the officer says, Professor Plum.

The girl opens the door and then hurries back to her mother, and watches the door. The backs of her feet press gently into the curve of her mother's breast.

A man steps into the house, looking around. I'm Officer Jake, he says, and this is Officer Philip. Officer Philip nods. Is your mother here?

The girl nods.

Is she asleep?

The girl shakes her head.

Then Officer Jake sees the blanket behind her and he crouches beside her. She watches him pull it back. The purplish color has spread up under her jaw and down under the V of her blouse. He shakes his head. He kneels and the other officer takes out his walkie-talkie. He says he has a 419 here, a 419.

Officer Jake kneels and tilts her mother's chin back. When did she stop breathing? he says.

Long time, she says.

One day, two days?

Then the other officer, she can't remember his name, is reaching his hand out to her. He asks if she has a shirt to put on because they need to go outside so Officer Jake can have some room.

* * *

The dogs have stopped howling now that the ambulance has been at the trailer long enough that the lights are as much a part of the field as the oil derricks' fires. The girl sits in her tire swing with her feet on the ground, waiting for her father to come get her. One of the sheets that covered the plants is now tied around her throat. When she came outside to give them room with her mother, she found the sheet wrinkled on the ground by the trailer skirting. She feels dumb wearing it, but she didn't know what else to do with it. It's damp from the dew, and she can smell the detergent beneath it, like when her hair gets wet and even if she didn't take a shower that day, she can smell the shampoo a little. The sheet drags against the ground beneath her.

By now there are two more police cars parked in the ditch and the ambulance is only lights flashing against the side of the trailer. She doesn't look into the lights or they follow her wherever she looks.

Strangers stand in her yard.

The radios in the police cars crackle on and off like the mosquito killer in the backyard when it has batteries.

The ambulance people are crouching around her mother in the

light of the door that also casts a square on the yard but stops just before reaching the girl's feet.

There comes another vehicle, up over the overpass and down the road, setting the dogs off again. She can see them running alongside the van until it turns onto her road. Then they fall back into the darkness. The van passes the driveway then stops, its red brake lights turning the girl pink. Then it reverses into the driveway, parking alongside the ambulance. For a second, its headlights draw the weeds and grass out of the dark. Then the lights shut off. A woman steps out of the van.

Officer Jake and the others meet her in the yard. They talk and nod and point at the trailer. The woman puts her hands on her hips and nods. They look at the girl. The woman comes over. She says her name is Allison and you must be Maydith. The girl peeks at her over the tire swing.

I like your cape, the woman Allison says.

It's a sheet.

The woman Allison smiles. It's a nice sheet anyway.

The girl shrugs.

Listen, the woman says, I'm going to need to go inside and see your mother. Would that be okay with you if I did?

I think she's dead, she says, and stabs her toe in the dirt and turns herself around so that her back's to the woman.

Okay, the woman says.

The girl keeps her back to her. When she turns around, the woman is already walking up the stairs and standing in the kitchen alongside the ambulance people. The girl can see between their legs to where her mother lies.

* * *

The sky is lightening and only the van, a police car, and her mother's car are in the driveway when the policemen come out of the trailer carrying a stretcher. It is her mother on the stretcher in the black bag. The girl has seen enough TV to know it. She hurries to the porch and moves the planters off the steps so that they don't trip and so the pots don't break. The woman Allison opens the back doors to the van, and the legs of the stretcher fold up as they slide it into the back. There's no room for the girl back there so she goes around to the passenger side of the van and tries to open the door.

Sorry, kiddo, a voice says behind her. You're going to stay here, I think.

The girl looks over her shoulder. Officer Jake is looking at her from around the back of the van. The doors shut, and the woman Allison comes around and looks at her, too. That's right, she says. Remember, your father's coming so it wouldn't be good for you to be somewhere else when he gets here.

The girl tries to open the door again, tugging at the handle. It's okay, the girl says. I need to go with her.

You need to be here when your father gets here. Officer Jake's going to stay here with you until he comes.

The girl looks at herself in the side mirror as she says, You can call him and tell him where I am.

Officer Jake says, Miss Allison will take good care of your mother, okay?

The girl's lower lip quivers. Promise?

He spits in his hand and holds it out. Shake on it? he says.

She looks at him and pulls the sides of her sheet-cape around her.

It's a bigger promise this way, he says. You do it, too.

She spits in her hand and holds it out. They shake. Eww, she says, wrinkling her nose and rubbing her hand against her leg.

It's gross, right? he says.

She giggles and grins wide, leaning forward.

That's a good kid, he says, and pats her on the back.

Then the van is pulling out onto the road. It's almost to the T-section, when the girl sees her father coming up over the overpass. As he slows to turn, the van turns, going the other direction.

* * *

The girl's standing on the low risers for the Christmas concert. She's wearing a green sweater and black jeans and loafers and red ball earrings. She's gesturing along with the song, trying to smile at the same time, but she keeps forgetting the motions. Her mother comes in through the cafeteria doors then holds her hands on the push bar so that the heavy doors don't shut loudly. She's late. She looks confused and she turns, standing behind the cafeteria tables where all the other children's parents sit, facing the bleachers where the children sing.

She's wearing purple earmuffs, and as she walks alongside the tables, looking for a place to sit, some of the other parents catch her eye long enough to give her disapproving looks. Maydith waves and her mother waves back. Then her mother's pointing at a place on a bench and the people sitting there nod and scoot over. Then she's sitting down, taking off her earmuffs, but she's watching Maydith the whole time.

Then the song's over and Maydith is following the other children off the risers just like they practiced, and then they're supposed to file into the hallway, and they do, but once they get there, Maydith turns around and runs back into the cafeteria, tapping her mother on the shoulder and then climbing into her lap. The cold is still on her.

I came as fast as I could, she whispers, and Maydith nods, leaning back against her mother's chest. She smells sweet, like shampoo and night.

* * *

The girl wakes up in her bedroom still wearing the sheet and her penguin pajamas. Her father is sitting on the bed beside her, leaning up against the headboard. His eyes are closed and he's holding her stuffed bear against his chest. She rests her head on the bear's head, her father wraps his arm around her so she can snuggle close.

Did you sleep okay?

She shakes her head.

If you're hungry I thought maybe we could go to the Dairy Queen, her father says.

Is Mom dead?

I'm sorry, honey.

Is she?

Yes, yes, she is.

* * *

Just before the girl steps out of the hallway and into the kitchen, she imagines her mother will be lying there on the other side. But there's only light and gold flowers. She wonders what happened to the pillows and blanket, then sees them folded on the couch in the living room beside her mother's purse. It's still four o'clock.

She opens the refrigerator and takes out the milk. It will expire in a few days. On the counter is the picture from when she was a toddler and climbed in the cabinet with flour all over her. Her father has the same picture on the refrigerator at his house, but she can tell by the grease splatters that it's the one from this refrigerator.

She opens the cabinet under the kitchen sink and sees the

other three squares of the peanut-butter and jelly sandwich in the trash can.

She pours a bowl of cereal and heads outside to eat it. She doesn't want to sit at the table, doesn't want to be in the kitchen. On the counter is the cell phone. It's unplugged and done charging. On the screen is what time it is, and the picture her mother took of the girl and her father at the pumpkin patch. Her mother had tried to take a picture of just him, and he started backing away, and then she was chasing him and he was off running and the both of them laughing. And he faked left like he was going to run into the cornfield maze, and her mother yelled at him, and he twisted and turned the other way, like when he plays tag football and the girl and his wife Sharon sit in the bleachers drinking hot chocolate from a thermos. He ran past her, picking the girl up on his way, and he turned, saying, Don't shoot, I've got a hostage. And they're laughing, all of them laughing.

THIS BOMB MY HEART

———

Out in the vast field, the girl kneels on the ground in her winter coat. She is digging a hole. It's cold, and she wears one of her brother's old coats under the wings he made for her when she lost her arm in the explosion. The skin is still pink in places, tender in deeper places. Her brother made the wings from sawing branches from a fallen tree and bundling them with rope. He picked Queen Anne's lace from the unplanted fields and the ditches, then carried it home to spread across newspapers on the porch, like their mother used to. Small breezes lifted at the pages, as though searching for news about the war.

Now and then he would look into the bedroom window where his sister slept, feverish, kicking at blankets and nightmares she wouldn't remember. When the flowers dried, he wrapped them around the branches with wire and sat on the porch step, painting them white while he waited for her to die or not die. And hate him forever, either way. Since it was his fault. Or the war's fault, but the war was too big, he decided, to take the blame for this. So big it almost wasn't responsible for its own deaths.

He drank beer at the kitchen table, drove their parents' car up to the gas station by the interstate to stock the shelves or ring up lottery tickets and gas. Mainly, people from town bought the lottery tickets, and people driving on bought the gas. There was a smaller, less expensive gas station downtown, but most interstate travelers didn't venture past the exit's cluster of fast-food restaurants and one hotel.

Before the accident, his sister often rode up to work with him.

Why don't you go play with your friends? he'd say as they drove up toward the interstate, the wind blowing through the open windows.

Pool doesn't open until one o'clock.

You could play in the park until then. Swing or something.

Maybe, she'd say, if she said anything at all. Often, she didn't. She'd always been a quiet kid, even before their parents died. Or maybe he'd been gone for so long that quiet was just the impression he had of her.

Kids don't tease you, do they?

About what?

I don't know. Our folks being dead, maybe.

No, she said.

But they tease you? he said.

I don't know, she said.

Because they do?

She didn't answer, though sometimes he would drop her at the pool, and she'd take the crumpled dollars he ironed out on his leg for admission and a snack. It was the same pool he'd grown up swimming in. One less diving board because some kid had dove into the concrete instead of the water. But, overall, it looked the same. Same chain-link fence, same faded yellow DON'T RUN on the concrete, same green chairs where mothers lay on their bellies, bikini tops unhooked. Only now the mothers were closer to his age. But mostly the girl stayed home or went with him to the gas station. That was okay, really, because he didn't like being apart from her, either.

At the gas station, she'd sit at one of the two booths where old farmers sat and cursed the weather, or maybe a family of travelers gathered while their mom peed. She'd write down all the different license plates as her brother switched on the gas tanks behind the counter cluttered with displays of beef jerky and sunglasses, and the metal oven that hot dogs rolled inside all day.

Maybe this will be the one, a customer would say about another lottery ticket.

May*be*, her brother would say, trying to sound hopeful. But on his break when she'd stand with him in the grass behind the gas station, he'd shake his head and say, Goddammit. Goddamn this town.

After her accident, he started bringing home glass figurines from the set of mirrored shelves that stood between the potato chips and movie rentals. He wrapped the fingers of her good hand around them or set them on her bedside table or the windowsill where the light came through. A crystal fish, a stained-glass mermaid, a glass mouse with wire for whiskers—red heart clutched to its chest. He thought the trinkets were meant for truckers to buy, gather up, and present to their family after months on the road, but usually the people from town bought them. They were small, beautiful, and inexpensive. And couldn't be taken back like refrigerators and couches, lended with the repo trucks that circled the streets like buzzards.

When her accident happened, he called one of the medics he'd been stationed with. Like him, when she'd come home, she hadn't known what to do with herself or the world, or if there was a difference, so when he called, she told her father she couldn't help sell real estate for a while and drove the lines of her car atlas until she found the town, the fields, the house, the damaged sister, and the soldier who called her here.

The first time the medic walked into the small bedroom and saw the little sister, the medic said, You have to take her to the hospital.

I know it's bad, he said. He showed her all he'd done.

You did right, it's just . . . she said, gesturing. The girl's eyes were closed, her cheeks flush, but her breathing seemed awake.

You said you'd help, he said. I told you her whole arm.

I know, but . . . she's just a kid.

Please, he said. They'll take her away if we go there.

Maybe they should, she thought.

You said it was an accident, she said.

It was, he said, though he found it harder to believe in accidents.

She pressed her hand against the girl's forehead. The girl moved against her, like a cat pushing to be petted. She smoothed the girl's eyebrows with her thumb. She turned away from the girl. But if she doesn't make it . . . she said, lowering her voice.

She'll make it, he said.

But *if*.

We'll take her to the hospital before that can happen.

Okay, she said.

She looked at him.

I promise, he said.

She thought if she'd known his parents, she might have recognized the expression. She hadn't known him real well when they were over there, just enough that they'd eat at the same table if they both were there. Their jobs rarely took them to the same place. His to dig up landmines. Hers to patch what she could.

The house he'd grown up in didn't tell her more about him, unless people are what they've lost. If so, she knew him well. While the girl slept, and mostly she slept, the brother and medic moved through the farmhouse like ghosts unfamiliar with who they were supposed to be, taking turns tending the girl and looking out the back door at the farm and the tractors that now tended it.

The brother and sister's parents were dead, but the house didn't seem to know it. Like the house from the woman's childhood when her parents divorced. Instead of immediately dismantling it, her parents would walk through it touching things. Picking a mirror up off the wall then setting it back on its nail. Running a finger down a line of books. Opening cabinets, standing there, shutting cabinets. One night she had woken to find her mother standing on the toilet, scraping at the wallpaper.

I never liked it, her mother said.

She knew her mother meant the wallpaper. It hurt her feelings anyway.

And now she found herself in another house, empty with things. The back patio lined with planters of brittle branches. The stillness. Even the sunlight seemed to press its palms against the lace curtains, the faded carpet, the kitchen linoleum as though feeling for the grief, so it could smooth it away.

* * *

The girl moves her spade along the edges of the hole to widen it. The empty coat sleeve is safety-pinned to the pocket because her plan is not to set off the landmine today. To set it off, yes, but not today. The coat smells like the basement. She took it from a plastic container her mother had stacked there, meaning to drop them at the thrift store, but never making it. When the girl's brother joined up, her mother said she was glad she hadn't given his things away.

The girl wears her father's old gray stocking cap rolled over her eyes and down to her chin. Under the cap, she has buckled one of her mother's belts around her eyes. It's one of those wide, elastic ones with a big buckle. From her brother's first tour when her mother joined the small fitness club downtown and worked out every other night. She has the belt wrapped twice around her head. Just to be sure.

What a sight, her father might have said.

Who are you supposed to be? her mother might have said. Like she was just inventing another strange character for trick-or-treating.

You're so weird, the girls at school would say. But they already say that.

Probably I look crazy, she thinks.

Maybe I am, she thinks.

But she is trying to prevent herself from seeing where she digs. Like when she and her friends would play hide-and-seek and she'd open her eyes the littlest bit, and look between her fingers the littlest bit, and see the direction their legs were running to. Not because she wanted to win, but because she feared never finding them, of looking and looking and they can see her but she can't see them, and they're all giggling with their hands over their mouths and rolling their eyes. Because what a loser. What a dork.

If she opens her eyes now, she'll see the sun around the belt like light around a closed door. Even with her eyes closed, there's a glow, but the stocking cap shuts that out, shrouding her in the darkness necessary to dig but not know exactly where she's digging.

When she and her brother buried landmines, they always looked where they were buying them. Now is different.

She was worried that she couldn't get lost behind her own house, so she practiced a few times without the landmine, and both times when she pulled off the hat and belt she was surprised to find where she was. The trick, she thinks, is walking while imagining herself in so many different parts of her life that when she stops, she's where she imagines and not where she is. So that when she removes the blindfolds, it seems her brother and mother just finished taking down the green string of lanterns from the back patio, her brother handing them down to her mother who carefully presses them into the box. The girl didn't hang the lanterns this summer.

No one notices the absence of lanterns except her, of course.

The nearest house is four fields away, and anyone who might drive by in the night probably wouldn't think about them unless they were brightly lit, just as they didn't seem to think about the family once they started disappearing, and probably would have forgotten the war if not for the pictures of local soldiers taped around the light poles downtown, yellow ribbons gone white, wire tearing out of them.

There I am, her brother would say when they drove past it. His picture was by the grocery store.

I think it's nice, her mother would say.

The girl didn't know what to think. When his picture first went up, she felt like a celebrity. That's *my* brother, she would think, as though announcing it to crowds. But passing the picture while he was home between tours made him seem less permanent. And the longer the war lasted, she started to feel embarrassed about it. Like someone was playing a joke, laughing at them that he still was over there while other soldiers were home for good, waving from fire trucks in parades or carrying children on their shoulders through the park. Sometimes, she thinks that's what killed her parents.

Abandoned houses lean this way and that along the country roads. Clotheslines still standing. A bowl of dead leaves on a kitchen table. Shoes under a bed. She used to wonder how the house's people had disappeared.

Like this, she thinks.

* * *

She can't trick herself into believing her brother's alive. When he died, all her memories of him changed, in the way that every memory became a story with his death as its ending, and in another way she can't quite explain. Memories changed that he had never been in. Like when she went to 4-H camp, and one night, the counselors led the kids past the lake and into the tall, dark trees. Someone was drumming, and a big fire crackled surrounded by logs and straw bales the children sat on. When the drums stopped, a counselor called the meeting to order, like a secret meeting of the highest order, instead of a group of sunburned kids sticky in mosquito repellent. The kids went quiet, and a storyteller with a bushy beard sat down and told a story about a man and woman starving way out in the middle of nowhere, in woods not unlike these woods, in a little house, and they were so hungry, but there wasn't food, until one evening, the old woman licked her finger and thought, how nice it tasted, and she began to nibble at her finger, despite the pain because the pain of hunger was greater. She nibbled at her hand until she was full. The next night, she licked her other finger, and broke it clean off between her teeth, and ate one finger after another until only the bones were left, and those she soaked in her soup. The little old man eventually did the same.

Her brother wasn't at the camp, didn't sit next to her, leaning forward as sparks of fire tripped against the dark. But now that he's dead, he seems to be there, both behind her and watching the starving couple eat themselves, but she'd never remembered it that way until he died.

Perhaps the memories haven't changed, but she has, and so the memories feel different because she remembers as a different self.

To forget he's dead would mean returning her memories to how they were before he died, but she can't remember how they used to be—except different, more scattered, unpolished, not cut as though to fit a puzzle for one box.

Of course, she tries.

He's not dead, she'll think.

Yes, he is, she'll immediately think.

Part of his death is her trying to pretend him alive. Like, but not like, when he was gone to the war, and she'd pretend he was on his way home, his tour ended early, and he didn't tell them as a surprise or if it didn't pan out, but he's nearby, just at the end of this road, turning onto it right now. She'd imagine it until even the cat seemed to strain to hear his boots in the gravel down by the yield sign, and she'd race out of the house and up the road to meet him, her jelly shoes rubbing the backs of her heels as they slapped against the black patches where the road had softened under combines, tractors, quarry trucks, the hot summer sun.

And he wouldn't be there.

Well, what did you expect? she'd think at herself.

She'd stand in the middle of the intersection, looking down the empty roads, across the corn and soybeans, then close her eyes.

Now, she'd think.

And open her eyes. Search the distance for him.

Then close her eyes.

Now.

Somewhere, a bird would be calling because there's always a bird.

Now.

* * *

One time he did come home as a surprise instead of the family picking him up at the airport, and she didn't hear him on the road at all, had no sense of his nearness even when the doorbell rang and it was him on the porch, holding the mail he'd taken from the mailbox on his way up the driveway.

Pizza coupons, he said, holding out a flimsy advertisement. And a letter from Grandma, looks like.

She stared at him.

Who is it? her mother called from the kitchen.

The girl jumped at him, yelling, and he caught her, lifting her up, asking why she didn't stop growing. Their mother came into the living room, wiping her hands down her jeans.

You, their mother said.

The old dog moved slowly down the stairs, tail wagging, chin gone gray.

Up on his shoulders, she could see the top of her mother's head, the tops of her ears, the faded blouse hanging from her shoulders, its buttons sagging in their holes. Her mother seemed small, suddenly. Old, suddenly. Her mother clung to him, but didn't shut her eyes.

For good? their mother said.

He swung his sister down and dropped her on the couch.

Dad? he said.

Out back.

He nodded.

Let me get him for you, their mother said. Because his heart.

His heart?

Their mother stepped out back.

What about his heart? her brother said.

It's too fast, the girl said.

Her brother sighed. The old dog knocked its nose against his hand, pushing his hand into petting.

Their father came out of the field, their mother behind him as though to catch him should he collapse.

He had a heart attack, the girl said.

Her brother clenched his jaw.

I'm not supposed to tell you, she said.

Then the screen door was opening and her brother and father were clapping each other on the back.

In one piece? their father said.

So they say, her brother said.

Her father didn't ask if he was home for good.

That night or another, she crawled out her window onto the roof like her brother taught her. He and her father and brother sat below on the patio, under the string of lanterns.

Her brother handed a shadow to their father, pointing, his voice a murmur: Out in the field, she heard. Run in circles, she heard.

Pretty bad? their father said.

Her brother nodded.

The two looked out at the field. The distance sounded like the locusts down by the creek.

When their voices came again, they talked of rain—too much—what happened last time rain like this—how much longer the farm could last. She'd heard the same conversation between her father and mother, between her father and the men at the diner where her father took her if she woke up before his truck reversed out of the driveway at sunrise.

The men and her father shook their heads and stared into coffee cups they held between earth-stained hands.

At the diner, the men never spoke of the factory where they moonlighted to keep their farms going. Her father had put his application in there, too. At the factory, they never spoke of their farms. And, nowhere and with no one did they say they feared their children chose the war to escape the factory and farm. That maybe they should do like the others and sell their land to one of the two families who now owned most of the fields that made the town, then gone to work for them. And somehow convince themselves that land doesn't belong to anyone. But if land belongs to no one, neither do their houses or memories or children. And that's too much to take in. Like heavy rain on dry land, and so everything whirls away, breaking.

Just the other night she had the old nightmare from the days leading up to their father selling off the farm. Of the terrible man who walks up the road toward their house. He wears a gray suit and shoes black as rain. He sneaks under the barbed-wire fences and into fields, then takes scissors from his briefcase and snips up the rows of corn and soybeans and rolls them into his briefcase, snapping it shut before disappearing back to the city where, according to her father and the men at the diner, farming now took place. She would wake screaming. Her father hurried to her bed. He said not to worry, that as long as he lived he'd fight off the monster.

But what about your heart?

I'll steal his briefcase and hit him in the head with it, he said.

She giggled. And you'll live a long time?

Sure, he said. What else have I got planned?

She smiled, and he did, too.

* * *

The skin on her thumb cracks open. It's colder and colder, like every year, the rains sweeping in after Halloween, readying the air for winter. It doesn't harden the dirt out back here like it does in the front yard, because the land back here has been worked a hundred years. The cold makes her move slower, though, numbing her fingers and chapping her hands. She pauses to suck the side of her thumb, the dirt around her fingernail turns to mud in her mouth. The ghost of her other hand also stings, and she lifts it to her mouth.

After she lost her arm, she kept reminding herself it wasn't there. After her brother died, she tried to use that hand to touch him. Because her arm wasn't there and now he wasn't either.

I am planting trees, she thinks. She isn't, but this is what she tells her body to keep it working. Trick it a little closer to its death.

Soil's more clay than anything, her mother would say—kills more than it grows.

Every summer she followed their mother up and down the few

rows in the grocery store's greenhouse, to round out the plants
that grew from seed along the windowsills of the laundry room,
which was much too hot in the summer and much too cold in the
winter. Her mother would stop and read the plastic tags that
identified the flowers and how to keep them alive.

Annuals are hardiest. Her mother taught her perennials make
promises without knowing the winter. That's the trouble.

And so, every early summer, she and her mother brought
home a cardboard tray of geraniums, snapdragons, and petunias
to plant, with the shovel her mother always threatened to replace,
its wooden handle gone gray and cracking.

When their mother died, the girl's brother came home for
good, and the flowers in the cardboard tray were replaced with
landmines.

She doesn't know where they came from, or whether her
brother had a soul—if, when he died, his soul fragmented inside
her like the shrapnel he, then the medic, dug out of her shoulder.

I'm sorry, he kept saying. I'm sorry, Jesus, I'm sorry.

One day the landmines were just there in the tray in the
laundry room—as suddenly as her brother returned home so it
seemed he'd never been gone—as suddenly as he died, like she'd
never see him again.

* * *

A few months before her brother died, he started selling off
pieces of the house. But lots of people weren't buying, what with
the factories shutting down, and houses for sale all over town.

They kept buying lottery tickets, though, her brother reported.
When hope costs only a dollar, one lady told him, you buy it.

He put ads mainly in the university paper in the city about
thirty miles away. Many of the college students were from around
here, but more were from upstate suburbs so weren't affected by

the loss of assembly-line jobs, and so could afford to buy from the tables of yard sales and newspaper ads.

Several months after her brother died, some young couple showed up on the porch, asking about the dryer. They'd tried to call a few times, the boyfriend said.

The couple was tan and held hands. She hadn't seen people happy in a long time. She stared.

Then today was such a beautiful day, the girlfriend said, shrugging.

A beautiful day, the girl said.

So we decided to take a drive, the boyfriend said.

A drive, the girl said.

The couple looked at each other.

Beautiful country down here, the boyfriend said.

My brother's dead, the girl thought.

So, the boyfriend said, is the dryer still for sale?

The girl didn't know. If your brother dies, is the dryer still for sale?

Maybe we shouldn't have come, the girlfriend said, looking at her boyfriend's face from chin to jaw.

No, it's for sale, sure, the girl said. He moved it into the garage, the girl said then walked out of the house, and off the porch to the garage.

The girlfriend gasped at the girl's arm, the one there or the one missing. Then covered her mouth, then pressed her forehead against her boyfriend's shoulder.

He's just at work, the girl said. Then squeezed between her brother's car and garage door.

Before she twisted the handle on the garage, and pulled it up, she imagined her brother would be behind it.

Of course he wasn't.

The garage door rattled back. Tools hung from above her father's workbench. Bags of her mother's potting soil were slumped in the far corner. Lawn chairs, the old tent, the Tiki torches her mother bought on clearance but never unwrapped.

It works? the boyfriend said, coming up behind her.

She nodded.

The girlfriend wiped her finger against it like there'd be dust, then pulled back the lid and leaned over it, then stepped back, holding her nose.

Something in there, the girlfriend said, taking another step back.

The boyfriend looked into the dryer.

Clothes, the boyfriend said. Moldy. You got a trash bag or something?

She went to get one.

Her brother's clothes. A pair of jeans. A flannel shirt. One T-shirt after another. Socks with holes in the heels. It was like watching him be put back together as the boyfriend lifted each piece of clothing out of the dryer before dropping it into the trash bag. The boyfriend carried the trash bag to the porch.

It's heavy, he said. Probably your brother should take it the rest of the way into the house.

Then he gave her the money, counting it into her hand.

I was about to make dinner, the girl said. If you wanted to stay.

Oh, that's okay, the girlfriend said. We have dinner plans with some friends.

Thanks again, the boyfriend said, waving as they climbed into the truck.

She waved back. As they diminished in the distance, she realized they were trying to get away from her. She left the trash bag on the porch. The trash bag grayed. Rain collected in the folds. Then wet leaves. Then snails. Then the hot sun dried out the leaves and snails, and the rain brought new snails to visit the shells of the dead.

* * *

When her brother returned to the faraway field, she asked her mother if he had killed people. Her mother said it was his or war's business, but not hers.

So she asked her father, who said, It's a war.

When her brother came home again, she followed him around the house, asking him over and over inside her head, Did you kill anybody?

She leaned against his car as he hunched over the engine, and she thought, Did you kill somebody?

As they sat on the couch, she watched his face reflect on the dark TV screen between commercials, and asked it, Did he kill people?

She pressed her cheek outside the barn door and listened to his friends while they smoked pot under the hayloft where they used to have sleepovers.

His friends wore docs and farm-looking boots. He wore his tan army boots.

She waited for his buddies to ask if he'd killed anyone. Because that's war. Killing people. But none of them did. One of them held up the pipe and said, So, does this help?

Help what? her brother said.

You know.

Oh, my war-fucked brain?

No offense, man, one said. They looked at the ground. At their shoelaces or the stains on the toes of their boots where they'd spilled beer some forgotten night.

Yeah, your war-fucked brain, said one of the guys. His voice loud. She felt herself blush.

Probably, her brother said, shrugging and smiling sideways.

No worse than you already were, another guy said.

Cheers to that, said another.

They laughed.

Someone cracked his knuckles.

Someone coughed.

There was this kid, her brother said, a little boy. He lived near a field where I was digging. Big job. Three, four weeks out. The boy's brother was in the war. He'd come over and talk to me in the mornings, after his chores. He had a dog. A mother. She'd send him out with a coffee for me, and he'd pass it over the fence. Nice kid, just a kid, you know. He'd told me it was going to be his birthday, and his mom was going to take him to the city. He was real excited. When they came home, gone all weekend, he runs out to show me a kite his mother had bought him in the city. He climbs under the fence and sits on my lap, leans back against my chest. Like it's the most natural thing. We sat there and he showed me the kite. Real nice kite, not some plastic dragon or movie character out of a bargain bin. But it wasn't expensive, either. Just well made. You could see all the patterns of the paper. Yellow kite. We looked at it for a while, just him and me.

He looked at his hands.

Anyway, he said. Then pushed his hands against his legs and stood up.

What happened to the boy? one of his buddies said.

I told you. He got a kite.

But what else?

He had a birthday, her brother says. He got a kite. Leave it at that.

So something did happen to him?

He had a dog, a mother, and she drove him to the city for his birthday and bought him a beautiful kite, and he showed it to me.

In the house, a light flipped on over the kitchen sink. Their father sat down at the kitchen table, holding his wrist. Then took the small notebook from his breast pocket to record the number as he had done since his heart attack.

She stayed huddled in the dark between the light of the house and the light of the barn.

Her brother walked out of the barn. Look at that moon, he said.

She looked.

Beautiful thing, he said.

The same moon was in the war, she thought, and it felt like she was having his thought.

Then he shook his head and headed toward the house. She didn't wonder whether he'd killed anyone. She watched his shadow, to see if maybe it had changed like he had, too.

* * *

It's morning, and their mother's at the stove turning pancakes. Their father's counting his pulse again. He records the number. He slips the notebook into his breast pocket.

Good? her brother says.

Fine, her father says.

What was it? her mother says.

Her father taps the table where his name and her mother's names are carved. When your mother and I were first married, he says, I carved our names into a tree.

And it was dying but you didn't know it, the girl thinks.

And it was dying, but I didn't know it, her father says.

What were the numbers? her mother says, pointing at his heart or little notebook.

So, to save our names, her father says, I cut down the tree and made a table out of it. Took all of a week to pull that tree down.

We bought the table at Sears, their mother says.

I made it, he says.

One minute, she says, we're standing in the store, and he's cleaning his nails with his pocketknife, waiting for the salesman.

Next thing I know he's carving the table. In the middle of the store. Your father.

It was romantic, he says.

Like he's Davy Crockett or something, her mother says.

We'd already bought it, he says.

By the mere fact of your carving it, yes. But no, we hadn't actually bought it yet.

The girl and her brother are laughing.

I had to carve it there, their father says, because, you see, kids, the bark around your mother's heart was too hard. When I met her, she pretended she was soft as pine, but I learned. Thick as cherry. And, children, remember, cherry isn't the whittling kind.

Talk and noise, her mother says, as she does after one of his stories, like the one about the doctors finding a bomb in his chest where his heart should have been.

You should have seen the doctors, he says, their faces, like they were breaking news. Said I knew all about the bomb. Course I knew. Had to stuff something in the hole after I gave my heart to your mother.

You really say that? her brother says, smiling.

Of course he said it, their mother says. He thinks a patient's job is to entertain. Doctors make your father nervous. Besides, I thought your heart was the bomb, their mother says to him, and your heart attack happened because I forgot I put your heart under my pillow and rolled onto it.

Same difference, their father says.

The girl imagines her father pushing his heart gently into her mother's hands, saying, Take care of this bomb my heart.

Doctors should make everyone nervous, her father says.

Doctors are here to save people, her mother says.

And that's why you can't trust them. Like a pack of bloodhounds come running into your backyard.

Bloodhounds? her mother says, rolling her eyes.

Then no one's at the table or in the kitchen. Because now all memories end with everyone where they were, but aren't.

* * *

Most of her memories of her brother are amber, like the glasses at the diner where they ate breakfast every Saturday after the doctor discovered their mother's cancer too late. Then their father died. Then their mother said, Please don't leave again. And the girl's brother said, Okay. So their mother said to the doctors, No more treatments. I can't take any more.

Then the girl and her brother were sitting in the funeral-home office again, with the undertaker and his catalog of caskets, and his son in a hand-me-down suit. Afterward, her brother drove her to the grocery and they bought slushies and drank them at a picnic bench outside. A few people stopped by with their carts and condolences. Sorry to hear. A terrible thing, of course. Can't imagine, of course.

Now what? the girl said.

You go to school until you graduate, he said.

Then what?

Get the hell out.

What about me? she said.

That is you. You fill your head. You get the hell out. Fall in love maybe. Have babies, maybe.

She laughed.

That funny? he said.

Sort of, she said.

I'll be a good uncle. Take them to the fair, spoil them.

Buy them kites, she said.

He looked at her.

She looked away.

Why'd you say that?

You could have kids, she said.

About the kite, why'd you say that?

It was stupid, she said. I'm sorry.

Anyway, he said, I've already got a kid.

She looked up.

You, kiddo.

I'm your sister.

You're everything now, he said. But he said it in the way that reminded her of him cursing the town. This goddamned town.

What about you?

You don't worry about me. Things happen. It's hard to know.

Are you going to die? she said.

Everybody does, he said.

She looked away.

You miss them, he said.

She nodded.

Me, too.

The sun felt good on her back. The grocery doors whooshed open when people stepped on the mats, and the cold air hit her in the face.

* * *

She would hear him crying in his bedroom. She heard him leave the house, the car drive away. In the morning, their parents were still dead. But at least he came back.

* * *

At first he wouldn't let her help him bury the landmines. But she just joined him one day, and after that, he didn't try to stop her. Early on, they didn't wear blindfolds or stocking caps rolled down to their chins when they dug the holes for the mines. Hearts racing and cheeks flush, they'd return to the field with the cardboard tray, then crouch side by side and pluck each one like an overfilled pastry and set it into a new hole—his tongue wedged in the corner of his mouth, her standing above him to block the sun from his eyes.

Once the mines were buried, in a line or a semicircle, they'd run back and forth, jumping over the dirt piles like he'd taught her to jump crawdad holes.

Jack be nimble, he called.

Jack be quick, she called.

When their faces were flush and they had a hard time catching their breath, he sent her into the house while he dug up the mines and set them into the tray like their mother removing her glass ornaments from the Christmas tree.

Back inside, her brother would open the freezer and take out two frosted cups. He poured himself a beer and her a soda, and they clinked glasses like he showed her. Maybe he sang a toast from the war, or maybe they talked or just traced their parents' names in the table.

What would you do if Mom and Dad were alive? the girl said, one time.

Both? her brother said.

She thought. Yeah. Both.

Move to Florida, probably.

Florida? she said.

Yeah. I like it there.

We've never been there, she said.

I went.

She tried to remember.

Between tours, her brother said. I went there instead of here. Nobody knew. I just went.

Oh.

Are you mad?

I don't know.

Did you see a mermaid? she said.

Aren't you a little old to believe in mermaids? he said.

She felt slapped. She opened her mouth. She closed it. She looked at the refrigerator. There was a little seagull magnet their grandmother gave their mother.

Yeah, I saw a mermaid, he said. Of course I saw mermaids. Lots. Every morning, they'd be out there on the shore when I woke up, sunning themselves and collecting the seashells that washed up in the night like coins.

Were they beautiful?

No, he said, but the place where I stayed was. Little town by the ocean. Lot of people who worked the circus live there in their off-season. Some mornings, they'd go down to the beach and practice. Tight-rope, juggling—the works. While fishermen walk up the dock with their silver lunch pails.

You should have joined it, the girl said.

The circus? Believe me, I thought about it, he said.

But you didn't.

Doesn't look like it.

Let's go, the girl said.

To Florida?

Sure. There's a map in the car.

You're in school, he said.

There are schools there.

You'll miss it here, miss your friends, your teachers. It's not good moving all around.

We could go for a little bit and come back.

Maybe next summer, he said.

There's a lot of young people down there, you know, she said.

Right, he said, laughing.

She smiled.

Because that's what their grandmother had said after their mother's funeral, when their grandparents came back to the house

before driving back across the state to their own. Their grandparents
sat on the couch, balancing paper plates on their knees.

Don't you have TV trays? their grandfather said.

We could eat on the table outside, I guess, her brother said.

Too cold, their grandmother said and raised a chicken leg to
her lips and pulled at it with her teeth.

What you need to do, their grandfather said, is sell this place,
move some place nice.

Lots of young people in Florida, their grandmother said.

Beautiful place, their grandfather said. Some ugly parts about
it, but ugly's everywhere. Can't escape that.

The girl tried to catch her brother's eye. All she knew about
Florida were the souvenirs decorating their grandparents' house:
the tiny crab claws and seashells and bamboo wind chimes and
the plastic coasters encasing sand dollars.

This is good potato salad, their grandmother said. Do you
know who made it?

Mom, the girl said.

Just the right amount of crunch, their grandmother said.

She used to make it all the time, the girl said. You've had it
before.

Their grandmother nodded. I'll have to get the recipe from you
before we leave.

* * *

The girl sets the small shovel by her leg and leans back on her
heels, rolling back her shoulders. They ache. The wings are heavier
than they felt when she first came out here. Her jeans are dirty.
She digs into the field she cannot see and will not see until after
she buries the landmine and has walked away. Sweat in her hair,
between her shoulder blades, damp in her scarf that she's tossed
to the side, her coat heating up like a greenhouse.

The hole is now deep enough that when she reaches in, her shoulder is flush with the plane of the field. She flattens her palm against the bottom of the hole, curling her fingers slightly because the hole is deeper than wide. Legs straight, she rocks back on her toes like a cat stretching. The backs of her knees burn, her thighs burn. The wings tip awkwardly. She carefully pushes her weight into her hand, rolling her fingers against the dirt, like when her father took her to the city hall when she was little, and the police officer rolled her fingers into an ink pad and then pressed them onto a piece of paper should someone kidnap her and drop her in a farming ditch.

The air on her sweaty skin is cooling, clammy. It's coming nighttime. She pours a little water in the hole.

She takes the mine from her pocket and sets it in the hole. She rocks back on her heels, resting her bottom on the backs of her sneakers.

She might walk through the field day after day, year after year, following the sled that death pulls until the rope frays and splits, and she can sit down on it. It's also the only way she knows how to keep living. Because she can't die and leave the ground like this, for some stranger to discover.

She lifts the dented watering can over the hole, its spout duct-taped on by her father after it fell off the porch. She pours the water against the side of the hole like her brother poured beer against the inside of a glass. At the kitchen table in the low light, he seemed calmest, like all the world was right as the frost on his glass disappeared where the beer hit and most of the house was in shadow.

* * *

He inherited the house and his sister and the corn and beans and the town and the oil derricks burning against the nights, pumping blood into bank accounts. He inherited all he had meant to leave

forever, even his face tied with a yellow ribbon to a light post on
Central Street, in front of the diner where he once sat as a little
boy with his father, with his first sweetheart, with his little sister,
her pigtails backlit by the diner window.

She liked how the amber glasses sparkled on the plastic
tablecloths and up the window they sat in front of. She liked
resting her chin on the tablecloth and turning the glass as she
peered at him through the ice cubes, as if he couldn't see her, as
if one of them was locked in an amber mountain.

Amber bulbs in the lantern that hung above their front door.
Amber beads on the string necklace someone gave her that she
could wrap around her neck four times, and still hangs down to
her belly button though she can wrap it only three times. She is
older now, her head larger, her heart, her pain larger, but the
necklace the same, making her childhood seem smaller than it
might have been. She isn't sure.

Amber memories, an amber childhood, a brother encased in
amber like a fossil in the mail-order archeology kit he had sent
her through the mail one Christmas.

Once, he brought a girlfriend with them to Saturday breakfast
at the diner, one of the girls who rode with the family to pick him
up from the airport and hung around a few days until she saw he
wasn't the same, or wasn't ready to propose, or wasn't interested in
driving with her to the nearest university and some party in some
apartment where the college boys leaned against doorways and
counters and smiled down at the girls in sequins and halter tops.

The girlfriend, who had evidently spent the night, sat in the
passenger seat of the car where the girl's mother should have been
sitting. The girlfriend looked into the visor mirror at herself, then
into the backseat where the sister sat. Well, aren't you cute?

The girl met her brother's eyes in the rearview mirror. His eyes
agreed he'd made a mistake, but could she just bear with him until
after breakfast? So she did and he never brought another woman

to the diner. Though there were still others who she might run into in the hallway on her way to the bathroom in the middle of the night, or in the living room, curled on the couch and wearing one of her brother's T-shirts.

You must be . . . the woman would say.

Yeah, she'd say, and pick the TV remote off the table and change the channel to whatever she wanted to watch.

He's told me so much about you.

I've never heard about you, she'd say, if she said anything. But usually she didn't, until the woman would start fidgeting and glancing down the hallway as though he were about to appear, even though they could both hear him snoring.

After he died, the women came around less. At first, she was glad, because she wanted to be his only griever. But then she got angry. Where was everyone? Didn't anyone notice him missing?

A few women came to the door and knocked. One woman kicked the trash bag on the porch while she waited. Another cupped her hands to the window by the front door. Then turned down the steps and crossed the yard, like the teenage girls who used to sneak into his room at night or midafternoon while she and their mother ran errands in town and their father walked through the fields, wondering how to keep it from falling apart.

A few of his old high-school buddies left messages on the answering machine, but once their mother died and he'd become the girl's guardian, everyone had all but disappeared. People let people disappear much faster than the girl ever would have thought.

* * *

Sometimes, they missed uprooting a mine, usually because he had a hard time saying it was time to put them back, always wanting to run one more time across the field.

Alone this time, he'd say, waving her back.

And she'd stand on the edge of the patio, clenching her toes and holding her breath as he ran, speeding up just like when he did pole vault on the track behind the high school. But this time there was no pole to aim at the edge of a mat as it bowed his lean body into the air.

One more time, he'd say as he walked back to her on the patio.

Okay, she'd say.

Until it was nighttime, and they had to work by flashlight to dig them up. Sometimes that night, or the next week, or a month later, a coyote would explode or maybe a cat, as though in heat, yowling and rolling circles in the dust. And then she did.

* * *

And all the king's horses and all the king's men, he's saying, and his face blocks the sun from her eyes, her bone and flesh curled back, blood freckling her cheek and forehead.

Little sparrow, he says. My little sparrow, he says.

* * *

She fills the hole with water so that the dirt doesn't fall hard and set it off. Anything can. It's fragile, or maybe just real, and all the bombs should be thought of as fragile. She pushes in dirt then waits as it sinks before pushing in more. Once the hole is full, she pats it down like her brother would.

In one of his first letters home that their mother read to the girl and her father, he wrote that the explosions reminded him of the stone quarry or what their mother called a sonic boom, which the girl thought meant the spray planes over the fields had flown too low. Then, when he got home and heard the stone-quarry blasts, she watched his face and tried to imagine the faraway fields.

* * *

The wind chimes clank from one end of the clothesline. It's time to put them away for winter. It's dark now, dark as the nights that her brother walked home drunk, shirt unbuttoned, shoes in one hand and the invisible glass he'd raise to the crickets.

She stands up, careful not to lean on the ground to help herself up. She turns toward where the house may be. She'll be safe when she bumps against the back railing, like swimming into the wall of the public pool, eyes closed, her shadow mermaiding beneath her on the cement floor.

Once she's safe, she'll open the screen door, its screens bowled by years of wind. And she'll walk inside, into the living room, up the stairs and down the hallway and into his room or her parents' room and she'll slip off the knit cap and unbuckle the belt and open her eyes.

* * *

As he stood in the field, he saw himself standing in a rainbow, and he turned, searching until he saw his sister standing on the roof of the house. She dangled the stained-glass mermaid from her fingers, raising her hand up and down as though floating it on an ocean of sky.

It was one of the trinkets he'd bought her from the gas station.

The sun flashed like a song through the stained glass, a colored web fragmenting his little sister's face with the lead-frame lines.

It was beautiful.

He stepped toward it and the mine went off.

* * *

His bed smelled like he was alive, like he hadn't showered in a few days, the sheet oily like his back. The room was dark, sheets draped over the curtains. When she fell asleep, she dreamed him in a field, playing drums. Soldiers sat around him, guns on their backs, clapping to the beat. Then the drums exploded. She woke up. And she did not wake up. Just as she didn't fully wake up after their mother came out of her father's hospital room and said he was dead. Just as she didn't fully wake up after the doctors said it was cancer, and she walked in on her mother laying naked in bed, staring at the ceiling, hands on her breasts.

Some days, the girl spent whole afternoons in his bedroom, turning his lamp on and off, wishing she could simultaneously walk past the house, see the light flashing and think the light was him or his ghost. Maybe living with his ghost wouldn't be any better—maybe then she'd have different questions and worries, but she would just like to see him again, outside of herself. She wanted new memories not of her making.

Several nights she awoke thinking his ghost was in the house, and one night it climbed through his bedroom window. She held still, clutching the bedspread. The ghost tripped on a chair. Cursed. Then climbed into bed. The ghost smelled like chemical flowers. The ghost threaded its arm down the girl's waist and up under her arms, against her chest.

I missed you, the ghost whispered in a woman's voice.

The girl lay still.

I been calling and calling you. The ghost whispered, pressed her thighs under the girl's legs.

Then the ghost was snoring, its breath a mix of peppermint and beer.

The girl wondered if she were the ghost. If she were dead, and had somehow become her brother. The ghost was warm. The girl fell asleep, into nightmares of her brother alive but knowing he was dead, and how angry he was, how angry he was to be dead.

When the girl woke up, the ghost was a woman in the crack of morning light. Lips crackled with wine.

The girl went downstairs to make breakfast. She tried to think what to say when the woman came down and asked where he was. It was almost noon by the time the woman woke up. The girl was watching cartoons on TV.

The woman sat down on the couch next to her.

Hey, she said.

Hey, the girl said.

I used to watch this one when I was a kid, the woman said.

The girl didn't know what to say, so she didn't.

Is he not here? the woman said.

No, the girl said. There's cereal if you want some. Or oatmeal.

Do you remember me? the woman said.

The girl shook her head.

Do you know when he'll be back?

The girl shook her head again. The woman looked at her. You got his eye color.

The girl hoped nothing walked over a landmine while the woman sat here.

The woman took a cell phone out and typed with her thumbs. Until a car pulled into the driveway and honked. Just tell them to come in, her father would say. Yeah, yeah, her brother would say as he turned to the door.

That's my ride, the woman said.

Okay, the girl said.

The woman shouldered her purse and pulled at her shorts. See you around, I guess.

On TV, a person shook her hair, happy with her shampoo.

* * *

Her brother watched the field. The girl watched his face.

He said that sometimes a landmine will go off in the faraway place, and when the soldiers go to find what's left, they find nothing, like a ghost set it off.

What do you think of that? he asked her.

She watched his face to know what she thought of it.

* * *

She dug though the shredded rucksack pocket for the red address book their mother gave him when he left the first time, their address already written into it.

You think I could forget? he said, laughing.

Of course not, their mother said.

Oh, he said. I get it.

What? she said.

It's like your version of a dog tag.

No, it's not like that, their mother said.

It's okay, he said.

It's not, she said, reaching for the book.

He pulled it back against his chest.

Seriously, Mom, it's fine.

You're not going to die, she said.

Maybe, he said.

You won't, she said.

By now the book was full of names, addresses to people she'd never met but who met him as he followed what the war left behind. Folded bar napkins, business cards, his familiar small, loopy cursive.

The woman who had helped put her back together was in there, the medic. She was on a glossy blue business card, a picture of her smiling with lipstick and a black blazer. Real estate. She sold houses.

The girl remembered the woman leaning over her. This will hurt, and I'm sorry, the woman said. The woman's T-shirt gaped at the neck so the girl saw her breasts. It reminded her of the orthodontist, leaning over her with his face mask, the thick black hairs in his nose.

You won't remember the pain later, the woman said.

And she didn't.

The girl took the business card to the couch and picked up the telephone like the game she and her brother played with old phones in the thrift store, raising them to their ears, saying, You'll have to talk louder, I can't hear you.

What?!

You'll have to talk louder, I can't hear you!

What?!

The girl dialed the phone number.

The woman answered.

The sound of the woman's voice, the deep realness of it in the girl's ear did something inside her, and she had to clench her teeth to keep from crying.

I need you to stop calling me, the woman said.

The girl held the phone closer to her ear.

Listen, the woman said. I can't do this anymore.

The girl set the phone back in the cradle, feeling it click.

* * *

Grief, a lamp burning for years inside an empty bedroom. Grief, the faded patch of carpet where the sun has burned every day of years.

How strange that, alive or dead, her brother didn't know when she was thinking of him.

* * *

He said, When it has rained and the ground is saturated to the core, and a landmine goes off, there's no dust, only clumps of wet earth. In drought, there's so much dust there isn't enough blood to weight it all back to the ground.

Between two tours he worked at the factory.

How it is? their mother asked him.

He shook his head.

It's not forever, their mother said.

It's like a fucked up high-school reunion.

The girl laughed.

Watch your mouth, their mother said. You don't have to talk like that.

Sorry, he said.

What's it all about? he said.

What's what all about? their mother said.

You know, he said, spreading his arms and looking around.

I don't have all the answers.

How about one? Even one would be an improvement.

Okay, she said.

Well, how can you keep going to church?

Their mother looked at the girl, then at him, then back at the calendar where she was writing in their father's upcoming heart appointments. They'd just come back from another doctor, and he was upstairs, having a nap. There was to be a surgery, follow-ups, another surgery.

Same as the sun keeps coming back, I guess, their mother said.

Simple as that, huh? he said, but his tone was hard, sarcastic.

Seems pretty complicated to me, their mother said.

He shook his head.

Their mother reached across the table and took his hands. She turned them over in hers, touching his knuckles with her thumbs. His hands looked like the battered wings of angels exhausted from crawling in forgotten fields then digging out landmines before the war ended and everyone went home except the people who lived in the field and walked across it to get their mail or meet a neighbor or chase a spitting grasshopper as it sprang over an unseen mine—until days or a lifetime after the war, while pulling a sled or pushing croquet hoops into the yard, someone stepped down. And the earth shifted. And the mine blew. A heart into the tree branches.

My baby, she said.

Not anymore.

She lifted his hands to her face and kissed the backs of them, then set them down on the table and looked away.

* * *

She crosses the field to the fence, resting her hands lightly on the barbed wire.

Depending on the direction she turns, she'll follow the fence right back to the house, or the fence will take her around most of the field before reaching the house.

Once she reaches the house, she won't return to the field for a while. Maybe she'll wait for one of the first winter rains that come one after another, dropping the temperature until the sky is white as the snow that will come any day. Maybe she'll wait until spring before she walks back onto patio and into the back yard that turns into cornfields. But she will walk before the farmers start moving the seed that will blossom only once.

Though she will not know where the mine is, she doesn't yet know that she will never forget it's out there. And when she realizes this, she will buckle the belt around her eyes and slip on the gray stocking cap and take the cardboard tray again into the field, burying but never exhuming, going out there until she doesn't cover her eyes. She will begin close to the house, digging around the doors and windows, mine after mine until the tray is empty, and if she does make it back to the house, she will finally be trapped there by her own death and no one else's.

THE FISH

———

She's asleep when he pulls over to make a reservation. The place looks pretty run down. Parking lot's cracking. A couple kids in turquoise polo shirts lean against the corner of the hotel, smoking cigarettes and watching him. The lot around the hotel is weedy, a large wooden FOR SALE sign on the edge of the road.

But that won't matter after dark, he thinks. That won't matter tonight. Hardly noticeable, maybe. He locks the car around his wife. The small bag he packed is in the backseat. He's pleased with the efficiency of it. He never packed for them before. He enjoyed it. She might say it was the novelty of it, and knowing he likely wouldn't again.

Regardless, once she finally fell asleep in the bathtub last night and he helped her climb out and shuffle to bed, it felt good to have a task after he finished cleaning out the tub. Not that he believed she'd still want to help her grandfather today, but the possibility sent him into the basement to do laundry, and then back upstairs to take down the overnight bag that they probably would have used for the delivery.

There used to be a little muffin store inside the hotel, she'd told him on when they drove past it on other visits to see her grandparents. And the muffins! she'd say. Mom and I would get these wonderful blueberry muffins in the morning while Dad was still asleep. Jesus, they were good.

We could stop, he'd say. Get one.

But she always waved him off. What if they aren't as good as I remember?

Inside the hotel lobby, he looks for the muffin store. From the hotel's disuse, it looks like he wouldn't stick around to make a reservation if it weren't for his wife's memories. There were nicer hotels across the street, but this one will please her. Hopefully.

No one's behind the counter. He waits. He looks for a bell. She doesn't like him to ring it. Rude, she'd say.

He walks down the hallway. The floor is made of tile that looks like fake rocks, large fake rocks. The restaurant from her memory is there, surrounded by a low brick wall. A tree rises out of the restaurant and up past the surrounding balconies of rooms, up to a skylight. Nothing's remarkable about the skylight. Glass and black lead lines. Sky the white gray of early autumn mornings. For a second, he imagines it's a ship porthole, and all of this is under water. He likes illusions like that.

The tree trunk is wrapped with string lights that, if they're on, are hard to see in the early morning light but probably are very pretty in the evening, especially if you're a kid. The grand piano is there, too. A few people sit at tables drinking coffee. Their expressions suggest that they're deciding whether their stay has been worth their money.

Just like she described. Strange how you can return to the site of people's memories without them there.

And the muffin store, or what was the muffin store. Against one wall in a row of storefronts built into the wall. Something about the stores feels closed for good. A faded green and white striped awning extends over one window. Faded from what? Skylight maybe. Or the light poles cemented in the floor across from the storefronts, to create the look of a boulevard, some French sidewalk motif.

The sort of gimmick, he thinks, that means the hotel has been trying to stay afloat for a while.

He returns to the counter. He checks his watch. Same time as the large clock behind the counter. There are two more clocks, supposedly showing the times of different cities in different countries. He tries to remember the time gaps. Six hours between here and England. A woman in turquoise shirt approaches the other side of the counter.

Can I help you? she says.

My wife's having a miscarriage, he thinks.

She tilts her head as though she heard him, but isn't sure if she heard him right.

Sure, he says. Her name is printed on white tape across a metal nametag.

High turnover, he thinks.

A room, he says.

Do you have reservations?

No, I need to make them.

She nods and starts typing into a computer. How many? she says.

One room.

People, she says.

Two and one on the way, he thinks. Not anymore.

It's me and my wife.

So, two, she says.

He nods, but she doesn't look up. She types more.

The elevator dings, and he turns to watch. Maybe his wife will step out, aged seven or eight, in the black and pink bathing suit from the picture of her standing in a hotel room, holding a balloon and a vase of flowers her older sister sent her as a surprise for her birthday.

Another woman in a turquoise shirt comes out of the elevator. She's pushing a housekeeping cart. It rattles against the floor.

Freight elevator's out again, she says as she passes the counter.

I told Carl a hundred times already, says the woman behind the counter.

Tell him again. Ask him first, does he have his listening ears on? That's what I say to my kids.

The women smirk then laugh. He wants to laugh with them.

Business or pleasure, the woman behind the counter says, after printing a stack of documents.

What's that?

The occasion for your stay. Business or pleasure?

One of those, he says.

The woman stares at him, not smiling. As though that part of the training wasn't covered, or she skipped that day.

He hopes his wife won't wake up in the parking lot, won't wander into the hotel looking for him, palefaced, weak. She said she doesn't hurt like last night. She lay in the bathtub, naked, the faucet running over her, waiting for him to bring the prescription the midwife sent him to get from Walgreens. The first Walgreens was closed, so he had to drive across town to the other. The pharmacist was nice to him. Because she knew, of course. Those drugs. The time of night. And probably it was all over him, though he'd tucked in his shirt on his way in from the parking lot.

The bleeding will last a while. Days.

But, still. She should be at home, not en route to help her grandfather move into a retirement community. She should be asleep. He should be asleep. Everyone, he thinks, should be asleep.

But when she woke up, she insisted they still go. He has to be out today, she said.

After living there for, what, sixty years? he said. How does one day make a difference?

It's in the contract, she said. The next people move in tomorrow.

It's just a contract.

I'm going.

It doesn't seem like a good idea.

What do you want me to do? Lay around here all day?

That's what I was thinking, yes. After last night.

She looked away, blinking.

He waited. He knew not to touch her or she'd cry, or tell him, Don't touch me or I'll cry.

The house felt so still around them. The sheet was white and patterned with clusters of blueberries. She'd changed the bedspread to a heavier one a week or so ago.

It'll be good to go, she said, looking back at him. Half smiling.

You don't have to prove anything, he said.

It'll be good, she said again, smiling harder. I mean it. Unless you want to fight me, she said. She batted his arm with her fists. Put 'em up, she said.

He knocked his fist gently against hers.

Good, she said. Now help me get dressed.

He laughed. But she wasn't joking.

* * *

She doesn't wake up when he gets back in the car. Once he reaches the city, he starts turning onto the streets that lead to her grandparents' house. Each street seems to deteriorate more. Colors fading, paint peeling, yards growing taller. Even the city bus seems more sluggish. He drives beside it for a while, feeling sad.

Are we there yet? she says.

Almost.

She looks out the window. It's good he's leaving, she says. Right?

Right.

The car smells like fast-food breakfast. The afghan her grandmother made her still covers her legs, bunched in her lap. The same grandmother who used to live in this house.

It still feels shitty, she says. If Grandma were still alive, they wouldn't be moving.

That wouldn't make it the right decision.

I guess, she says.

When they pull up in front of the brick house, her grandfather's sitting on the porch swing. The old man waves when he recognizes them. The large pots on either side of the porch are empty of the flowers her grandmother grew in them.

We don't have to stay the whole day, he says.

I know, she says.

If you start to feel bad, just tell me. I'll take care of it.

I'll be fine.

Yeah, yeah. Just if you start not to be fine.

She waves up at the old man, who's standing now, shielding his eyes from the sun even though the porch roof still casts him in shade.

He rolls down the window. Should I park in the alley?

The old man shakes his head, and cups his ear. Smiles.

Just get out and ask him, she says.

Here or alley? he shouts again.

There's good, the old man shouts back.

Across the street, a few people sit on the stairs of a house. Their windows are covered in sheets.

Don't tell him, okay? she says as her grandfather watches them get out.

Did he know you were?

Yeah, she says. He seemed down one day. I thought it would cheer him up.

Did it?

She nods. It was nice telling him, she says. Her eyes are getting watery.

They'd read that it might be better to wait until the second trimester to make the announcement, and they'd agreed to wait, but it seemed for a while that each day he came home from work, she'd told another person. I thought we'd agreed, he said. It's hard to contain this joy, she said. And he knew what she meant. He'd told a few people at work, just enough that everyone knew fairly soon.

He wonders where she put the list of baby names they'd worked on together one morning. They'd gone out to breakfast. That was a good morning.

* * *

Her grandparents' house had sold in no time. No surprise, really. A beautiful house. Brick, one story but with a basement and attic. Tall ceilings, tall windows. Well maintained. Craftsman, the realtor said when she first walked through the house, taking notes.

I'm not going to lie to you, the realtor said, houses like this, no matter how well they've been kept, aren't going for much in this neighborhood right now. In a different neighborhood, it'd be a different story. A house like this, I could get you twice this, easily. She pointed at the number she'd written down.

We could wait, the old man said.

Waiting won't change much, I'm afraid, the realtor said. At this rate, waiting is the worse-until-better scenario, and I can't promise that the better will happen.

You look a little spent, her grandfather says to her when she reaches the top of the stairs and steps onto the porch where she once roller-skated, because the sidewalks, even then, were being pushed up by the heavy roots of the giant oak and sycamore trees.

He has always found something threatening about trees doing that.

Didn't sleep so well, I guess, she says. She shrugs then stands tiptoe to kiss the old man's cheek, even though she's as tall as him.

Good to see you, the old man says, reaching for his hand. Old man used to be a door-to-door salesman and still has the handshake.

Good grip, the old man says. Just like always. Ever think about going into sales?

Don't think that I have.

Good man, says the old man and squeezes the back of his neck. He opens the front door, and steps back to wave them in. Let me show you what I've been up to.

Up to? she says. We're here to help.

Can't say that it's done, he says, but it's pretty near it. We'll be able to break early for lunch. And before you argue, he says, wagging his finger at them, I'm buying lunch. Got a special down at the deli right now, heck of a sandwich.

* * *

The house is incredibly empty. So empty there's an echo to their voices when they talk.

We were going to help you with this, she says.

What else do I have to do, huh? her grandfather says, gruffly, but clearly pleased at her response.

I don't know. Watch baseball. Go to the store. Visit your friends.

Not many of those around here anymore.

I mean, it's great, she says. It just seems like a lot to do by yourself.

Do you need to sit down? her husband says.

Where? she says, looking around. The entryway is stacked with boxes. The living room is empty of furniture. The couch and matching recliners. The lampstands. All of it. And the dining room. The long table with its eight chairs, too. The buffet. The family pictures that were on the buffet are on the carpet, leaning against the wall.

There's one chair left, the old man says. In the kitchen.

I'm fine, she says. But the old man is already walking away.

It won't be as hard a job as I thought, she says.

That's good, he says.

Maybe I should have stayed home, after all.

He wants to agree. Instead, he says, No, it's good you're here. He's glad to see you. It's important.

You think so? she says.

Here you go, the old man says, crossing the house with the old wooden kitchen chair. He sets it behind her. Pats it.

Almost let them take this, the old man says.

Who?

Donation truck. In fact, I did forget, and had to get them to take it out of the truck. They were nice about it, though.

I thought you were going to sell the furniture, sell as much as you could anyway.

Too much hassle, the old man says.

It was worth a lot, she says.

Then let it be worth a lot. I've no need for it.

It's not exactly free, your new place.

The old man shifts from one foot to another. His smile wavers. I didn't know I was making a mistake, he says.

It's fine, she says. I just. It's fine.

When you feel rested, I want to show you the backyard. That's what I've been working hardest on.

I'm fine, she says.

Take your time. Two of you now, he says.

* * *

They follow the old man through the house and onto the back stoop where, at one time, the milk was delivered.

I don't understand, she says.

The backyard is covered with holes. About half are filled, some with potting soil. The birdbath is still there, but as though to mark where one of the gardens was. A shovel leans against it.

Did someone take Grandma's garden?

It's in the garage, her grandfather says, pointing at the leaning structure at the back of the yard, alongside the alley that runs behind all of these houses. A few black plastic pots of flowers sit on the stepping stones. The old man points at them. Just a few more left, he says, and I'll have it all.

I still don't understand, she says.

I'm taking it with me, he says.

You're taking it with you, she says. The garden?

Her garden.

Grandma's flowers. All of them.

That's right.

She nods, slowly.

It's a small room, remember? she says. I mean, it's a nice apartment, but it's small.

I'll make room.

There's not a patio or balcony, she says. Won't they need sun?

There's windows. They've got a sale on plant stands, I saw. Figured I'd wait until I was moved in to go buy them.

She looks at her husband. He shrugs.

I mean, she says. Maybe you can take a few, but.

She's clearly waiting for the old man to respond with her thoughts. To have a realization about the flowers.

But, he says.

Well. You can't just take *all* of them, she says. Not just because there isn't room, but because when you sold the house, you sold the yard, too.

I didn't sell these flowers.

You did, she says. Sold means everything in and around the house. Sold even means the new curtains we bought for the showing.

Hell if I did. They're Evelyn's. My wife's, he says. *Your* grandmother's, he says, pointing at her like a traitor.

She holds up her hands.

Not anybody else's, he says.

Out front of the house, a car drives by, its bass thumping loudly.

* * *

Now, she's in her grandparents' bedroom, and her grandfather is out getting some fresh air. He's not sure what to do, so he's sitting on the lone kitchen chair in the living room, reading an old newspaper. An article about next week's junior-high jazz concert and spaghetti supper. But next week is now this week. So, yesterday. Last night. They missed it.

Because there was blood in her underwear.

Then her voice calling out to him from the bathroom. And he's rushing in. And she's on the toilet, holding a wad of toilet paper in her hand, holding it up to show him. That's blood, she says.

It's so bright, he thinks.

She wipes again. Shows him. I keep trying, she says. But it's never just white.

He uses her phone to call the midwife.

In the background, his wife is saying, Should I bring the toilet paper with me? Ask her.

Sure, the midwife says.

So they do. In plastic baggies from the kitchen drawer where they also keep the wax paper and aluminum foil.

Do you hurt? he asks her as he helps her down the stairs of the house.

Not yet, she says.

Into the car.

His wife cradling her belly across town, though she hasn't started showing yet. Cramps, she says.

The midwife meets them at the front door. They follow her into the small room. His wife sits on the bed. She takes the baggies from her purse. The midwife holds them up, looking.

Then leads them into the ultrasound room. It's an old machine, but does the job. That's what she'd said their first appointment, when they saw the baby in there, not even a baby yet. When the midwife had trouble dating it, moving a small plastic wheel this way, then that way. This many weeks or this many weeks. When did you say your last period was?

I have long gaps between my periods, his wife explained.

Well, you're definitely pregnant. There's no question about that.

Then the drive home. And how excited they were.

Then the drive home last night, not even two months later. His wife leaning her head against the passenger window. Purse in her lap. The traffic lights kept changing. Other traffic followed the rules. A few people waited at a bus stop. How can that be?

Then they are home. She lies on the couch. He brings pillows in from the bedroom.

Do you want to watch TV? he says. If there had been plants in front of the couch instead of a TV, he thinks he would have asked her if she'd like to water the plants.

That'd be alright, she says.

How do you feel?

I don't know what's happening, she says.

I know.

It's going to get worse, I guess.

That's what she said, he says.

Okay.

He sits next to her. She lifts her feet on his legs. He offers her the remote. She shakes her head. You choose, she says. Something with people laughing, she says.

* * *

He sets aside the newspaper. Must have been dozing off. Because he has a swimmy feeling in his head. The last story he was reading, about a new cub at the city zoo. The rise in visitors may be what keeps the zoo from shutting down, after years of mismanagement.

He stands up. He stretches. This way, that way. It feels good. He calls out her name, but she doesn't answer. Maybe she fell asleep, too.

On his way to her grandparents' bedroom, he glances in the backyard. Her grandfather is back there, bringing his foot down on a shovel. Sheen of sweat on his forehead. There's something noble about it, he thinks.

Her grandparents' bedroom is empty except for one twin bed. It's a beautiful bedroom, mainly because one wall is windows looking into the row of trees that divide this house from the neighbor's. It's a small gap between the houses, close as touching, really.

You don't see windows like that much anymore, the realtor said.

Original to the house, the old man said.

Beautiful, the realtor said. When you buy curtains for these windows, she said, turning to the granddaughter, make them light, sheer.

Gets pretty cold in the winter, the old man said. Need thicker curtains to keep in the heat.

Of course, the realtor said. These would be just for show. For the eye.

The old man peered at her like he didn't understand.

I was just reading, the granddaughter said, about how some people bake cookies on days that people will be coming by to show the house.

The realtor nodded. Some do that, yes. Staging. Some realtors even hire families.

What? the old man said.

Actors, his granddaughter said. To pretend they live there.

What's wrong with people? the old man said.

Probably the actors don't move quietly through the rooms, explaining that now isn't the best time to show them what was supposed to be the nursery.

The leaves on the row of trees are changing, bright reds and yellows. When the dresser stood here, the mirror reflected them like those photographs of water where it's hard to tell which is reflection and which is casting it, so you have to decide first, then look to see if you're right. Both skies can't be reflection, surely.

The lightness of this bedroom. He wishes he knew how to recreate that.

There's a pile of clothing on her grandfather's twin bed, still on hangers.

She's in front of the closet, nearly in it, staring up. For a second, it's easy for them to imagine them into younger versions of her grandparents. Just married. Having just bought this house, the moving truck on the way. So much possibility in the changing leaves.

Would you look at this, his wife says.

He checks the back of her jeans for blood.

She points up at the closet shelf.

He moves close enough to touch her. There's a patch of sunlight on the carpet.

She gestures toward the top of the closet, and he expects to see all of the old man's hats from his salesman days, when people opened their doors to strangers and offered them iced tea. He'd meant to ask the old man if he could have one or two. Hard to find hats like those, these days.

The hats aren't there. Instead, the shelf is lined with small, round plastic containers. Inside each is a fish.

Maybe these were under the hats all along, the man thinks.

Fish, he says.

Fish, she says.

Well, would you look at that. He takes one down. The jar is just big enough that his fingers don't fully meet. It looks like one of the containers you buy macaroni salad in from the grocery deli. There are holes in the lid.

The fish moves from his movement, its fins waver. He tries to hold his hand still. She looks through it on the other side.

I can't tell if it's dead, she says.

He carries it to the windows, then crouches as he sets it on the window seat. He waits there until the water calms. The fish doesn't move, doesn't fight the water. It floats back to the bottom, on its side.

I used to know what they're called, he says.

I can't think of it, either, she says. She combs her hands back through her hair. It will get thicker, she told him one night as she stood in the bedroom doorway brushing her hair. How's that? he said. Hormones, I guess. Prenatal vitamins. Happened to my friend, too.

He wonders if her hair did get thicker. He can't ask now.

He returns to her side at the closet. Are they all the same kind?

Looks like it, she says.

He starts to count them.

Twenty-two, she says. Twenty-two. I counted.

He counts them anyway, silently. Not because he doubts her.

Are they all? he says.

Dead?

He takes down another. The fish in this one is dark reds and burgundies. Part of it has disintegrated in the water. Floating bits. The longer he looks at it, the more he feels like he's looking away. He stacks it onto the one he's holding, balancing them against his chest as he reaches past her for a third. Then a fourth.

If you drop them, she says.

He carefully walks them to the window seat.

She sits on the bed while he carries container after container to the window seat.

What would he be doing with all these fish? she says.

Maybe he got lucky at the carnival. The fish toss, or whatever it's called.

With the ping-pong balls?

He nods.

You're joking, she says.

Yes, he says. Maybe he's been selling them door to door.

Like a scam or something?

I wasn't thinking scam. Just. He's lonely, isn't he? Since your grandmother died. That's why the move to the new place, right? So he'll make friends.

That can't be it.

He shrugs. He likes the idea of the old man laying out a suit each morning, choosing a hat, carrying a large briefcase of fish up the sidewalk. Knocking on a door. Excuse me, ma'am, but have I got a deal for you. Children following him all over town. Hey, mister, what you got there?

Only exactly what you didn't know you needed, the old man says, bowing so deeply that he scrapes his hat against the ground when he takes it off.

Man, the trees this year, he says, looking at them through the containers, sudden backdrops to these small, watery worlds.

They're beautiful, she says, not looking toward the windows or even their shadows in sunlit squares on the carpet.

A square of stained glass about the size of his hand hangs in the window. It's different blocks of color. A souvenir, probably. The way it doesn't quite fit. He touches it. It clatters against the window. He steps back.

What will we do with them? she says, looking up and down the row of containers now on the window seat.

We could put them back where we found them, he says.

Sage advice, she says.

Thank you.

Though not much of a housewarming present.

No, he says.

What's he doing with twenty-two dead fish? I mean, don't answer that. He keeps everything my grandmother ever touched, so this isn't such a surprise.

Her grandfather has been so dutiful to his dead wife that he'd even cycled his dead wife's clothes out with his, back into the Tupperware containers he kept under the bed, where the grandmother also used to keep the Christmas gifts she was sewing over the course of the year. Ornaments for the great grandchild, Christmas stockings for the newest babies. A sweater for his wife's mother. A cross-stitch of flowers like the ones that used to hang on the walls of this bedroom. Those are gone, too, he realizes.

I don't like it, she says. Dead fish where his hats should be.

He laughs.

It's not funny.

It could be, he says.

She shakes her head.

Hey, he says. Why don't we take a break? Have lunch? He's probably wearing himself out there digging up her daisies.

What a thing to say, she says.

What?

That's what people say about dead people, she says.

He thinks of their baby. No, it wasn't a baby yet. Is she thinking of it, too? He looks at her.

Digging up daisies?

That's right.

I don't think so, he says.

Digging up the daisies is right, she says.

Raising the daisies? he says, as though to himself. No. Watering the daisies. That's what it is. Watering the daisies.

That's not it, she says.

Watering the daisies. Because they're dead.

You're dead, she says.

Then give me a kiss, why don't you? he says and walks on his knees to where she sits on the bed. He rests his cheek on her leg.

Our baby's dead, she says.

Yeah, he says.

The sun through the windows behind him is warm on his back.

* * *

They sit on the porch steps, balancing paper plates on their legs. Her grandfather sits on the swing, her grandmother's pink gardening gloves folded beside him. Pink and yellow tulips on the front, little rubber dots on the palms. There's streaks of dirt on the old man's cheeks, the side of his neck. Where he must have rubbed the sweat away in the garden.

So, what's with the fish? the man says to the old man.

What's that? the old man says.

Rye bread, she says. Never liked it as a kid, and now I can't get enough.

Found twenty-two dead fish in your closet, the man says.

Oh, those, the old man says and takes a bite of his sandwich. His face is covered in white bristles. Probably he packed his razor already.

Where are your hats? she says.

The old man chews, looking out over the porch wall.

The fish are dead, Grandpa, she whispers, as though the neighbors shouldn't hear.

I know it, he says.

You know it?

Nearly dead when I bought them. A few were.

And you still bought them, the man says.

Sure, the old man says. Bought an aquarium, too. Did you find that?

She shakes her head.

Bottom of the closet. Saved it back because maybe you'd want it for the nursery or something. Help the baby sleep. Water sounds. Your grandmother used to have a noise machine and swore by it, though I didn't tell that she went to sleep any earlier.

Twenty-two fish is a lot for any tank, I'd imagine, she says.

Only a few were alive when I set it up.

Oh.

And the few left killed each other. Fighting fish. Guess they were all males that was left. That kind of fish don't do well with its kind.

Seems like the people who sold them to you would have told you. Or given you a brochure or something.

Them? They don't know nothing about fish. Nobody who sells anything these days knows anything about what they're selling except how much it is. And even then the cash register has to tell them half the time.

And half the time it doesn't even know, the man says.

Ain't that the truth, the old man says.

It's just a lot of fish, she says.

That's what I thought, he says. There were more than that. Shelf after shelf full of dying fish. The cashier didn't even know they were selling fish, much less dying ones.

They were dying in the store? she says.

That's right, he says. Nice girl, though, got on the loudspeaker, tried to send somebody to meet me there. So, I went back and waited. Waited a long time, but nobody came. So I bought two. But all the ones I had to leave weren't doing any better. I'd only gone because I'd run out of shampoo, but got turned around, found the fish. When someone finally comes, he doesn't seem that concerned. I tell him, if this were my product, I'd be concerned. He says he'll see into it. I say that's not good enough. He says I only work here. Can you believe it? I go back next day and same thing. Same fish hardly making it. And a stack more by the sink hardly making it. So I filled the cart with them. What else do I have to do with my day? That's what I figured.

I kept some of them alive a while more. It's a nice tank. Top of the line.

Probably you couldn't have done anything, she says.

Sure, I could have. That's why I tried. Living things you keep alive. That's what you do with living things.

Well, they're dead now, she says. Nothing to be done but throw them out. She's taking their plates, stacking them one on top of the other.

Help me, she says to him. The least you can do is help me. Then she's walking into the house. A fork falls off, splattering mayonnaise up her leg. Goddammit, she says. Her grandfather stands to help. I've got it, she says, bending down. Then she's in the house.

It's hard on them, the old man says, nodding toward the house. He nods.

* * *

It's late when they reach the hotel. Ta-da, he says as he pulls into the parking lot.

What's this?

Thought we could spend the night here.

I can make the rest of the drive.

He reaches across her and opens the glove compartment, hands her the hotel room swipe cards. Already made a reservation, he says.

She smiles. Okay, she says. Is that what the bag in the backseat is about?

I packed efficiently, he says.

I'm sure you did.

He wants to tell her about doing laundry in the basement last night. The cold bare floor. The way the inside of the washing machine seemed like a pregnant woman. How when he moved the laundry from the washer to the dryer, he had a strange feeling like he was delivering it. He found a pack of cards in one of the overhead cabinets where she keeps the detergent. He'd sat at the table while he waited, playing solitaire. Game after game, even after the dryer buzzed.

He offers her his arm as they approach the sliding doors. She takes it.

It's a different woman in a turquoise shirt at the counter. She watches them. He waves like he knows her. She doesn't wave back.

It's still here! his wife says, pointing at the gift shop. It's dark, closed sign on the door.

I bought a ceramic heart from there, she says, with my name on it. I'd forgotten about that. She pulls away to peer against the dark window. A rack of postcards by the door. Pictures of leaves changing, of regional landmarks, of cornfields, soybean fields— pictures for people not from here to send to people not from here.

And the elevator, she says, pointing again.

Makes sense it's still here, he says.

Funny guy, she says.

The freight elevator is broken, though, he says. You know how Carl is.

What?

He laughs.

One of your inside jokes with yourself?

Yep.

The sound of a piano playing drifts from the restaurant. The lights are pretty in the tree.

The tree! she says.

Their room is on the fourth floor, so they take the elevator. She passes her hand over the walls. They're black and turquoise marble, 1980s luxurious.

She leans against the gold railing. I used to ride this to every floor, she says, then get out and run around the floor and ride the elevator to the next. It was wonderful.

Where were your parents?

She shrugs. It was different then.

Will we let our kid wander a hotel?

Of course not.

Then they watch the light count up the floors. Because they accidentally acted like they had before the miscarriage. Filling the pauses in a day with "what will we do" scenarios.

You think he'll be alright? she says.

He'll be fine.

Your grandpa?

Yeah.

He'll be fine.

All the flowers fit, she says.

They did, he says. They laugh. But it had made the man uncomfortable, all those plants in the new apartment. How it smelled like earth by the time they left.

I'm hungry, she says as they walk up the carpeted hallway

toward their room. The closer they get to the room, the damper the air feels.

Swimming pool is on our floor.

Oh, she says. Too bad you didn't pack my swimsuit.

Should I have?

No, no. I can't swim anyway, for several weeks, I guess.

They turn up the next hall. At the end are the doors to the swimming pool. Foggy. There's the sound of children yelling.

You think it's still open?

Restaurant's still open.

I'm hungry, she says.

We could order a pizza, he says, lifting their room swipe card that has a picture of a pizza on it and a phone number.

Sounds good. I guess it doesn't matter what I eat anymore.

They probably have sandwiches, he says.

Studies show extra cheese solves everything, she says.

Research study?

So I've heard.

It's a running joke between them. Another research study out to reach conclusions that everyone already held to be true. Just out: more people buy ice cream in summer than winter.

Their room has two double beds.

This is wrong, he says.

This will be fine, she says. She turns on the lamps as she moves through the room.

I'll be in the bathroom for a while, she says.

Do you want me to go with you? he says.

She shakes her head. No need now, she says. She shrugs. She'd done that at their wedding, a few years ago. When the preacher said, Will you take this man, she shrugged. Everyone laughed. Of course, I will, she said, and wrapped her arms around him. It had been a good day. Everyone dancing at the reception afterward, in an old barn that had been converted into a restaurant years ago.

There'd been a DJ with his stand of flashing, colored lights, and the speakers on black stands. There were three package options, and they'd picked the middle package, whatever it was. At the time, it'd seemed of vital importance. He'd fallen asleep one night with her holding the paper of options, reading glasses on the end of her nose, a pen pressed against her bottom lip.

We can't afford to have more than one of these, she said.

Okay, he'd said.

So you have to love me forever.

Okay.

She shoved him.

Well, what do you want me to say? he laughed.

That you want to make babies with me.

Don't have to be married to do that.

Good point, she said and set the paper down, her glasses on top of it. Well, that's a relief.

He drops down on the nearest of the double beds. A section of ceiling above the TV is spackled in a way that doesn't quite match the rest of the ceiling. Water damage.

* * *

The pizza is there when she comes out of the hotel bathroom, a white towel wrapped around her hair, and holding another white towel around her middle. It gaps in an upside down V down her torso. She laughs at the table. He's covered it with the sheet from one of the beds and turned off all the lights except for the lamp above it. It's set with the paper plates.

Extra cheese? she says.

Absolutely, he says. He pulls her chair back.

Don't mind if I do, she says, sitting.

He takes one of the napkins and tucks it into her towel.

You're ridiculous, she says.

I love you, he says.

I love you.

He takes the plates to the dresser where the pizza box sits. He fills their plates. He brings back the liter of soda, a washrag draped over his arm. He hands her a cup. She laughs. She pulls the plastic off it.

Our finest, he says.

Aged to perfection? she says.

He bows.

They eat, now and then looking through the window and at the tree trunk rising through the air.

A lot of women don't even know they've had one, she says.

How's that?

They think it's just a normal period. Maybe like a worse one than usual.

Like they don't know they were pregnant?

Right.

Hard day, she says.

Hard stuff, he says.

Will you hold me after we're done eating?

Sure, he says. Of course.

She nods and looks back out the window. It's pretty, she says.

It is, he says.

* * *

It was a good idea to come here, she says. It's morning, and they're sitting in the restaurant downstairs. The continental breakfast is set up in steam pans over Bunsen burners on one table. Scrambled eggs, sausage, gravy. A basket of biscuits. An industrial coffee pot and trays of white ceramic cups.

I think so, too, he says.

They smile at each other.

Maybe we can stay another night.

He thinks about it. I guess we could.

Let's do it, she says.

It feels so daring, he says.

I know. Why does it?

They laugh. It feels unforced.

When he comes back from making the reservation, she's reading a newspaper. He moves through the line, scooping the scrambled eggs onto his plate. He takes more watermelon this time.

Baby born at the zoo, she says as he sits across from her.

I read that yesterday, he says. He watches her face.

Cute, she says, and holds up the newspaper so he can see the picture of the cub.

Yep, that's the one, he says.

I went to that zoo once, as a kid.

Nice zoo?

I don't remember. I just remember the elephants being in this big, echoey room. These black bars. A sign to be careful. And everything else seemed made out of concrete. And how loud they were.

How do you feel about zoos?

She squints. Looks up at the skylight. I guess they're pretty awful places, really. Like circuses.

Do you want to go?

Maybe, she says.

They laugh. Because it's so fucked up, all of it.

They read for a while more. Maybe, she says, we could stop by and see my grandfather. See how he's settling in.

He seemed fine.

He did, didn't he? I feel sort of guilty, though, being this close and him not knowing, thinking we're at home.

We're on vacation now, he says.

Is that what we're calling it?

Sure, he says.

Cheers, she says, and raises her coffee cup.

She's right. It's nice being here like this.

A couple children come running into the restaurant, lifting the silver lids and peering over.

Eggs! the boy exclaims.

You hate eggs, the girl says.

Since when? the boy says.

Since *always*, the girl says.

Sausage! Dad, look, sausage!

Hey, would you look at that, the father says, moving on lean legs. He's wearing similar plaid shorts as the boy. The mother is wearing a visor, her hair in a ponytail. She rubs the man's back. Oh, sausage, yum, she says, in a way that makes her family laugh.

He sees his wife watching.

Let's go on a drive, he says.

The boy's standing tiptoe and ladling eggs on his plate.

You don't like eggs, his father tells him.

I love eggs, the boy says.

Let's go, he says, standing up and lifting her elbow as he does.

We should put those signs in our room if we're staying another night.

What signs?

About not washing the towels or anything. To save water. The environment. I didn't leave them out because we were leaving.

On their way to the elevator, they pass another family, this one with a baby wrapped around the front of the woman's chest. The couple is holding hands.

She turns around, grabbing his sides to keep from toppling into him. She's looking this way and that.

There have to be stairs, right? she says.

He points at the EXIT sign.

The stairwell is hot. She climbs in front of him. Before they reach the top of the first flight, she's breathing heavily. The pregnancy book said that she'd start losing her breath as the pregnancy continued. On account of something. He can't remember.

There are no windows.

Why don't we take a rest? he says.

She nods, but keeps climbing.

Above them, a door swings shut, and there's the sound of yelling, then the slap of bare feet. Slow down! one child yells.

Last one's a rotten egg! another child yells back.

You'll be in so much trouble if you lose me again.

You weren't even lost.

Was so.

I'm going to do a triple flip.

Oh, yeah? I'm going to do a triple-quadruple flip.

Not if I do a triple-quadruple-double flip.

There's no such thing.

He looks up and sees the tips of the children's fingers sliding up the railings. Then the door slams again, and all is echo.

She stops with one foot on a stair above her, and leans back against the railing and wall. Her face is pale with streaks of pink up her throat.

Where are they all coming from? she says, panting. She closes her eyes, but raises her chin like she's looking up.

He thinks of when they were looking for a house to rent, how suddenly he noticed every FOR RENT sign in every yard and window. Even signs that weren't FOR RENT signs. It lasted for several weeks even after they'd moved into the house. Now he hardly notices them, but they're surely still there. Maybe it's the same.

Let's get off here, he says, and pushes open the door.

They walk along the balcony, glancing over it down into the restaurant. A few doors have silver trays with empty bowls and crumpled napkins on them. Several more have DO NOT DISTURB signs in the key slots. A housekeeping cart is near their door. For a second, his wife thinks it's parked at theirs. She walks faster.

It's okay if we miss it, he says. If they accidentally clean our room.

It's not, she says.

It really is.

I don't want her to know.

Know what?

There's blood on the toilet paper, she says.

Didn't you throw it away? he says.

Yes, but.

She doesn't know you.

It feels different if we were leaving today.

But when they reach their room, the cart isn't there but parked a few doors down. Good, she says.

Inside, though, the beds have been made. The trash cans are empty. The sheet on the table from last night's dinner is gone, too.

We didn't make it in time, she says.

It's as if we were never here, he says.

Maybe there's some comfort in that.

She slides her arms under his, presses her face against his shoulder.

He thinks of the aquarium in the trunk of the car. The picture of the aquarium pasted across the front, filled with beautiful fish, wavering seaweed, neon gravel, and behind it all, an ocean backdrop that makes the water seem bright blue instead of the green stripes down a nursery wall, where a child sleeps in a small bed by a nightlight, her parents just beyond the door listening, listening.

THE LIGHTNING TREE

———

The cabin feels empty when she wakes up, like it has just been cleaned or they locked it up and returned home, somehow forgetting themselves here. She touches her neck. Her heart like a leaf in the wind. She turns to the other side of the pillow and reaches across her husband's side of the bed.

He isn't there.

There's been a chill to the air the past few days, the end of summer. They probably won't come up here again, even if she does end up back in the hospital.

She raises up on her pillows, watching her arms as she does, as though to encourage them to hold her. Too thin. At first, when people didn't know, they kept complimenting her. You've lost so much weight! they said. How pretty you look, they said. What's your secret?

She looks out the window. The lightning tree rises out in the field like a scarecrow, though the field hasn't been planted for years. Her husband grew up in the cabin, on this farm. It used to be bigger, when his great-grandfather settled it, but has slowly been sold off. She guesses he'll sell the rest of it once she has left, though they haven't talked about it.

They started coming up here after her first jaunt in the hospital, which is what she called it. Jaunt. Now she has ended up there so many more times it's a tradition, and a tradition to drive from checking out at the hospital up the long road to here.

The first day he brought her out here, long ago, he held her hand in the shy but sure way of young men in love, and led her past the collapsed barn and to the lightning tree that, as a boy, he'd hoped might save his brother's life.

It's beautiful, she said.

Older than Moses, he said, like his father said, and he imagined saying to their child one day.

They ran their hands over the blackened trunk. It had been struck so many times that she almost expected to feel electricity humming beneath it.

Isn't it rare for the same tree to be struck so many times? she said.

It's a magic tree, he said.

Magic? She smiled sideways at him, but he was looking up at the branches.

That's right, he said.

What's it do?

It shows impossibility.

* * *

She plucks her fingernail against the quilt, staring at holes where the needle once punched through the fabric, shadows of where thread held the pieces together for a long time.

She listens to the house until she can hear him. In the mudroom. His fingers forcing the thick buttons of his coat through the buttonholes. She imagines it as vividly as though she can see through the wall. Because she purposely memorized him doing this as she watched him combing his hair, sweeping the kitchen, buttoning his coat. When the doctor predicted blindness, she began trying to memorize the world as though it, too, would fall away with her sight, like some inner and outer eclipse.

She kicks down the quilt like she still has that kind of energy. Her heart speeds up. Her breath shortens. She tries to stay inside of it, calm.

Not right now, she thinks.

You're fine, she thinks.

Calm. So calm.

The front door shuts. His boots cross the porch.

She lies there for a long time before climbing out of bed, nightgown untangling from her legs as she reaches toward the ceiling. Looking at her fingertips. Tree to sky.

She makes her way slowly through the cabin. He's outside, probably fixing something. That's what he mostly does up here, especially now that she sleeps so much, though she tries not to. He doesn't like it up here. She does.

The cabin is good because it's all one floor, rooms close together, and not much furniture to dodge or trip over. Feels like she's always knocking over things at home, a vase as she reaches to lean on a table, candles off the mantle, the umbrella rack by the front door. Their house a labyrinth that she'd somehow built.

She passes by the picture of the hog hanging from a tree. It's a small picture, black and white, no bigger than her hand. The hog's hanging by its legs and is split down the middle.

They always seemed so much bigger strung up, her father-in-law said, when he saw her, looking at it.

Is that right? she said. She'd never seen anything like it.

You recognize that tree? he said.

She shook her head but then she did.

That's back before it got struck.

How do you have a picture of it?

Don't know who took it. It's always been right there, since I was a kid.

She leans in now, examining the hog closely. It doesn't bother her like it used to. Her death makes her feel like examining everything, like everything's a grasshopper she might have caught as a child, its stuck leg snapping against her thumb.

She imagines waving the flies away from the hog, but they'll return, darting across the hide, moving in and out of the dark empty place where its life had been. Or some of its life had been. She isn't sure exactly where life was. Maybe that's why people believe in souls.

When she was a young girl and thought of her mind, she imagined it as a black foggy space empty of what she hadn't learned yet. But no matter how much she learned, the fog was still there, and still is. Maybe it was god.

So dramatic, she thinks. Always so dramatic. Why would you imagine your death to be any less?

She'd grown up in a house full of pictures. Family pictures, prints by well-known photographers, besides the photographs her father took. But her husband has only a few. There wasn't a camera, he said. She didn't even know how to respond, having spent much of her childhood driving around the sunset with her father, taking pictures of the world brushing against it.

And the pictures that do exist, her husband doesn't much remember. There's the handful of stern relatives who died before he was born, one of the cabin in its younger days, the one of his mother and father in a three-legged race, and the portrait of his brother and him sitting on a concrete stoop. Knobby-kneed, squinting, arms around each other's backs. She'd had that one matted and framed for his birthday a couple years ago. It hung in their bedroom for a while, but he'd brought it back to the cabin.

She doesn't know how or exactly when his brother died—only that they were young and he shouldn't have. She's never asked.

They've been married long enough to know he will eventually tell her. Or he won't.

She holds the frame of the front door. She closes her eyes and stands still, so still, until she feels herself disappear. Just like this, she thinks as she imagines herself as his next wife standing here, wondering about the dead wife. What that part of his life had been like. He sometimes goes to visit the grave. She would watch him go and come back. He'd touch her shoulder as he passed by her, maybe pause and kiss the top of her head. She wondered if he did that with the dead wife. She feels generous for letting him go to the grave.

* * *

The rocking chair is on the porch, right by the front door. She sits, pulling on the blanket that she leaves out here.

It's not long until he comes out of the barn wearing shorts and a T-shirt. Maybe it wasn't him putting on his coat, after all, that she thought she heard. Or maybe she fell back asleep without knowing it, and now it's much warmer. She's wearing jeans, a sweater, and one of his black knit hats that she's always borrowing because she never can find hers.

You're up early, he says.

It's nearly noon, she says.

I'll go make you some toast.

I'm so tired of toast.

Can you do jelly?

She rolls her eyes, as though it were a silly question. She wishes it were.

Watch out or they'll get stuck like that, he says.

Then I won't have to think because I'll see all my thoughts.

Clever.

Toast is fine, she says.

Toast du jour, he says and kisses the top of her head on his way to open the door. Nice hat, he says.

Thanks, she says. She watches the storm door close behind him. The second or third time they came up to here after the hospital, he fixed the front storm door.

What do you think? he said when she crossed the threshold.

You didn't carry me, she said.

No, he said. Look. And pointed up at the coil. He pulled open the door then let go. It slowly wheezed back into the frame instead of slamming with a bang.

You fixed it, she said.

I did, he said. You asked me to.

Did I?

You made a big deal. It was windy one night, and you kept waking up.

Thank you, she said.

I thought you'd be pleased.

I'm tired, I guess.

Then he started fixing things around their house, too. He glued together the teapot, tightened the banister so the railing didn't shake, and bought new cabinet pulls to replace the ones that kept falling off.

So, what's going on? she finally said.

You've been asking me to fix these things for years. So I'm doing it. I thought you'd be happy about it.

This part, she said, this fixing part, is supposed to come after. After what?

My funeral. It's like living in the house after my funeral.

His shoulders sagged.

If everything changes before I die, then I'll die not knowing what anything means.

I can stop, he said.

No, she said. I'm an asshole. I'm sorry.

You only say that when you're trying to end an argument.

You don't like to argue, she said.

I don't have to fix anything.

It's good. You have to keep busy. This affects you, too. I forget that.

She knows her death makes him do what he does, but doesn't know whether she should feel responsible for it. She has never thought of death as hers before, a possession.

But she doesn't like coming home from another doctor's appointment or hospital stay or even a haircut to a more mended house. A new latch for the gate. All the nails in the deck that were sticking out now hammered flush. The weathervane oiled so that she can't hear the wind turning it. The house quieter than it has ever been. She hadn't realized how much of their lives had been the sound of breaking.

* * *

He hands her the toast on a small glass plate. She can see the blanket on her lap under the edges of the toast. He moves to leave.

What are you fixing today? she says.

Kitchen chairs have a wobble, he says.

A wobble, she says.

I noticed it the other night.

It could wait.

I'd like to get to it, though.

You could sit with me a little.

It'll be nice to have dinner at a table without fearing the chair will collapse beneath you.

I've never worried about that, she says. Have you?

I guess not, he says.

She smiles. So does he.

She takes a bite of the toast.

He sits on the porch stair where he sits with his brother in that picture. She wonders if he thinks of that.

I think I'd like to do it today, she says.

He doesn't answer or look at her.

Did you hear me? she says.

He nods.

Well?

It won't end up being how you imagine.

That's not the point.

Isn't it? he says.

Let me try, she says. You don't have to carry me back if you don't want to.

Of course I'll carry you back, he says. Why would you even say that? Just to get your way?

Maybe I'll end up walking around the world, and that's what scares you.

He takes his hat off, and moves it from one hand to the other.

I'll bring souvenirs, she says. Chocolates. Postcards. Magnets. Shot glasses.

Okay, he says. If you walk around the world, he says, how will I find you?

I'll come right up behind you. She laughs.

You're breaking my heart, he says.

* * *

Of course, they knew it might be more than a routine checkup. But they talked like it would be routine. Probably nothing. Just overreacting. Do you want me to go in with you? he said as they drove to the doctor's office.

It's fine, she said. Of course, if it were something awful.

Of course, he said.

But it's not.

Right, he said.

Then she didn't come out after an hour. Two. He interrupted the secretaries gossiping behind the counter. They seemed annoyed. There were baskets of flowers on the counter. One woman asked what her name was.

Spell it.

Okay, I'll call back.

Then a nurse came out and called his name. He raised his hand. She took him to a door that didn't lead into an examining room, but to a small, blue office with a heavy desk. His wife looked up then back out the window. There was condensation between the panes of glass. A plant. A clock. The doctor welcomed him in, gesturing at the empty chair beside her. He'd think of it again in a few months when the money started tightening and they went to the bank about a loan. The banker welcomed them into his cubicle, gesturing for them to sit at the matching chairs across from his desk before sitting down.

But the doctor sat on the edge of his desk. He was a young doctor.

It could be nothing, the doctor said.

She wiped her nose with a tissue. It was already wrinkled.

Then they were leaving the building, his wife zipping up her coat with the tissue still in her hand.

He opened the door on her side of the truck. The seat was cold. The truck's defroster was broken. With the end of his fist, he wiped at the frost inside the windshield. He was intent, and the frost curled off in shears on the dashboard.

We don't have insurance, she said.

That can't matter, he said.

It's bad timing.

Always is.

When he's an older doctor, she said, he'll probably sit behind the desk instead of on it.

You noticed that, too?

Yeah.

She picked up one of the frozen curls and held it by her ear.

We could get some coffee, he said.

That sounds good.

He rubbed at the glass.

She scratched at the window. People die all the time, she said.

He checked the defroster. It seemed to be on.

* * *

One night when they were very young, hardly married, she fell back on the bed and closed her eyes and said, Okay, pretend I'm dead. What do you do?

If you're dead, you can't look at me, he said.

Right, she said. It's hard to hold my breath.

Why are you holding it?

So that if you look at my chest, it's not going up and down.

I don't think that death is holding your breath, he said.

She didn't answer.

So, she's dead, he said, as though to an observer.

But she was grinning and holding her eyes shut so tightly, her smile all the way to her ears.

Are you heartbroken? she whispered.

I am, he said.

I can't hear heartbroken in your voice.

Maybe I'm always heartbroken, he said.

Okay, your turn, she said. You be dead and I'll mourn you. She rolled out of the bed and pushed him toward her place.

Close your eyes, she said.

People hardly ever die with their eyes closed, he said.

Really?

Really.

I don't like that, she said.

He didn't answer.

Oh, are you dead?

* * *

I'm going to go see about those chairs, he says. If that's alright
with you.

And you'll help me when you come back? she says.

I don't know.

What do you mean you don't know?

You're not going to walk around the world, he says.

I just want to see how far I can walk, she says.

Why? We both know you can't make it from here to the tree
without having a seizure.

You can't be mean to me, she says.

I'm not trying to be. I just don't understand.

She feels one of her rages coming on. She makes fists and heat
pulses in her arms and her muscles tighten, and she wants to
take her fists to everything, windows and walls and mirrors, until
glass rains against the floor as though it's her she's broken. The
rages were worse early on. More of them. She didn't tell him for
a while she was feeling it, but he said he already knew.

It shouldn't be okay to feel hate, she said.

You're fine.

No, I'm not.

I imagine you feel all sorts of ways.

Stop being so generous.

He didn't answer.

It's not hate if it's okay. Let me hate. Why won't you let me
hate?

You can hate, he said.

It's not up to you.

I don't like to argue, he said. You know I don't.

But why? Why don't you? It probably has to do with your brother.

And you only bring him up when you're trying to get your way.

She didn't answer.

My parents were fighters, fighting all the time. Throwing shit. Breaking things.

Like what? she said, even though she knew.

He shrugged. Anything that breaks. Beer bottles. A bowl, a cup. One time, Mom threw a stack of love letters out the window that he'd written her during the war. My brother and I didn't know what they were. Dad knew. He asked her to go get them. She wouldn't. Can't you hear it's raining? he said. I'll never forget that, how quiet he said it. Can't you hear it's raining?

She still refused to go get them. It rained the rest of the night, puddles everywhere next day. And the letters still out there, in this thick blue ribbon, like she must have cared about them. That confused me. How could she be the one to tie them and the one to throw them?

Sun came out and baked them dry. But they both refused to pick them up. My brother tried to, but Mom said no. I don't know if she expected Dad to pick them up. Or he expected her to. He'd walk past the letters like they weren't there. My brother and I started daring each other to take them because we knew Mom and Dad were watching them, no matter how they pretended not to.

We'd do any number of tricks to get near them. Cartwheels. Walking on our hands. He even did a backflip off the porch rail. Probably that was when he was practicing to run away with the circus. Every single time, just as we went to scoop them up, Mom or Dad would see us and yell, and we'd drop them. By autumn, the letters were brittle, rippled. By winter, the ink a blur. By spring, he was dead.

Your brother.

My brother.

Just like that.

Just like that. The world one way, then never again. My parents didn't argue after that.

What happened to the letters?

I don't know. They didn't matter.

* * *

After lunch, he helps her inside to take a nap. He lies in bed with her, arm over her waist. But it's too heavy, and she has to ask him to move it.

Tell me another story, she says.

I don't know any.

About your brother.

Why?

Because he mattered to you, she says. But there's something else, too, though neither of them say it. How he's become more present sine her diagnosis, and even more since they started coming up to the cabin.

Maybe it's because of the cabin, or because she watches him so closely now. So close he feels haunted by her, like she has brought her ghost into the house to show it around. He worries that all her memorizing may not work, and doesn't know how to tell her without making her mad. She's mad a lot now. One night, he tried to tell her but he couldn't. That he'd forgotten the sound of his brother's voice.

It feels different than the ghost his brother left. That ghost appeared suddenly, as though being pushed onto a stage without knowing its lines, and so it clung to everyone in the family, asking for help, to give it memories of the boy so that it might understand.

He can tell she doesn't realize how closely she follows him. With her eyes. Her words. Her shadow. It unnerves him to be so constantly aware of himself through her. Of her stare, her breath. Of not being able to save her. Of her leaving.

And that he would be the ghost she left behind.

Did I tell you about the time my brother learned he had a heart?

Her eyes are closed. Tell me again, she says.

He walked with his chest puffed out like a tough bird. He was so proud of having a heart, and went around telling everybody and pointing at it. And nobody dared tell him we all had hearts.

After he died, I walked in on my father alone at the kitchen table. He was drinking water. He asked did I want some. We sat there drinking the water. He drank his fast then went to the sink for another. I'm just so thirsty, he says to me. I've never felt so thirsty.

He feels her breathing against him. He tries to remember the old, good feeling of their chests rising and falling against each other, how he'd try to match his breath to hers. Now there are pauses in her breathing. He holds his breath in the pauses, listening for hers.

* * *

He daydreams again and again of that day he carried his brother out to the lightning tree. His brother's face was so pale, the shadows under his eyes. He wore white pajamas with tiny blue boats all over them.

I've got a plan to save your life, he told his brother.

Okay, his brother said.

Okay. Do you need any help?

Naw, I got it. I'm just telling you so you know.

Thanks, his brother said. Trying to smile.

After his brother died, he got it into his head that he'd bring him back to life. He decided he'd need those boat pajamas. He looked all over his brother's room. Under the bed, through drawers. Then in the hall closet where his mother kept the hamper.

His mother came up behind him. What are you trying to do? Tear up the house right after the nice ladies from church cleaned it special just for us. They didn't have to do that.

Where are his pajamas?

They haven't fit you in years, his mother said.

Where are they?

What's gotten into you and your father about those pajamas?

He has them?

Got them out of the laundry earlier this morning. What's this about?

Where is he? Where's Dad?

Out at the barn last I saw.

He ran out there, past the sheets hanging off the clothesline, past the hogs at the trough. His father wasn't in the barn, but out behind it, by the woodpile. His father looked up. His face gaunt and drawn. He held a matchbook, was folding it in front of a match.

Don't burn them, he said to his father, reaching to stop his hands.

Then he was suddenly on his back, on the ground, staring up at his father, and his father looking down at him.

You don't tell me what to do, his father said. My son is dead. You don't tell me what to do.

I'm going to bring him back to life, he said.

A thought passed over his father's face. Then it was gone. You'll do no such thing, his father said.

Out at the lightning tree. I just need his pajamas.

That's grief that has you. Look here, his father said. We're going to burn these. Put them in our memory like everything else. Otherwise, we won't be able to stand it.

The pajamas were laid out across the mess of wood. The boats floating over the fabric. A gentleness to how they were laid out. He started to cry. His father went about starting a fire.

* * *

So, I'll just leave one day, she said. And you don't have to bother looking for me. I'll just go. And maybe it will be because I'm dying, and maybe it will just be because. Then you won't have to deal with an ending. No funeral, no fake flowers. I'll just leave one day when it seems right.

That's unending, he said.

No, it will be fine, she said. Just like our dog. When he went missing, remember? And you found him?

You're not a dog.

I know I'm not. I'm saying *like* that. And not like the dog but what he did in the end.

They'd gotten the dog as a puppy soon after their wedding. It was strange to see the dog age with their marriage. He never knew what it meant.

When they brought the dog to the cabin to visit his parents, they always leashed him or kept him in the house because he was a city dog, not a country dog.

I don't see the difference, she said.

Country dogs are just . . . he tried to explain.

Country dogs die, too, don't they? Get hit by tractors, cars, and so forth.

Yeah, but.

Well, he deserves to run free, too, she said. He'll come back.

Just because you want him to come back doesn't mean that he will come back. He doesn't even come back at the dog park half the time.

He will, she insisted.

And she was right.

Until after one of her long hospital stays, and they brought the dog up here, and she let him off the leash. At first, the dog hung around the cabin. Napped in the shade of the porch or the barn.

Maybe you were right, he told her.

Of course I was. She smiled, but her face was pale. Dark circles under her eyes. That gone look. Like his brother.

In the morning, the dog was gone.

He'll be back, she said.

He's old, he said.

You think he's left to die?

Maybe.

Like me?

Not like you. You're not dying.

The doctor.

The doctor sits on desks. The doctor doesn't know anything. The dog will be fine. Maybe he just got turned around.

Because he can't hear the weathervane, she thought.

He'll find its way back? she said.

Sure, he said.

The dog didn't return that night. She stood in the yard calling for him, but it wore her out, though she pretended it didn't.

He found the dog in the windbreak, by the small creek where he and the dog sometimes went to think together, the same creek where he and his brother had played as boys, the creek near the tree where he had found his brother who had gotten confused one night and wandered right out of the house. Like some hypnotized bird. Like a swallow inside a flock of swallows, a boy inside a flock of all the other people dying around the world that day, following death in strange swirls that can only be seen from space.

The dog was torn up pretty badly, lying in the creek, breathing ragged. He never told her that part. Never would. Not a thing to tell. He tried to move to see him but didn't have the strength. So he carefully stepped around the dog, and knelt in the creek so they could see each other.

He rested his hand on the dog's shoulder, lightly enough that the dog seemed embarrassed by it. He lay there in the creek for a while after, until his sobs came out as short, fast breaths—his lips tight on each other. He thought of her, of his brother, of the dog. It was cold in the creek, but the sun was warm. How strange, he thought, that the sun is warm.

* * *

He finds her not very far out of the backyard, clearly heading to the lightning tree, and beyond that the rest of the world, which is field as far as he can see. Threads of her sweater are caught in the sticky weeds. He sits down beside her. He brushes his hands against the grass.

She stares up at the sky.

What do you see? he says.

He sits there for a while more, knees pulled to his chest, letting his arms hang off his knees. No differently than when she made a surprise picnic but needed to use the toaster, and she threaded two extension cords out the kitchen window and across the yard to the blanket.

He watches her chest fall and rise. He listens for pauses.

You're breaking my heart, he says.

She doesn't answer.

It's difficult to pick her up. He almost thinks he can't do it. It feels lonely already. Lonelier than he thought it would. He carries her toward the lightning tree, careful not to trip over the roots.

Help me, he says.

THE MISSING TIME

———

Thomas comes home from searching. His clothes are damp from night and dark morning, fields, windbreaks, and the howling of coyotes and hope. He doesn't let go of his flashlight. He doesn't intend to stay long. Long enough to eat, long enough to stand in front of the kitchen cabinet and then realize that he hasn't opened it or taken down a bowl. Long enough to remember why he's staring, why he has to go back out. Because Sam went walking. Now he must walk, too.

He finds himself staring at the cabinet pull. It's white porcelain with tiny blue flowers on it. The glaze is finely fissured.

From the kitchen he can see across the living room. The bedroom door is slightly cracked open. His wife Nell is sleeping in there. He has looked enough times to imagine her as though seeing her. The way her body rises over the bed, the way her eyelids flicker when she's moving into deep sleep. He crosses the living room. He stops at the foot of their bed. Yes, she is as he remembers. Or at least, he can still fit her into the forms of his memory.

Dawn is slipping through the sliding-glass door and under the blinds. The world hasn't yet turned enough to let the light reach her through the dark. But it will, and it will keep turning. And the darkness will come back like a breath.

He plays the beam of his flashlight over her toes then up her leg, first the outside and then up the inside curve of her calf, her knee, up through her nightgown, up to the rounded bulge of her belly and then up over her heavy breasts.

She is so large now, large as the earth and the baby who sleeps, too, inside her. The baby will die. Will live, age, and die. She and he alone decided that—somehow. Or maybe they didn't, but if they take credit for giving life to the baby, then they have to take credit for the death, even if the deaths their own parents gave them happen first.

He stands still, and moves the flashlight only with his wrist. He crosses the light up her throat, over her hips, her cheeks, and lays it still on her eyelids so that, for a second, he is the giver of the stars she would see if she opened them.

I'm alive, she says quietly. She doesn't open her eyes. Thomas realizes he has been outlining her as he would outline his brother's body if he finds him dead.

I know it, he says.

Are you in? she says.

Not yet, he says.

You need to sleep.

I know it.

You know a lot tonight, she says.

He turns off the flashlight like a fact. He climbs into bed beside her. He rolls against her. She is always so warm now. She touches his back, and he can feel the wet of his shirt against her palm and the stress in her arm. She hasn't woken relaxed for years.

You can wake me up? he says.

In two hours?

What time is it?

I don't know, she says.

One hour, he says.

She reaches into the bedside drawer where she kept the basal body thermometer all the years between the first miscarriage and this pregnancy. Now she keeps the fetal heart monitor there. He hears her squirting the gel on her belly. He fights the sleep like darkness and dawn. When he hears the *washa-washa-washa* of the baby's heart, yes, a baby now, not a fetus, not an embryo, a baby now, closer to the earth now, *washa-washa-washa*. And her body relaxes. And sleep comes over him like the beam of a flashlight hovering over the ground and showing the weeds. Just outside of the circle of light must lie a dead brother or a scared brother or a brother hunched in a ditch, eyes wide and a week's worth of beard and dirt covering his face. But like in life, in sleep there is only darkness inside the light, and blue flowers on a cabinet pull.

* * *

Thomas wakes up and then hears the knock that woke him.

The knock is slow. Decided.

He lies in bed on top of the sheets, unable to remember what he dreamed, only the feeling.

Nell's side of the bed is empty. There's a glass of water on her bed stand. Her jar of prenatal vitamins. It's summer now so she isn't on the extra vitamin D anymore. They were both taking it. Like last time, but the baby didn't make it into summer or from embryo to fetus.

The knock comes again. Then Nell's bare feet crossing the living room. He can sense who is knocking in the way that people sense things but don't say they do. And because he knows who's at the door, he imagines that he's wrong—that it's really the angel his father said would appear down at the creek when someone in the village was about to die. An angel knocking on the front door, on the porch in wet clothes and rumpled wings, mouth set.

His father would take him down to the creek when he was a boy, and they'd wait in the dappled shadows for her. He imagined the angel looked like Jackie Zeffers, the poorest girl in his class. Jackie Zeffers with her blue winter coat, puff gone out of it, and her dirty face and neck and her blue, blue eyes. Jackie Zeffers who always wore a brown belt and kept a comb in her back pocket from the photographer who gave everybody a comb on school picture day. There he'd wait for Jackie to step through the poison ivy and wild raspberry trees and down onto the sandy bank where the creek ran too close to the sewer lines for most parents to feel safe about their kids playing there. She'd unhook the bloody wings from her back, and carry them into the creek, balancing on the rocky bottom.

Missed her again, his father would say at the breakfast table, slapping the obituaries with the back of his hand.

And when their father began dying hard of the cancer, Sam started walking alone to the creek. Their mother had been worried about it. I don't like it, Thomas. Not attended like that.

He's a grown man, Thomas said. He knows how to swim.

I still don't like it, she said. He's not a good swimmer.

He's a fine swimmer.

Someone should be with him.

Isn't God with him?

I'm ignoring what you said, his mother said. Then she sighed. You know your father wouldn't like him going down there like that.

Then Dad should tell him, Thomas said, as though his dad wasn't in a hospice bed in the back of the house, as though his mother deserved to be punished for how this life was turning out.

His mother sighed. If Sam could live with you and Nell for a little bit. Even a week, just so he got out of the habit of walking down there.

Our yard isn't any farther from the creek.

Maybe it's just the pattern, the routine. Maybe being around your father, the nurse coming and going like breakfast. Death always on his mind. That angel you and your father put in his head. It was alright for you two, with your stories, but it's not the same with him. All these years I been telling you to be more careful what you say to him. Haven't I said again and again, he don't understand regular? Don't I say take a little more care?

She was punishing him, too, maybe. Trying to. Each of them with no one to blame, but needing someone.

This isn't about the angel, Thomas said.

Of course it is, she said. Why else would he be going down there except because of that story? He wants to know if your father's going to die, when it's going to happen. When? He says to me over and over. When Mama, when?

What do you say?

I don't know what to say. I say when God's ready.

Maybe it has nothing to do with that.

The other night he tells me not to worry because he hasn't seen the lady with wings and so Dad's not gonna die. So Dad's not gonna die, Thomas, that's what he says to me.

Doesn't sound like such a strange thing to think. No stranger than God, really.

I've been remembering when your aunt died. You probably don't remember, you were so little. But I'd wake up from these nightmares about her. She was so mad, so angry at me for not saving her life. And I'd lay there in the dark clutching the sides of my mattress, to keep from running to the cemetery to dig her up. We didn't live far from it. And I knew it was wrong, but the urge didn't care. And I think to myself what if Sam wakes up from a dream like that but about your father? And so he wakes up and it's nighttime and none of us know where he's gone.

They sat in the stillness of the house. Dust floated. The same pictures on the walls. The couch faded over the years from the sunlight from the window, which seemed impossible because the house always felt so dark. Thomas imagined his mother putting on her gardening gloves and carrying the shovel over her shoulders and walking down the road toward the cemetery in the dark. But he understood what she meant when his father died and he woke to the same thought lit by moonlight and ache. Because what if he dug up the grave and his father wasn't inside it after all? Then his mind would have been right all this time, that it was impossible to have a dead father.

Their mother packed Sam's bag, and he lived with Nell and Thomas. And Sam did stop walking to the creek. He helped Nell around the house or sat on the porch strumming Thomas's guitar or asked if he could feel the baby kick or would put his ear against the baby heart monitor.

Then their father died, and Sam returned home to live with their mother and took back up walking to the creek.

Maybe he's just pretending Dad's alive again, Thomas offered.

The boy isn't capable of it, his mother said.

He's a man.

Boy or man, she said, he doesn't understand pretend.

Or, Thomas said, he doesn't understand that Dad's dead since you keep talking about him alive in heaven.

I didn't say I knew where heaven was. I didn't say it was in the creek.

All death is pretend, Thomas said.

What's that mean?

I don't know, he said. And he didn't. Did you explain to him again that Dad's dead?

And break his heart all over again?

* * *

Nell's murmuring to whomever is at the front door. If it's Jackie Zeffers, in her old blue coat, gray sneakers, and angel wings, Nell doesn't sound surprised. But not much ruffles Nell, really.

Thomas imagines his brother Sam is there, too, standing behind Jackie the angel. Jackie takes Sam's arm in both of her hands, pulling him gently forward as she steps back, like their mother does when Sam's scared.

There's the sound of Nell, coming back through the house, passing the kitchen full of casserole dishes left by curious visitors, toward the bedroom, her bare feet scuffing against the dusty wooden floor.

She appears in the bedroom doorway, and presses her palms against either side of the frame. Her elbows angle down toward her bare feet. He watches her look at him.

It's Don? he says. Don's the town's only full-time policeman. The other policeman lives in the next town over. With the search, more have come in. But he knew it would be Don who came to the house.

He won't come in, she says.

You offered? he says.

I did.

Did he tell you?

He wants to talk to you, she says and pushes the ball of her right foot against the floor, raising up on it and then lowering herself. And then she's rolling up on her left foot, the bones creaking, and then onto the ball where she stays, waiting. It is an old ballet habit, but since she has been pregnant, the sound makes him imagine the baby in the darkness of her placenta, shadowed by the veins branching around it, as though the veins creak. And now with Sam disappeared, the sound has also become the sound of twigs under Sam's tennis shoes.

Seems like he'll be on the porch until you get there, she says. Whether you hurry or not.

He wants He wants to ask if they found Sam. But no. She won't say. And no reason to say what will just lead to her talking around, just so he can talk around. They can talk around, that's no problem.

Can talk around all day, never say anything. Talk around until they're two strangers. Always easier to deal with a stranger's hurt. And then, once they're strangers, he can say, I think Sam's dead. And she can say, Yes. Yes, probably he is.

Tell him to come on in, he says, opening his eyes.

He won't come in.

Right. You said that.

I'll tell him you'll be out in a minute, she says, turning. She stops. It's gonna be fine, she says.

The way breath is fine?

Is breath fine?

Sure, he says. Sure it is.

Then I don't know, she says.

I know you're beautiful.

She smiles then comes to stand beside him, letting her fingers trail over his face. If it's over, let it be over, Thomas. Let it fine be that you didn't find him.

A cruel thought occurs to him, but he doesn't say it because he doesn't mean it. It's just the meanness fighting sorrow.

* * *

The last time Don came to talk to Thomas was when Thomas's Dad was early sick and Nell was taking her temperature every morning but no longer telling him the numbers she recorded in her little notebook. Sam was the reason for Don's visit that time, too. He had been arrested and was up at the police station.

What do you mean he's *still* there? Thomas said as they stood together on the porch.

Your mom was meaning to come get him, Don said. But word is your father's. . . . Well, I figure she has reason to keep forgetting to come. Thought it might be better to tell you.

How long's he been there?

A day, two days is all. He's okay, of course. Seems to be pretty content, actually.

Does anyone else know?

Just me and Alan and Widow Haley, of course.

Widow Haley?

And that's when Thomas learned Sam had been picked up for exposing himself. Widow Haley was the one called in about it.

He what?

Weren't any kids there, just Widow Haley, who made the call, but—

Jesus, Don.

There's protocol, Thomas.

Of course. She saw him, though? You know Widow Haley, he's—

Last time—

Last time?

Teenagers mooned him right back. Don squinted up in the sun so as to make his smile seem part of it. Thomas laughed then felt a twist of guilt about it. That acidy feeling climbing up his throat.

Probably should have told you sooner, Don said, but your mother said she'd take care of it and your father laid up the way he was. And there didn't seem to be any harm in it. But, you know. Happened in another county, a retar—a man like your brother and a little girl.

Sam wouldn't—

That one lived with his parents, too, and the parents said he didn't know no better. And maybe he didn't. Way I see it is a man's a man no matter how slow he is. But a little girl, well. Can't have that.

Certainly can't have that, Don.

Certainly can't have that.

* * *

Thomas steps out onto the porch. It's bright outside and he squints. Don's there, standing on the last step. Don nods at him as he takes off his police cap. His shoes are edged with drying mud and what looks like sand.

Think it's going to rain again? Thomas says.

Don looks up at the sky. Don't know, he says.

Supposed to have a couple more, I guess.

Good for the farmers probably, Thomas says. Or maybe Don says it. If Thomas didn't, Don would have. Since Sam's disappearance, he has consistently irritated himself at having a wealth of ready-made answers. He wonders if people make their way through life just resaying what they've heard others say. If the sky looks this-a-way, say this. If someone says, Rain, then answer, Good for the farmers. If someone says, No rain, then answer, Good for the farmers. If you're a farmer never say the rain will be good unless you follow it with a reason why it isn't such a good thing. Too much of a good thing.

A whole system of ready-made responses.

Your brother, Don says.

Go on.

Out in the creek. 'Bout a mile from your Mom's place.

The bridge was washed out, Thomas says.

Thomas follows the young policeman across the lawn to the edge of the field where Don decides that they will stand, or perhaps the events that have led to Don being here cause them to stand there. Thomas looks at Don's shoes again. Sand caked on the soles. Must have come here first thing after finding Sam. It was good of Don to do, Thomas thinks.

My mom know?

Thought it'd be better for her to hear it from you, Don says.

Probably right.

Don't know why he was down there, Don says, but from the looks he walked alongside the creek for a while, maybe even the length of day.

The storm, Thomas says.

Creek's high. He gets turned around. It took him quite a ways, nearly six miles. He's banged up pretty bad. We'll know more after the autopsy.

Autopsy.

Got to have one with a death like this.

He's dead.

I'm sorry, Thomas.

You think someone had something to do with it?

Messing with him or something?

Something like that, Thomas says.

No, but law says maybe we can't know things like this just by a feeling.

He drowned, then?

Looks like it.

Thomas holds out his hand. Don takes it. Thanks, Thomas says. We really appreciate it.

Need to identify him, Don says.

Oh.

Won't take but an hour, or less than two.

Thomas nods. Let me get my coat, then. Thomas turns back toward the house. Nell's on the porch, up on the balls of her feet, her hands lightly touching the porch railing. Caught in his eyes, she stays like that, her bare legs lean and tan, her back straight, her shoulders drawn behind her. His brother's death passes between them. She lowers her feet, and he starts back to the house. It's too hot for a coat, but he doesn't know what else to do when a brother dies.

* * *

Then he's beside Don in the police car driving up the soft asphalt
road, his jacket folded on his lap. They pass the creek. When the
car doesn't slow, Thomas realizes that his brother isn't there
anymore, that he'll have to go there alone another day, and that
today, they're going to the hospital in the city where most of the
people in the county are born, and die.

Probably Don wants Thomas to say something, and will speak
once he does. Thomas feels bad for not speaking to Don, but he
has nothing to say. Even though Thomas and the policeman are
about the same age, he has always felt older than the man. But
here, like this, he feels much younger and knows what it must be
to need to be told how to feel. He's glad that Don doesn't press
him, and feels the wisdom in it.

When Don pulls the car into the back of the hospital parking
lot and cuts the engine, he drops his hands from the steering
wheel and looks off across the sheet of asphalt toward the
rectangular brick building.

Nell and I toured the delivery floor a few months back.

Good people there, Don says. Both of ours were born there.
Hear they're remodeling.

Yeah, one side of it was shut off, plastic.

Seems that's coming up here pretty soon, the baby.

Another month.

So any day could be, Don says.

Guess so, Thomas says.

You'll be fine. Don examines his hands on the steering wheel.
Thomas, he says, it's him in there. It's Sam. We all know it's him,
but law says that kin's got to identify the body. It's a paperwork
situation, really.—Don nods at the parking lot.—Now, it's fine
with me if this is as far as you go. Gonna see him in the casket
anyhow. Ask me, the whole thing is for big cities where nobody

knows nobody, but I know you, and you know me, and I know that that's your brother in there.

Thomas looks at his own hands, clasped as they have been, on the coat folded in his lap, the fake lamb's wool edging his coat collar. His words surprise Thomas, like a storm in a creek, breaking the country bridges and rushing the silty banks and drowning the tiny red bugs that, despite their unimportance to the world, always captured his brother's attention. His, too, but whatever Sam had an interest in seemed more important, more noteworthy.

Maybe we should pray, Don says.

If you say it's him, no prayer's gonna change that, Thomas says.

Okay.

Thomas opens the door and steps into the parking lot, through the back door of the small hospital. Then Thomas and Don are entering the elevator that lowers them into the basement, to a small room with two plastic chairs that remind Thomas of the chairs in his father-in-law's dry-cleaning business, the ones by the gumball machine.

Don apologizes, It's usually faster than this. Don shifts back and forth, and Thomas can tell that it would calm the policeman for him to say something. But all he can hear is the fizz of the florescent light above the metal table.

Thomas sits down. It's cold. He goes ahead and puts on his coat and slips his hands into his pockets. He kneads the lint between his thumb and knuckle. When was the last time he wore it? He can't remember, but it seems important to know, now, on this day.

Maybe it was when he took Sam out to see their father's grave, to help him see that their father couldn't be down at the creek. But, no, it seems like he had it in the car for one of the summer concerts at the park band shell. Nell and he have taken Sam every summer Thursday since he was a boy. It was the first time they didn't let him dance. Ever since he was a kid, he'd liked Michael

Jackson and their mother had found two baseball batting gloves at a yard sale and cut off the fingers for him to wear. It didn't matter what the song was, Sam would strut his strut into the patch in front of the band shell where maybe one older couple shuffled together as a few children twirled or reached for lightning bugs or bent over, looking through their legs and smiling at their parents. But not this summer. Not after the arrests.

You're twenty years old, Sam. No more dancing. Sam tried to stand up anyway, but Thomas held his arm to his chest. No, Sam. That's it.

Nell spoke up. No more Michael Jackson. It's not suitable for a man your age.

I'm a man like Thomas.

That's right, Nell said. Does Thomas dance like Michael Jackson?

Thomas doesn't like Michael Jackson, Sam said.

No more dancing, Thomas said.

No more, Sam said.

No more Sam is Michael Jackson.

No more Sam is Michael Jackson. Sam leaned forward on his elbows, resting his face in the palms of his batting gloves and drumming his fingertips against his cheeks. Something about it irritated Thomas. He asked Sam to take off the batting gloves. Nell gave him a look. Sam resisted. C'mon, Thomas said.

Sam shook his head and clutched his hand over the back of his other.

And it suddenly made Thomas mad, the vulnerability of Sam doing that instead of clenching his fingers, which would have better prevented Thomas from taking off the gloves.

Take them off, Thomas said.

Sam shook his head.

Now.

No.

Thomas could feel it was a small, unnecessary cruelty, but now he had to be consistent, didn't he? He couldn't now say never mind.

Nell looked away, chin on her hand.

Of course he should have let Sam keep wearing them. But he didn't. He made them all fold up their chairs and leave the concert. Marched the family back to the car, Sam saying, No, no, no the whole way and wringing his hands. Nell probably thinking it was supposed to be a nice time, a return to routine after the death of Thomas and Sam's father, a break for their mother who said she might use the time to do the crossword. Maybe she'd make some iced tea.

Don is standing up, answering the door with whispers. Then he shuts the door and says it will be a moment, that he'll stay with him long enough for him to identify the body—then I'll step out, and you can stay here as long as you need. Just knock when you're done.

That won't be necessary, Thomas says.

Either way, Don says. The way he says it reminds Thomas that Don knows much more about this, and that he should listen, and so he thanks him. They wait.

Then Sam is brought in. His skin has been patted dry from the creek, and Thomas silently thanks whoever did the kindness. His face is clean shaven, and it occurs to Thomas that he has imagined his brother having been alive for the missing time, his black beard growing as the sun moved and his chest moving with breath as he waited to be found. But, no.

Thomas stands above his brother, and if Don is still in the room, he doesn't know and doesn't think of it. He forces himself to press his hand lightly against the angry red and purple streaks around his brother's throat. He had slipped and fallen into the creek, or walked into the creek and then slipped, or maybe he'd even lain down in the creek like he and Thomas used to, looking into the canopy of leaves and sky. But this time a storm came, and after the drought, the earth couldn't take it in, and the creek filled, and swept Sam a long way before he tangled on the roots of a tree.

His eyes would have been panicked. Would have scanned the creek for Thomas to appear. He would have yelled, Thomas! Thomas! Out loud or in his head. And maybe heard the sound go nowhere. Shut down by the trees, the air, the water, as abruptly as their father's hand damping the guitar strings.

Thomas closes his eyes and feels himself in the distance. When he opens them, the streaks are still on Sam's skin. Of course they are, he thinks. What a stupid way to die, he thinks, feeling the insult but not the tears, though those will come, too, mad, indignant but obediently following the curves of his face.

Then a voice says, Yes, that's my brother, and Thomas knows it must be his own voice, far away as it sounds.

When his mother was pregnant with Sam, Thomas went to one of the ultrasounds. The screen showed his brother floating inside the dark of her. He'd seen Sam's brain through his skull. This was before the results of the amniocentesis, his father calling to tell him about the chromosomes, but that it looked like his mother wouldn't end the pregnancy.

Why would I? his mother said later, daring them to answer. If there's one thing I've learned, life isn't a beauty pageant. Boy needs a home same as anybody. Boy should see the stars.

Not long after, it was Nell in a small office that looked little different than the first, and a young ultrasound technician who might have been the same one pushed buttons on a keyboard. But the *washa-washa-washa* of the baby's heart didn't come. Nell looked at Thomas. Thomas looked for the volume button. He waited for the quick flash of light that marked the heartbeat before it could be heard. The beat had been there last time, now it wasn't. How strange that hearts work that way.

It hurts him to think of it, and so he thinks about it harder in order to deepen the hurt. How much of grief is punishing oneself into grieving. As though one can never grieve equal to the life. And one must grieve for that, too.

* * *

Thomas holds an old clipboard and signs the lines on the papers, confirming the body death took was named Sam. Sam's not missing anymore. He waits for relief to follow the thought, or disappointment, or anger, but there's only the scratch of the pen against the paper and in the distance a humming air conditioner and a woman's voice saying she'll be a little late tonight but you go on. The woman sits at a desk in the corner. She's on the phone. And Thomas imagines it's Sam on the other line, hearing her say exactly what Thomas is hearing on this side of the air-conditioning, the safe canisters of pens and paperclips and assortment of picture frames.

But she shouldn't tell Sam to go on because he's going on to the creek, and he'll die if he goes. But, if she's talking to Sam, the storm is over and it's a different life Sam has with her, a different Sam. He's alive and his only problem is that his wife will be a little late home from work, but he's going to go on. Where to? To a game with his brother Thomas. That's right, they're going to go set up lawn chairs at the men's softball diamond and watch a game. Because if we're dreaming, it might as well be 1982 and so the men's softball league still exists and is winning games across the state.

Just one more page, Don says.

Thomas nods then looks again at the clipboard. The woman isn't on the phone anymore. She has her back to him, and she's on the computer, scrolling through a spreadsheet with her one red fingernail pressed to the keyboard button. She stops now and then, looking for something. Maybe his brother's file. Has she seen Sam, his body, or maybe just his name on the file? It's too late for her to fall in love with him, wish herself into the last years of his life, to kiss his cheek as she straightens his tie. What a stupid death. Stupid, stupid, stupid.

You're doing a good job, Thomas, Don says.

Thanks.

That's all now.

Okay.

On the way out of town, Don pulls into a fast-food ice-cream place. The one from their childhood is long gone. They sit in the drive-thru. Don orders two sundaes. Hot fudge okay with you? he says to Thomas. Thomas nods. He hasn't had a sundae for years. Probably the last time was with Nell, but what if it was with Sam, and he doesn't remember?

The teenage boy with a face of future acne scars hands the ice cream through the window. Thomas takes the plastic cup from Don, and Don runs his tongue against the red spoon. It's strange to see someone's tongue like that. What does it all mean? How can it even be the case that he just saw his dead brother and now he's eating ice cream in a police car while his mother is in a house she still hasn't completely cleared of his dead father's belongings, and she has no idea he'll be there soon, parking under the old oak tree he swung in as a boy, to tell her Sam's dead.

Are you sure it's him?

Yes, he'll say. Or nod.

You saw him?

Yes.

How? She'll say, bringing her hands to her mouth.

And he'll have to tell her how the storm raised the creek and he lost his footing or something.

But I just bought him those shoes, she'll say. The tread was good.

It was slick probably. Or something and the creek carried him away until the necktie around his brother's throat snagged a tree, or a tree snagged him.

By his necktie?

Yes, mother.

I don't remember which one he was wearing that day.

The blue and yellow one.

The striped one?

Yes.

That was your father's I think. Or maybe I got it for him. I just washed it the other week.

They said we can pick his clothes in a few days. Did you hear me, Mother?

What will I do with them?

You can wash them maybe, and hang them back in the closet.

Okay, she says. Okay, I could do that. And you're sure?

Yeah, it's him. It's Sam.

And she leans against him, her forehead against his chest, her hands on his arms, and she's pushing against him like a child trying to find sleep in a pillow.

* * *

Thomas was very small when, on a hot day in summer, he had wished it was winter. It was a wish that would return each summer, a little more lightly with each passing year, but this was the first summer it had come to him, hitting him with yearning that he may have never felt before that time—felt in the way that he could have asked what it was and someone would have understood to answer him. It was the same yearning he would feel, though more fleetingly if he didn't dwell, when there was a TV special with a magician who could fly, but wouldn't say how. It's *that*, that desperate, overwhelming desire to be able to defy reality. And because it was that, it was perhaps the first time Thomas had felt what reality was.

It is little surprise, then, that he felt it the first time in the middle of summer when the air's so full of heat that it wrings the body, so greedy for more and more water, that it takes from everything, leaving plants dry as fabric.

That summer, little Thomas stood bare chested and sunburned beside his wading pool, and he wished it were winter, that when he opened his eyes, it *would be* winter—regular, flat winter with the cold fields and the people in the village in their awkward winter coats, and the cinnamon smell of his mother's decorations, the flashing colored lights taped in the window, the pinecones in a bowl on the kitchen table, the wreath of chestnuts and red ribbon, his sweaters, his father digging out the Christmas records and snapping his fingers, and the mailman delivering cards printed with a snowy countryside dotted by small, perfect farmhouses as sleighs jangled by, and a small, dark-headed bird sat on the foreground fence. The more he imagined winter, the more he didn't want to open his eyes and find himself still in summer.

His mother found him in the backyard, weeping in his wading pool.

What is it, Thomas? Did a bee sting you?

He shook his head.

Are you hungry?

He tried to tell her he didn't want to be in this day anymore.

Open your eyes, Thomas. Just tell me and I'll make everything better.

But how could she pull snow over the fields like the colorful hot-air balloons spread out in the grass at the small airport where his father took him each summer? Then he remembered the hot-air balloon festival wouldn't come for another year, the heavy wicker baskets with silver tanks that puffed fire into the balloons, the fabric rippling and growing larger until they raised off the grass dragging the baskets against the field, as the people hurried to climb in before the balloons took off.

He wept as his body lowered into the pool as though on balloon strings, arms weak at his sides and the veins in his neck bulging as he yowled.

His mother went back into the house, calling for his father.

What's wrong with him? his father said.

Who knows? his mother said. He won't open his eyes.

When his father came out, Thomas forced the crying to a hitch but kept his eyes shut.

What is it, son? his father said. Bug in your eye? Let's have a look. He felt his father's fingers against his eyebrow and cheek, about to peel open the eye to see.

It's not winter, Thomas said.

What's that?

Thomas's chest hitched faster, fighting new tears so that he could speak only one word at a time. It's. Not. Winter.

His father laughed, but Thomas doesn't remember that or how his small shoulders began to tremble. His father crouched down. You're right, Thomas, he said. It's not winter. You're right on that.

I want it.

Winter?

Thomas nodded.

It will be, his father said, and pushed the tears across the boy's cheeks. But he didn't tell him he had to open his eyes.

That night, his father woke him up. Be quiet or you'll wake your mother, he said. Thomas blinked up at him. He went to Thomas's closet and pulled down shorts and a T-shirt and tossed them on his bed. Hurry up now, he said and left. Thomas scrambled into his clothes and the cool summer night.

His father sat in the car and Thomas started to climb into the backseat and onto his booster seat, but his father said no. In the front with me, kiddo. Thomas grinned. So did his father. Then they were driving the country roads.

The ditches and bugs flashed by in the headlights and the radio lights glowed on his father's face and hands. Here we go, his father said as he turned onto another road. Both sides of the road weren't planted. He drove a little bit farther before pulling into the middle of the road and stopping. He turned off the car.

See, Thomas? It's winter, his father said. See the black ice on the roads?

Thomas looked. The moonlight shined on the slick asphalt patches, and if he didn't look directly at the fields but through the sides of his sight, the fields seemed covered with a light snow. But also in his peripheral vision was the glow of the radio on his and his father's bare legs that stuck out of their shorts, and in the distance, crickets.

His father waited a while before turning the ignition on, the headlights returning the night to summer. Thomas waited for his father to say something else, but he didn't. They drove home.

It's like that, Thomas says to Nell.

She's resting her cheek on the pillow, watching him.

That's the closest to how I feel.

Like you want it to be winter?

He tries to say yes, but his throat thickens with tears, and so he stops.

* * *

Thomas goes to the creek and kneels on the sandy bank, the damp creeping into his thin pants and against his skin. The sand is tracked by birds and the shoes of police and probably the coroner. Down where the water laps, there's a sort of impression in the sand where Sam was probably pulled out, stood over, assessed.

He leans back on his heels. Now would be a time for God to speak. And maybe a good time to hear whatever God had to say.

A bird moves through the branches. Thomas looks up. It jumps from one branch to another. The leaves shift. The sun flickers. His mother might have taken the bird as a sign. Of anything. Of Sam being okay now. Nell would have, too. But of the baby being fine. You don't think Sam . . . that it's an omen?

Of what?

I don't know, she said but pressed the tips of her fingers against her belly.

The baby will be fine.

First your dad, she said. Now Sam. What if?

Thomas imagines that the same bird shifting through the branches as Sam lay below, lost. Or from years ago, when Thomas and Sam would lay on the bank looking up, or turn damp castles out of the wax coke cups they'd saved from the softball concession stand, or eat sandwiches while waiting for the angel to arrive, parting the weeds and the poison ivy with her bare hands.

You think she's on her way, Thomas?

Maybe.

Sam's baggy jeans are scrunched up at his knees and expose the white athletic socks their mother lays out for him each morning, along with a clean undershirt and underwear.

And if she comes, somebody's going to die.

If she washes her wings.

Right, Sam says, if she washes her wings.

That's what they say, Thomas says.

She needs to clean them.

Yes, Thomas says, and if she doesn't, then they say it means someone in the village is going to die.

I hope we don't see her. Right, Thomas?

People gonna die even if we don't see her.

But if we see her, we'll know early?

That's right.

I still hope we don't see her. Because we don't want anyone to die, right, Thomas? We don't want anyone to die.

That's right, Thomas says and looks over at his brother's face. At the flush cheeks, the soft lines of his body, the concentrated seriousness, and eventually, the black bristles of a beard. A beard. As they lie on their bellies on the creek bank, it strikes Thomas that Sam has had a beard for a while now. That it's going to keep growing in.

Out of surprise of the obvious, Thomas says, You're a man now, Sam. Sam looks up from the water and rests the side of his face on his folded hands and smiles. I'm a man, Sam says.

Yes, you are.

I'm a man like Thomas, Sam says, grinning.

Sure are.

I'm a man like Father, Sam says.

Like Father, too.

Father is a man. Sam is a man.

That's right, buddy.

I need a wife. I'm going to get me a wife.

Oh yeah?

Yeah, a wife. Gonna get me a wife. The girl at the pharmacy wears a yellow dress. The girl works there, and she wears a yellow dress, Thomas, and I'm gonna ask her to marry me.

Thomas tries to think of who Sam's referring to. Probably Deena Sweitzer, the pharmacist's granddaughter.

Shouldn't you take her on a few dates first, see if you like her?

You ever seen her, Thomas? She wears a yellow dress. Ever seen my girlfriend? You want to go meet her? Go and meet my girl?

Does she know she's your girlfriend?

She said yes. She has real pretty face, a nice face. I'm a man now, Thomas.

Yes, you have a beard and everything.

And a wife, I'll have one of those, too, like you and like Father because she's going to say yes. My girlfriend's going to say yes. Like Nell. Right, Thomas?

Thomas wants to congratulate Sam, encourage him, wish him luck. But he doesn't. Later, he overhears his mother agreeing with Sam that the pharmacy girl is pretty. Thomas knew why their mother encouraged it, of course.

It was hard not to wish for Sam what everyone else seemed to have, whether they wanted it or not. And so now and then his mother, and sometimes Thomas, and sometimes Nell, talked to Sam like he could date a girl in a yellow dress. If Sam had been interested in a boy in a yellow shirt, no one would take him seriously. Sam being gay wasn't in their mother's vision, since being gay wasn't an identity that survived in small towns, much less being like he was *and* gay. Sam had never broached the subject, far as Thomas knew. But if he had. Well, if he had, then their mother likely would have said, That can't be.

What did it matter now? Thomas thinks. Sam's over. Dead and here's the end of his story. You're alive, and Sam's dead, Thomas thinks.

Sam found the angel washing her wings, and maybe he tried to stop her.

Stop thinking, Thomas says.

Maybe the angel saw him and stood up and held out her arms to him.

Sam, Thomas says. His voice feels damp in the creek.

It matters who Sam actually was, Thomas thinks, because they had, for the most part, told Sam who he was. And Sam took part, too, of course. But how much they had shaped the story of who he could be, what he could accomplish, how smart they seemed to think he was. And they felt guilty about it, but they also felt like there couldn't be much harm in it.

After all, treating Sam like that was treating him like anyone. Thomas's mother had encouraged Thomas, hadn't she?—pretended that he was capable of more than he was, that his life would be so much different than his father's or hers, even though she surely had known better. Surely, she knew the chances were greater that Thomas would remain in the village than go to the university. That he would not become the big city businessman, or the fancy lawyer like on her crime programs. Which sort of lawyer will you be? she'd say as they sat in front of the TV sharing popcorn.

What would have been so wrong with asking him what kind of father he'd be? What sort of husband? Will you be the distant sort like your father, or the closer kind like one reads about in the magazines? Most all the men in the village were fathers and husbands. Surely she had known that was his likely trajectory.

The longer Nell's pregnancy lasted, the more he realized how much of the world his parents saw that he hadn't, like that Greek who'd calculated the size of the world by how far he could see. When Thomas was searching for Sam, he kept thinking about that man, how he would have seen further than Thomas could.

Sam's dead, Thomas thinks.

* * *

Nell's in the recliner when Thomas returns from the creek, after staying there into the night. She doesn't like it, but hasn't said anything yet.

It's late, she says. Her eyes look groggy, like his coming in the door woke her.

Not too late, he says.

Don't want to be tired for the funeral.

Guess not.

The fetal monitor is on the floor where it must have fallen from her lap. That she has it in the living room makes him think she didn't intend to fall asleep here, either. They've never said it, but he doesn't like how often she uses it. It makes him nervous. Evidently, she has tried to keep him from worrying by not telling him how often she's listening in on their baby.

You're awake, he says, pretending not to see the monitor on the floor.

She nods.

Baby keeping you up?

Maybe a little of that, she says. Aren't you tired?

Not too bad, he says.

She sees he's lying but leaves it. She opens her arms to him. He crouches by the recliner and rests his hand on her belly.

The first night he went looking for Sam, after a day of them driving every country road from the village center to the first sphere of surrounding villages, he'd been so thick with energy that she felt it in her throat like the heartburn before the miscarriage. As the days passed, that same energy had begun to unwind inside him, become heavy as a dead snake on a roadside, a snake that eventually dries up there, until it's as light as a cornhusk that blows across the road in drought or early autumn.

Tell me about it, Thomas.

I have these dreams, Thomas says, looking up at her.

Yeah, she says and waits.

Sometimes.

Go on, baby, she says.

Well, I don't want to wake up from them.

Okay.

She waits. He sees her see the monitor on the floor. She looks back at him. Should I worry?

No.

Okay.

Surely it will get better. When the baby comes.

It's coming, isn't it?

I think so, Thomas. I think this time, yes, he or she's going to come.

That's good.

It is.

He rests his cheek on her thigh. She cups her hand against his face, his ear. Like her hand's a conch shell, he listens for the ocean. He hears the creek.

* * *

Thunder rolls inside the clouds passing over the vast field, and inside the dream he thinks, *It's finally here*, as though the summer storm hasn't come yet. He turns toward the cornfield, ready for it to turn green under the beginning rain. People walk through the rows backward, in a line like mourners, wearing suits and floral polyester dresses, bodies swaying with each step toward the creek.

A rush of rain sweeps down, splattering the people's cheeks and the lenses of eyeglasses and faces of wristwatches. Thomas looks down at his own watch. He expects to see Sam's watch with the green band. Because this is a dream. He's sure of it. But it's not his brother's watch or his father's, and it hasn't stopped either. The second hand ticks forward twice, three times—enough to assure him that it will keep advancing.

The women's dresses press against their thighs, curl up, show ragged slips, varicose-legs above in sagging pantyhose held by rusted garter clips. Like birds tossed from the sky, the men's hats tumble off their heads and turn over the field. But they don't seem to notice.

Across the way, at the farthest edge of the field is the windbreak of trees. Even though that's not where the creek is, Thomas knows the creek is *there* in this dream. White shrouds cover the trees and flap like sheets from clotheslines. Lightning presses against the sky, illuminating the branches beneath the sheets. The shadows of the leaves gather from their branches into the shape of a man standing on one tree limb as he reaches up for another.

Lightning then the sky goes dark again, but there's enough sunset behind the dark clouds to see the mourners take another step back. The men's dress shoes and the women's heels sink into the wet ground, and as they lift their feet, small clods of mud crumble down.

Lightning illuminates the shadow of the climbing man is farther up the tree and reaching out as though to balance before moving onto the limb of another tree. Sam?

The sky goes dark. Thomas steps from his backyard into the field. The field is scattered with dirty wide puddles.

In one of the dirty pools of water floats a white athletic sock. Sam's.

Does that mean Sam's already dead? Or about to die? Or he came back to life and is going to die again.

He looks at the sock again, but now it's his brother's silver medical bracelet that he wore because of his heart. The same bracelet that caught on the roots of the tree and drowned him. No, Thomas, that's not right. It was his necktie. But that was the first time he died, last time was the bracelet. In another dream, Sam's walking through a cornfield maze like they set up at the orchard every autumn, and Thomas is running through it, chasing Sam's giggle before lightning hits the husks and sets them on fire. In one corner of the maze, Nell sits on a chair. Her belly is made of glass and a bird is inside it, flying into it like a window again and again.

It's bad luck, isn't it? she says.

Thomas runs into the field. The lightning comes again. The climbing man isn't there. It's cold and windy. He waits for the lightning to come again. Either his brother has fallen or the light from God's eyes that makes shadows on the earth has gone out.

Then Sam is there, and they're sitting in a cove of shade trees. He gestures for Thomas to come sit by him, and Thomas does.

Let's sit here, Sam says.

Thomas nods. It's peaceful here with him, safe in the shade, and they speak to each other, and it feels so good to be with him again. Let me remember this, Thomas thinks.

* * *

Nell insists on ironing the shirt before they leave for the funeral. He says not to bother. He already has it on, buttoned down, tucked in.

You wear a wrinkled shirt today, Nell says, and they'll take it as a sign that you're not thinking straight.

I'm not thinking straight.

She smiles as though it were a joke, and takes the shirt from him and unfolds it over the ironing board.

He watches her work the iron against the cloth, leaning her weight through her arm so that the muscle twitches almost imperceptibly. Steam hisses, her arm flexes. He wonders if the baby can feel the heat, can distinguish her heat from the iron's heat.

When Sam was little, she sometimes took him to work with her at her father's dry-cleaning store. He liked the gumball machine by the counter but was scared of the big room with the washers and the racks of clothing. He'd press his hands to his ears and squint his eyes and begin to yell as though trying to find himself among the larger sounds of the machines.

When she peels Thomas's shirt off the ironing board, she holds it between them, hooking the collar off her index finger. Heat radiates off it. He takes it from her, slipping his arms through the sleeves.

Are you going to speak? she says.

He shrugs.

No one expects you to, she says.

He nods.

If you want, I could fake going into labor in the middle of it.

Oh yeah?

Sure.

It's still early.

Nobody knows that, she says.

Yeah.

I'm just joking.

I know it, he says. I'm trying.

I know you are. She takes his hand and presses it against her belly.

My wife's dress is light blue with white polka dots, he thinks, and my brother is dead.

There, she says. Feel it?

He waits. The baby's head rolls beneath his hand.

She's turning over, Nell says. Are you stretching? she says, looking down.

Somersaults, he says.

Circus child, Nell says and smiles, resting her hand on the back of his.

I *am* trying, he says.

I know you are, she says. He was a good brother, she says. Your father. Sam. But we can still have a good life.

I know it, he says.

Do you? she says. She looks at his eyes, as though they're in the way of his thoughts.

Ready to go? he says.

* * *

The air is heavy in the church. The raised windows do little to decrease the stifling sweat and exhalations. Nell threads her fingers through his and walks up the aisle toward the front where his mother sits. Same place she sat for his father's funeral. Maybe the same dress, too. Black with splotchy orange flowers. Nell will remember. Sam's casket is in the same place, too. Closed. Good.

Thomas can feel the congregation around him like trees, elbowing each other, nodding at him. The strange feeling of celebrity that comes from being the relative of the deceased. Of course, everyone in the village followed Sam's disappearance. The TV news from two towns over aired Sam's picture—Missing Man—and then the footage of the creek in the distance when he was found. A few people recorded the news and brought the recordings by the house like casseroles. The village doesn't usually make the news except during the annual autumn festival, which might not happen this year because rumor is it's just too expensive.

Almost all of Thomas's schoolteachers are here, and Sam's— most of them the same, except a few more from the special program, though that's not what it's called now. A few families from the summer camp upstate that Thomas's mother drove Sam up to every year since he was about three years old. Thomas nods at them. They wave back. His eyes water. Because they didn't have to come. Or because he didn't expect them. Or because they carry more Sam memories. Sam in those palm-tree swim trunks. Sam splashing into the pool.

Even if Thomas wants to pretend Sam isn't dead, he can't since everyone from his whole life knows that Sam's dead. And Sam's somehow part of everyone. How to dig Sam's death out of all these brains?

Sam's casket stands in the same place his father's was, too, in front of the pulpit. Probably the same skirting, too. Same stand. But this casket is beige, a cheaper casket, the cheapest in the funeral home catalog.

I just didn't expect two funerals, his mother said to the funeral director.

You don't have to apologize, he said.

She wiped her forehead. She kept doing that. A tic Thomas had never seen before.

Thomas knew it shouldn't matter, the price of a casket. But it did. And it made him angry. Nell would probably tell him that's how he copes. By getting angry instead.

At the back of the church sits Lorna Farris and her daughter Marie. Marie had been paralyzed in a wreck on Six-Mile Curve. Lorna and Nell had been cheerleaders together in school, and the accident happened around the same time as Nell's miscarriage. Thomas thinks Nell sought out the friendship because she needed someone with grief who wasn't him.

The resurrected friendship lasted about a summer, and Lorna would come over with Marie. If Sam were there, he'd sit beside Marie, her arms velcroed to the wheelchair arms, her head arched slightly back and to the side. As sounds came out of her, Sam would nod as though she'd spoken clear as day.

From a distance, the two looked like a young courting couple from midcentury, Sam in one of his neckties and leading the conversation, Marie listening politely, in another new outfit—a splendid pale green dress or a lavender blouse and white slacks with perfect creases that belled at her feet, which were carefully fitted with matching slippers.

Other girls Marie's age were walking with boys around the park pond or sitting on picnic tables at the abandoned drive-in restaurant or, late at night, driving to the superstore in the next town over and strolling up the bright aisles hoping the boy they'd marry would appear but flirting with whatever boy appeared.

And I can't blame them, Lorna said. A few girls from Marie's class still come by, though less and less. I take her to the games, to the movies, so that they'll have stuff to talk about.

I feel like, Lorna said, everyone's just waiting for me to catch on and disappear.

Catch onto what?

I don't know. Like. Like that she's not the same Marie. But she is. Her body changed, but. I mean, her experiences may be different, but I feel like people think this new Marie should be locked up somewhere, like that old asylum in Ashmore that we used to drive out to for a good scare.

We were just kids, Nell said.

But people didn't change their thinking. Seems like nobody likes to see broken things. People don't keep broken vases on their tables.

She's not broken.

I know that, but I'm talking about people around here.

You can't think like that, Nell said.

But I do and feel like such an asshole, right? Because what was supposed to be scary was Marie. I was running around that asylum afraid of my own daughter.

You didn't know. How could you have known?

Lorna laughed. Once you have a daughter, a child, it's like you've always had one.

Nell was quiet.

Joe doesn't say much. He's angry a lot. He stopped carrying his gun in his truck because he's afraid he'll shoot somebody. I mean, he won't. But he just doesn't trust himself anymore. Anger like that, Thomas thinks. Yeah.

Please rise, someone says.

They stand.

The funeral is still happening. That's right, Thomas thinks. I'm at my brother's funeral.

Nell holds an open hymnal. He reads the words the people around him seem to be singing. The organs play. All in sync. Music. How strange.

They sit down.

The preacher approaches the lectern. He baptized Sam when Sam was eleven or twelve. The other night when he visited Thomas's mother's house to discuss which verses would be read, who would speak and when, the preacher said he'd probably say a few words about Sam's baptism. How excited Sam had been after all those weeks in the confirmation class. After the baptism, there was cake and punch in the church basement. Sam stood up by the punchbowl so that people couldn't help but shake his hand, pat his back. With every congratulations, Sam would say, I'll see you in heaven!

The person would chuckle and say, I hope so, Sam. Or, you sure will. But Thomas saw a few people as they turned away, the doubt, or wink like they were in on a secret they were keeping from Sam.

Thomas didn't believe in God, heaven, or any of it, but he'd be damned if the people who did believe in it all imagined Sam not there too or, worse, welcomed through the pearly gates as some other version of himself, which wouldn't be Sam at all.

I went to the creek, the preacher says, looking at Thomas.

His mother wipes her forehead.

Nell holds the sides of her belly. Thomas wonders if their baby's asleep. If they hadn't lost the first baby, she'd be sitting between them, maybe coloring in a book, her tongue concentrating in the corner of her mouth. No, the child would be older. Not a child anymore. Time keeps moving after tragedy, but the memory always feels as though it must have been just three, four years ago that it happened. He wonders whether Nell thinks funerals are no place for children. Some people think so. Would they have argued over it? Will they?

Or maybe Sam wouldn't be dead if their child had survived. Because one difference changes everything, though it's hard to survive thinking that way for very long.

What a stupid death, Thomas thinks. What a stupid death.

* * *

After the funeral, he goes for a drive. When he gets home, Nell's sitting on the top porch stair beside one of the white planters. She's plucking the drooping and shriveled purple blossoms from the petunias and tossing them into the garden edging the house.

Haven't kept up with them, she says. Dirt streaks her breasts and her forehead. She looks up at him. Usually, he'd take her into his arms, maybe lift her braid over her shoulder—at least sit next to her. He doesn't. She picks up the small watering can at her hip and tips it above the planter.

He goes into the kitchen and opens one cabinet after another, not knowing what he's looking for until he finds himself looking at a coffee mug. He takes it down and sets it on the counter. The screen door wheezes open then bangs and Nell walks into the kitchen. She looks at him.

We're out of coffee, he says.

The drive didn't change anything then?

No, it's still summer, he says.

She's tired in the eyes.

I'm sorry for all this, he says.

I cared for him, too, Thomas.

I know you did. Sure, I know you did.

You act like you're the only one with a right to feel about it one way or another.

He looks back at the mug empty on the counter in front of him. His brother's dead and they're out of coffee because his brother went walking and then he went walking and she'd brewed a thermos for him every night and then he'd brew more when he woke up and went walking through the day, crossing the roads and the fields and passing through the town and the diner where people were having coffee instead of helping search for Sam, and Thomas would scream, *Help me find him!* in his head, as he walked by, on past the photocopied pictures of Sam taped to the windows and around light poles. Missing Man. But he isn't missing anymore. Now he's buried beside their father, and there's no more coffee. He will go get some. Facts, facts, facts.

You want to go with me? Thomas says.

You need to sleep. No sleep once the baby comes.

Are you having contractions?

Nell shakes her head. The wrinkle alongside her lips is deeper these days, more worried.

I'm sorry, he thinks.

I'll be right back, he says.

How much more can we take? he thinks. Fuck, fuck, fuck.

He drives to the grocery, but when he gets there there's other vehicles in the small parking lot. The Taylors' minivan, the Hendersons' station wagon, Phil Oakley's old truck, and five or so other vehicles he'd know if he looked closer. Probably the people from those cars are meeting in the produce aisle right now, or the frozen foods, reaching for a box of dreamsicles with one hand while reviewing the funeral, how bad Sam's death has been on the family, such a happy guy Sam always was, and their mother, poor thing. A shame. Sure is. But at least there's the baby to look forward to. It's a real blessing that baby. How long have they been trying? Nearly a decade seems like.

Longer, Thomas thinks. He drives back onto the main street that becomes a highway to the next town. Same highway he drove every other weekend when he'd met Nell. City girl, he'd call her. He remembers going to one of her ballet recitals, her last one. Groups of little girls danced before her, watching each other's feet, trying to smile, and then Nell came out, her face heavy with makeup to cover her acne, and she danced alone in front of a blue curtain, and when she jumped, her toe shoes knocked against the stage. When Sam was little, she'd take out her old toe shoes and dance around the house with him in her arms, and he'd pat her cheeks, laughing when she spun.

The superstore parking lot is large and mostly empty. He usually avoids the place because the lights are so bright and the place makes him anxious, like he's lost in a garish carnival. But alone, tonight, he feels no different than any recent day. If anything, a respite.

After he finds the coffee, he doesn't go straight to the cashier, but walks up and down the other aisles, letting his eyes slip over the colors, the prices, the tired faces of the late-night workers who ferry huge cardboard boxes and crates across the aisles. Their faces make him sad. Thomas turns away, until the lights and things to buy distract him from their lives.

On the way out of the store, he stops in the entryway, which is lined with windows and along them, quarter machines filled with gold watches and tiny plastic people with painted faces and temporary tattoos shaped like hearts and skulls with handcuffs coming through their eye sockets. There are a few heavy arcade games with cartoon airplanes that flash on and off as they fly up the screen, and explode.

In the path of the exit stands one of those claw-machine games, its large glass cube half full of stuffed animals packed tightly together under a mechanical claw that hangs above them.

Thomas reaches into his front pocket for a quarter that he would have given Sam. Before he slips it into the small glowing red slot, he assesses the claw and the herd of cows and frogs and a few gorillas and aliens with stitched smiles and tufts of neon-colored hair. The back of the glass is up against a window overlooking the parking lot where insects mutter around the tall lights.

He feeds the machine the quarter. The lightbulbs flicker on with a giddy, mechanical song. He pulls the lever, and the metal claw jerks forward on its track. When it hangs just over the animal, he waits. The song ends. The claw descends. Its prongs come together weakly, scratching at one of the animal's forelegs, before wheezing back up, jaws empty as it follows the track back to start.

He searches his pocket for another quarter.

The song begins again, he pushes the lever, the metal hand drops, and comes up empty and slightly trembling.

Which one you trying for? someone says behind him.

Thomas turns. An old man stands beside him, looking into the claw game. He holds two gray plastic bags and, under on arm, a block of paper towels.

Thomas points. The old man leans in. What is it?

Thomas shrugs. Looks like the easiest to get.

The old man nods but hunts the glass cube for a more vulnerable animal. What about that one there? he says. That ostrich or something.

I think it's a giraffe.

Looks like a keeper, the old man says.

It's all neck, Thomas says.

Go for its wing. Over there, see?

I don't know.

Sure, sure. That'll do her.

Thomas nods and slips in another quarter. The music goes, the claw drops, the claw returns, the music ends, and the lights blink to silence.

Thomas imagines the old man driving the long dark road to home, probably one of the a small, one-story houses on every street, with large white planting pots on either side of the front door that his wife filled dutifully every spring with purple and white petunias.

The old man will park in the driveway, under the security light that hangs off the garage where maybe a basketball hoop once was, for a son who ended up using it only a few times while the man and his brother used it the most because they'd always wanted one growing up, and so on more summer nights than you'd think, the man's brother would come over, and while their wives visited, they'd play deep into the night, hurling the ball over each other's heads, darting away from each other, backing up against the other's chest, jumping and rebounding and cursing each other between laughter.

Then the man and his brother would sit on broken lawn chairs that Sam keeps meaning to fix but never does, which Thomas kids him about, and Sam punches him in the arm, grinning. They open their beers and say things that will become important like the memory of summer air in winter.

What's it like to know how your life turned out? Thomas wants to say to the old man.

The old man sets down his bags. Let me try, he says.

I'll have to go get more quarters, Thomas says.

The old man waves him off and takes a rubber coin purse from his pocket. He squeezes it open and wiggles his finger around until he finds a quarter. He feeds the machine without looking then leans against it.

The lightbulbs flicker, the music begins, and the old man maneuvers the claw until it's above the giraffe.

There you go, Thomas says.

Almost, almost, the old man says, his body gone still with focus.

The old man rubs his bottom teeth against his top lip. He gently pulls the lever toward him.

Looks good, Thomas says.

The claw drops, pulls up nothing.

Goddammit, the old man says and reaches for the coin purse again. This time when he pushes the quarter into the slot, he calls out, This one's for Old Maurice, you old son of a bitch, and he's dragging the lever hard then jerking it this way and that. The claw drops, shuts on the back leg of a pink animal and pulls it into the air, and as the claw swings the smiling animal, the old man's cursing up a storm, and Thomas looks over his shoulder, expecting a cashier or somebody in a blue vest to warn them to quiet.

Just before the claw reaches the chute, the rabbit falls back down onto the others, staring out, unaware of the two men staring back or at their reflections.

What a game, Thomas thinks.

Then he remembers Nell, who is at home, maybe sitting on the edge of the bed with her nightgown pulled up to her breasts and the fetal monitor pressed against her large, bare belly. Her feet against the floor. She is listening, listening, her eyes closed in the dark warmth of the night.

Yes.

THE WANDERING HOUSE

––––

The girl knocks on the wooden frame of the door. Dogs start barking, the shapes of them knocking against the curtains in the front window. But the curtains are held together with safety pins to keep the cold out. Thick plastic covers the windows, duct taped along the frames. Like every winter.

She waits on the porch. She can hear the boy coming through the house just like Riley used to. Though he usually sent Jack down to greet her.

Not much has changed. The sound of the TV walking through the wall of the house. Or probably the window. Thin windows. It's an old house. Riley taught her how to tell the difference between original windows and new ones. See the way the glass sort of wavers in the sunlight when you look up at the right angle? New windows don't do that. The difference between hand-blown and factory-made bottles. Pointing at the mold line. See there? Look at the lip. See the difference? He wanted to have an antique store one day. He'd even picked out where it would be, in the small, red brick building downtown by the train tracks, where Bell's Jewelry used to be. The white letters still in the brick. He'd tried selling some of the bottles and vases he found out in the woods at the Saturday auction. But the auction's better for picking, he learned.

People round here can't tell the difference between an eye and a glass eye. She'd laughed. They both had. Because that was before the explosion.

Of course not much has changed. The porch swing's still broken, just sitting there. The door's blue instead of red. Because in the larger daily reality where much of the world takes place, or at least where she used to take place, not so much time has passed. Some of her burns are still fresh pink. The deepest ones. The doctor said sometimes the ache never fully goes away. Because it's not just skin that burned off. It's nerves that deep down.

The dogs are bouncing faster against the curtains. The lock slides. Did they used to lock their door?

The front door opens, slowly. A tiny dog's face appears at the bottom, yapping. She tries to remember which name goes with this one.

Jack is standing in the crack of the door. Riley's little brother.

Hey, he says to her, then hooks the dog by the neck with his ankle, like a vaudeville cane, pulling the dog backward as he steps out on the porch. He shuts the door behind him. His socks are white with gray toes. Riley wore black socks with gray toes. Oh my god, she thinks. Is this what you're going to do the whole time?

So they let you? Jack says.

Yeah.

And it's okay for you to be out like this?

She shrugs. Mom probably doesn't think so. But this is important, right?

He nods. I meant the doctors.

They're not the boss of me, she says, winking. But of course she can't wink that eye anymore. She taps the palms of her mittens against her legs. Yeah, it's fine, she says. Hey, your door's blue. Looks nice.

Yeah. Mom read something about red doors.

Some spiritual thing? she says.

Not really.

My mom stopped going to church, too.

Oh, it's not like that, Jack says.

What's it like?

She read on the internet somewhere about red doors being code for meth houses.

The girl goes still. Don't react, she thinks.

So she went down to the hardware lickety split, Jack says, talking faster, and next thing you know we've got a blue door. She didn't want you to feel uncomfortable.

That doesn't sound like her, she says.

Jack grins. Well, I made that part up. She painted it before they found him.

You think it's Riley.

Before they found whoever it is. It's not the first time they found someone that might be him.

I didn't know.

Yeah. More and more bodies. Kind of like the meth billboards that started showing up. Like every time there's another body found on the side of an interstate, in another field, beneath snow, another billboard goes up. Or billboard, then body. Hard to know how long the people have been missing based on when the newspapers find them.

Chicken or the egg, she says, lightly. She hates the billboards. There's one on the interstate on the way to the hospital and she holds her breath when they drive past it, like it's a cemetery.

Some lady from a nonprofit had somehow gotten her cell number. Probably from the local news station after they ran the story when it first happened, when they didn't know any of the details outside of the footage of the skeleton of the house on fire, and so they got all the details wrong. Like that she'd done a rape kit. That Riley was at large. It wasn't like that at all. And Riley may be out there somewhere, watching the segment, thinking she was accusing him of rape. But of course he isn't out there. She knows he isn't. He was running ahead of her. He was the closest when all of a sudden.

The lady from the nonprofit asked if she'd be interested in doing a commercial.

I'm not an addict, she said.

Of course not, the lady said.

I mean it, she said.

Think it over, the lady said. Think about the lives you could save.

She hung up. I already think about that, she thought. That's what she should have said to the lady.

Anyway, Jack says. It didn't seem right to tell you about the others that didn't end up being him anyway. Your mom said you needed to focus on recovering.

I'd never heard that, she says. About blue doors.

Red doors, he says. Probably more in the cities than around here. If it's even true.

You think it's him? she says.

Didn't see it was snowing, he says, looking past her.

I can see it, she says.

I didn't mean . . .

Oh, she says, I thought . . . She gestures at her eye.

He shakes his head, looking away.

It's okay to look, she says. It doesn't bother me.

He looks at her.

She looks back.

Her thickly knitted hat, the pom-pom, the new skin grafted over her cheek, from a square from the inside of her thigh. Her left eye melted shut, eyelashes growing at different angles, like black stitches coming unthreaded.

How long did you want me to look? he says.

Smart ass, she says.

It's good to see you, he says.

Who is the you that you see? she thinks. But she can't deliver it in a way to make him laugh, so she just follows him inside.

* * *

She steps into the entryway.

Riley and Jack's father is sitting in the same old orange recliner, back to the door.

That you, Vix? he says, trying to look back over the headrest.

None other, she says. She tries to stand on the small doormat, to keep her snow boots from dripping onto the floor. Riley's snow boots are just inside the door. Gray with red piping.

I've been wearing them, Jack says.

Sure, she says.

Their father adjusts the crocheted doilies on the arms of the chairs. He rocks in the reflection of the TV. She walks closer. He pushes his palms against the chair arms, starting to lift himself to standing.

Please don't, she says. She holds out her mittens.

The same fake ferns stand in a line across the entertainment center. The same school pictures of Riley and Jack. You're framed now, she says.

Jack follows her gaze. Yeah. Mom bought a box of them at the auction house.

Same brown carpet. Same coffee table with the glass top. Same gold sunburst clock on the wall. They have no idea how much it's worth, Riley said. How much? Dunno. Two hundred. Maybe five. Pretty good shape.

Come stand where I can get a good look at you.

Oh, let's not do anything we'll regret, she says, lightly. She's learning the jokes that come with her new face. The jokes to make everyone else feel at ease.

Now, don't you say it.

But when she stands in front of him, in front of the footrest where his ankles are crossed, she sees how he hesitates. Sees him have thoughts. Sees him not say them.

Told you, she says.

Pretty as ever, he says. Your folks able to make it?

My folks, she says.

That's right, he says.

Folks was one of Riley's words. Not that words belong to anyone. But sort of. She'd never heard anyone use folks until she met Riley. But she didn't move here until first grade, and that's late, late enough for everyone to remember her family's not from around here. Which became more apparent after the explosion. Or maybe the town turns everyone into a stranger when something bad happens. Otherwise, it would be harder to talk about them like that. Or maybe violence just erases a person, and the town talks to keep the person there, present.

Jack's hanging her coat on one of the wooden pegs on the wall by the door. He points at her scarf. She shakes her head. She feels safer wearing it. About exposing a bit of herself at a time.

Nah, my folks stayed home, she says. I rode my bike. She reflexively turns toward the picture window where the bike is parked on the outside, by the old tree. Used to be a tire swing there, but she'd noticed coming in the fat black tire on the ground.

Pretty cold for a bike ride, a woman says. Riley and Jack's mom.

The girl turns to the sound, until she's facing the window the woman sits in front of, on the couch.

Not too cold once you get going, the girl says. Don't look at the curtains, she thinks. Once, their mother had caught her staring at the thick plastic over the windows. It ain't pretty, but it's warm, the woman had said. Right, the girl agreed, flushing. Meaning no harm, of course, but not knowing how to undo it. Because she did think the plastic was ugly. She doesn't know if she's allowed to think anything's ugly now. What that means for her.

The dogs are curled like furry pill bugs on the throw pillows. One on the woman's lap, chin over her forearm. She's wearing a spring white dress splashed with bright flowers, gathered in the waist, the skirt flaring over her bare knees. She's wearing black socks and the black skid-proof shoes from work.

That's a pretty dress, the girl says.

I thought I should wear a nice dress, the woman says. For the occasion. Your mother would wear a nice dress if you'd gone missing and now were found.

I once was lost, the girl thinks. But now I'm found, she thinks. A voice from church. Riley lost, but now he's found. Maybe. That's why she's here, isn't it? Because if he's found, now she will know. And then she can figure out what to do with that, or not figure out but have it at least, not picture him wandering the country roads like a vanishing hitchhiker.

Thank you for inviting me, the girl says.

Oh, Jack's the one who thought you should come. I said you probably shouldn't.

It's a lovely dress, the girl says.

Heard you might not be getting out soon as now, the mother says.

Lucky I guess, she says.

Like bamboo, the mother says.

Bamboo, the girl says. Right. When you visited the hospital. I'm sorry I couldn't speak to thank you.

Riley's mother had appeared at the hospital room door as the girl laid in her hospital bed, holding another clump of hair that had just sloughed from her scalp.

The burned hair smelled awful, but she couldn't say that or anything because of the breathing tube. Or, at least, not in a way her mother understood. Any time she tried, her mother summoned the nurse because she thought she was in pain. As though her mother imagined a pain that came and went, or moved in waves.

She held out her hair for her mother to throw away, but her mother didn't take it. She felt her mother stand up.

You shouldn't have come, her mother said.

Has Riley been here? It sounded like Riley's mother.

Vix will be fine, her mother said.

That's not what I asked, Riley's mother said.

It's what you should have asked.

I came right after work. Came as fast as I could. I still have to work, don't I?

The girl imagined Riley's mother in the dollar store's uniform: scratchy yellow polo shirt and black pants. How she'd take her shoes off as soon as she came through the back door, untucking her shirt. It was too long and went nearly to her knees. Anyone else want an iced tea? she'd say, pulling the pitcher from the refrigerator, a plastic cup from the stack by the microwave. Already have one, Riley would say, and the girl wouldn't say anything.

What is that? her mother said.

The girl tried to imagine her hospital room. A stack of magazines for reading. Maybe a bag of candles for lighting, something to align the universe.

Oh, this, Riley's mother said. Just came in a shipment. Bamboo. According to the little tag here, it's good luck. Guess you don't have to water it much or nothing.

You can't have plants in here, the girl's mother said, her voice shrill and moving around the girl's bed, bumping against the foot of it.

The girl groaned.

Dammit, her mother whispered. Sorry, baby, her mother whispered. Let me take care of this.

Has she said anything about Riley? his mother asked.

And then the room felt empty. No voices. Just the same distant sounds. There were less screams in the burn unit than the girl imagined there might be once she was in there. Probably because of the breathing tubes.

The girl thought of Riley and Jack and her in the dark car, the lights of the dashboard illuminating their faces as they sped up the country roads, headlights pushing against the dark, against the weeds and animals lining the ditches. Jack sat in the back, but leaned between the front seats. Riley was driving their mother's car. A brass angel clipped to the air freshener. Never drive faster than your guardian angel can fly, it said. Riley's mother had put one in everyone's stockings the previous Christmas.

Cornfields and bean fields flashed by. It was a wonderful feeling, going fast down roads they usually walked or bicycled, down hills, around corners, over Troll's Bridge, out to where Riley thought the Slave Cabins were, but they couldn't really see them in the dark if they were out there.

Then Jack said, Slow down, patting Riley's shoulder. Slow down.

A deer?

She looked. But it was just more of the same they'd been driving by all night. See that? Jack said, moving to the driver's window, his forehead against the glass.

You think it's a porch light? Jack said.

Oh, I get it, Riley said. Well, I'm not falling for it.

I'm serious, Jack said. His voice sounded serious. Look, he said. You see it, Vix?

Riley pulled over. The brake lights glowed red in the rear windshield and the side mirrors. She could see the exhaust smoking red on her side of the car.

Of course, the car was there when the ambulances arrived. So if Riley ran away, why didn't he take the car?

Turn off the headlights, Jack said.

Riley hesitated. It's dangerous.

Just for a second, Jack said. Not forever. Just for a second.

He cut the lights, and it felt like closing her eyes it went so dark.

She peered into the darkness. They'd see someone coming around the curve, but that car would see them too late.

Turn them back on, she said.

I think I see it, Riley said.

A porch light? she said. She tried to see the direction his face was turned, finding his cheek in the moonlight. Her eyes were adjusting, but she could still hardly see the difference between where night met the dark fields and windbreaks. If there was a porch light out there, surely she should see it.

This isn't funny, she said.

No joke, Jack said.

Hell if that was there last time we came around, Riley said.

I don't remember it, do you?

Their voices were getting excited.

Plenty of houses have porch lights, she said.

But don't you see?

Not a porch light I don't.

Pull forward, Riley. Maybe she's just at the wrong angle.

Shouldn't be any light out there, Riley said.

What do you know about it?

There's a dump site back there. He pointed, hitting his finger against the window. I go looking back there. Found a couple good bottles. Not like the usual medicine bottles, dime a thousand those. But nobody lives back there.

Maybe somebody's holing up.

No sheds out there. Nothing to live in. If that's a light, it's a porch light.

You think Kyle Orff really saw it like he said? Out when he was checking traps?

He's a liar otherwise.

But did you see his eyes when he was telling it? Seemed to believe it.

Turn the headlights back on, Riley. Please.

Probably just somebody out there dumping stuff, maybe. Flashlight or something.

Maybe. Strange time of night to be doing that.

I heard it's not even a whole house. Just like a staircase and a roof hovering there.

No, it's a whole house.

How do you know?

Why would it only be a partial house? What's scary about that?

Mamie Harris's mother told us that her sister seen The Wandering House when they were kids before they lost the farm, so they were living out in the country at that point, I guess. And they seen a house where there shouldn't have been one, or at least there hadn't been one for their whole lives until that night. Her sister snuck out the window and started walking toward it, but Mamie was scared, so she stayed put. When her sister got back, she was white as snow, I guess. Wanted to know if Mamie had seen them. Mamie didn't know what she was talking about. I guess all these ghosts started walking beside her sister the closer she got to the porch light, and out ahead of her, but they didn't see her at all. At least she didn't think so because she felt some of them walking through her, like they were taking something from her. Feel my heart, she told Mamie. And Mamie put her hand on her chest and could feel it beating. Faster than she'd ever felt a heart beat. Then her sister had two miscarriages when she grew up.

What's that got to do with the house?

The ghosts took those babies.

There wouldn't have been any babies to take when she was what, thirteen or fourteen?

Jack shrugged.

Maybe she was pregnant, Riley said. Sort of strange family, you know.

Who are they?

Mamie Harris? You know Autrey Harris, like a couple grades younger. Big glasses, same pair of jeans every day.

Smells?

No, you're thinking of Harold. That's a Cooper, but Coopers are cousins to Harrises. Not much better, either.

Granddad saw The Wandering House, didn't he?

Said he did.

You never told me that, she said.

Plenty of stories you don't know, he said, smiling.

Saw it right out in the field across from his house. And it wasn't a hotel or a house but a church, because it had one of those . . .

Steeples.

Steeples, right, and his father was standing by the door like an usher or sumpin, and see he'd never met his dad because his dad kilt himself. But there was his dad standing there, in a real nice suit, all brushed and he smelt of aftershave like the kind in the bottle his mother kept after he'd died, to remember him by, and he stood there looking at his dad trying to figure out if his dad had kilt himself yet. If time had changed somehow. Because his dad looked so young and good-looking. And so happy. Like he didn't know he'd kilt himself or that he was going to do it. And then his dad reached for the door, and gestured like it was time to go in, and just as he was about to follow his father inside, the church sunk into ground and all that was left was him holding a door by its knob.

I don't know about all that.

No, but I think he saw his dead father.

Could have dreamed it.

I'm gonna go take a look, Jack said.

Hell if you are, baby boy, Riley said.

You think I'm too much of a baby to do it?

I think you're a dumbshit if you do it. Riley laughed.

Ah, let him go, she said. He won't go far. We'll be able to see him if we turn the lights on.

Oh, baby will get scared and come running back in no time.

You just watch, Jack said. I'll go all the way up to the porch. I'll ring the goddamned doorbell.

Listen to him. Baby saying grown-up words.

Sure, I will. Let me out. Jack was reaching from the backseat, his hand appearing in the front, hitting along the armrest as he searched for the door handle.

Riley punched him in the arm.

Jesus! Jack said, pulling his arm back.

You don't talk like a baby. He might do it after all.

Don't be so hard on him, she said.

Then Jack's arm thrashed out like a snake, wrapping around Riley's neck, pulling him against the seat as Jack reached with the other arm to open the door.

Riley was grabbing at his arm, grunting for breath but laughing, too, and slapping his other hand over the seat at Jack's head, hitting his forehead and ears, pulling at his hair, and then the door was open and Jack was tumbling onto road and Riley was falling forward against the steering wheel, gasping for air.

Jack picked himself up. She imagined headlights roaring up, knocking him dead just as they saw him. Just like that. But, of course, no headlights came. It was a sheet of black, and they were hid somewhere inside it.

Jack flipped them off and crossed the road into the ditch.

Let him go, Riley. Give him some air.

He'll come back, Riley said.

Sure, he will. She unbuckled her seatbelt and leaned over the stick shift, against Riley's chest. She could feel him inhale. He liked the way her hair smelled. It's just my shampoo, she'd say when they were together, alone. But still, she liked how he reacted. Every time. His hand fell down her back as she leaned over him. His thumb falling down the shallow stairs of her spine.

She felt her breast against Riley's shoulder. His breath in her ear. He reached under her, shifting into first, letting the car pull forward, the back of his hand sliding against the inside of her thigh.

That was pretty suave how you did that, she said.

Did what?

So that we could be alone, she said.

You don't see it?

She laughed, low, feeling good, feeling glad she snuck out of the house to go driving.

Then she did see it. The light.

The Wandering House, Riley said.

* * *

His bedroom is the same, the mother says.

I'm just getting up to use the bathroom, the girl says.

I just wanted to make that clear, the mother says. That it's the same as it always was.

The girl nods. She shouldn't have come. Jack's still by the front door, so she can't make a break for it. Not with any grace, anyway. Maybe after she uses the bathroom. She can invent a stomachache. Cramps. But then Riley's mother would call bluff and offer her a heating pad. Something about the woman needed to punish her. Because Riley hasn't come back.

And so maybe it has to be okay, the girl thinks. Maybe she can be that for the mother.

Is it still down the hall? she says, because maybe the woman thinks she's not going to the bathroom, maybe she thinks she's going to sneak up to Riley's room. Which she'd like to do.

Bathrooms don't wander, the mother says.

She's Riley's girl, she hears Jack say. You're not supposed to be like that. She's Riley's girl.

She hurries up the hallway to keep from hearing the woman's response.

Macramé planters hang from hooks in the ceiling. More fake plants. Past the stairs that lead up to Riley's room.

Riley never liked her hanging out here. It's a shit house, he'd say. I like it, she'd say. You don't have to love the house, only me, he'd say. Done, she'd say.

In the kitchen is the sour smell of stale ketchup, counters stacked with cups and plates with food smeared on them, overfull ashtrays on the small kitchen table that's covered in newspapers, papers, cans of ballpoint pens, brown paper fast-food bags.

Just in here, Jack says, right behind her. His breath against her neck.

Thanks, she says. Opening the bathroom door. Her counselor says there's nothing to be ashamed of.

Except Riley's gone.

Her counselor asked if that made the girl feel shame.

She said that word was as fine as any.

The counselor said, have you ever heard of survivor's guilt?

The girl said, You didn't say there'd be a quiz.

The counselor waited.

My dad has it from the war. Mom's accusing him of it anyway. Usually when he has nightmares that wake her but don't wake him up. Mom thinks that's what he dreams about.

Is it?

The girl shrugged. She woke to his nightmares, too, to the moans coming out of his chest.

I'm sorry, Jack says. I thought you'd want to be here.

I would. I do. It's fine.

Do you still hurt?

Here and there, she says. Here and there.

He reaches past her, around the wall to turn on the light. Like Riley would have done. In a few more years, he'll be Riley's age. And maybe when his voice changes, she'll hear Riley's in it. Or at least how she'll remember Riley's voice. She never thought to record it. And Riley's cellphone was the per-minute refill-card kind, so he never bothered recording a message or checking messages because they wasted minutes. Which is why, also, if he's alive, he can't be tracked. Which, her best friend says, is plain shitty if you ask me. Because you lost your face for him. And he walks off.

I didn't lose my face.

Her friend said, Part of it.

He lost plenty, the girl said. His family. His home. Us. And he couldn't have walked off. He was closer to the house than I was. The closest.

A go-nowhere life working at that factory just like his dad, or worse, sweeping floors at the dollar store like his mom.

He had plans, the girl said. We had plans.

You would have broken up like everybody does.

That's a helluva thing to say.

I'm the only one who tells it to you straight, and that's why you love me. Remember. That's why.

The fact was the girl didn't really like her best friend, but it's true everyone treats her differently. Like she'll turn to ash if they say the wrong thing. As though words caused the fire and not a man who saw them from where he stood in the house. Because it wasn't The Wandering House. A wandering house, yes, but not The Wandering one.

The bathroom is small, barely the width of the bathtub that sits behind a plastic shower curtain stamped with gold seahorses. Her mother has the same shower curtain, in blue, and with matching seashell-shaped soaps in the ceramic dish by the sink.

For several years, the shells stayed wrapped in plastic—in case of company, her mother said.

When company finally came, it was people bringing food as condolences, trying to sneak looks past her mother to where the girl might be so they could see what they'd heard at the diner, grocery, hair parlor, church. How half her face was missing. No, the whole layer. No, most of her forehead, both cheeks. One cheek and her chin. Chin was fine. But no nose. No eye. Terrible thing to happen, especially to a girl. And one so pretty, at that. No fair queen, but pretty, sure.

Next to the toilet is a green glass wine bottle, corked. Like the one Riley packed for that picnic. She touches the tip of the cork, then picks up the bottle and rests it on her knees. He brought just enough for two glasses. Two small glasses.

Well, good, she said, because as you know, my uncle's an alcoholic.

God rest him, Riley said.

I know, right? Why does my mom say that when he's not even dead? That's what you say about dead people, right?

They laughed, cross-legged on the picnic blanket they'd spread on the concrete platform by the park pond where people sometimes stood to fish. She caught her first fish there. A bass. Her father threw it back.

The girl finishes peeing and searches for toilet paper. She finds a thin roll in the cabinet beneath the sink. She waits to see if she's going to cry. Then wipes, careful not to let her knuckles glance against the patches inside her thighs where the doctors took the skin they grafted onto parts of her face, shoulders.

Steal from Simon to pay Paul, her father had said, after the doctor had explained how the procedures would work.

Saul, her mother had said.

Is it? he said.

Pretty sure, she said.

Saul or Paul, doc? her father said.

The doctor looked up from his clipboard. What's that?

Her father clapped the doctor on the back.

The TV is still going loud in the living room. Jack said they weren't specific about when they'd call. Just that they would. She traces the embossed plastic of the seahorse on the shower curtain.

For a second she imagines darkness behind the curtain, the darkness that surrounded that house out in the country as they approached it. How much darker the dark became when the house exploded. Just like that. Up in a flash. How bright the light was against Riley's face as he turned toward her.

The darkness she woke from, found herself in as strange voices moved over her. The lights from the fire trucks swirling against the night sky, lighting up the clouds. When she was very little, she thought everything disappeared at night. The sun, the clouds, shadows.

She pulls the curtain back. A green tub with a corroded faucet. A shower chair. Riley's grandmother must have moved in, after all. A pair of women's underwear hangs off the faucet, curlicues of elastic around the thighs. She tries to find something amusing about them. She could put them on her head and wear them into the living room. Pretend they're bandages. Something Riley might do.

But there's nothing amusing about them. She hates how goddamned human everything is. How hard it is to hate people. That woman out there, Riley's mother, hates her, but here is her underwear. And there on the sink is the thin pad of soap she used to wash the blood out. Just like her own mother does and she does. Because they're humans. So damn human.

* * *

When the girl opens the bathroom door, Riley's grandmother is standing in the kitchen, her back to the girl. She has cleared a space at the counter, rubbing half of a lemon on a squeezer. She can't hear very well.

In the living room, Jack's sitting on the floor now, back against the couch, legs stretched out. He points at the rocking chair. She points at it. He nods. She sits.

Now, the grandmother is coming into the room, carrying a metal tray with a pitcher of lemonade and glasses. She makes her way in front of the TV and to the coffee table.

Do you need any help, mother? Riley's mother says. She's holding the black socks in one hand and painting her toenails with the other, the heel of her foot against the edge of the coffee table.

Oh, no, no, she says, bending slowly over the table, so slowly lowering the tray, the glasses quaking on it. The tray's covered in a painting of large, pink flowers. She points her jagged finger around the room, counting the faces. Then the glasses. Then the room again. One short, she says.

I can get it, Jack says. He stands, arcing his back, pressing his hands against the back of his hips.

Watch it, the mother says, capping the polish to keep it from spilling.

The phone rings.

The father fumbles for the remote control, knocking it to the carpet.

The phone rings again.

The girl tries to follow the ring with her good eye, without turning her head, without making too much motion.

The mother reaches over the couch to the side table, past the lamp made of plaster cherubs that stand with harps. A reproduction, Riley told her. Reproduction means a copy worth nothing. Unless you like looking at it, of course.

The mother lifts the receiver to her ear. It's the old kind, plugged into the wall behind the side table. Probably the same outlet they plug the vacuum into. Silly thought to have.

This is she, the mother says into the phone. Yes, the lady of the house. Yes.

It's probably a wrong number. Probably some kid states away wanting to know which candidate she plans to vote for in the primary. Or maybe Collections, like the phone calls her own mother gets now, about the hospital bills, the procedures, the cost of the bandages, the nurses, the shots, the oxygen. The numbers all of it adds up to. Overdue.

It must not be a wrong number, because she's still holding the phone.

They watch her as though they can listen through to what she hears.

And you're sure it's not his teeth? the mother says. He had three cavities, she says.

The mother crosses and uncrosses her ankles. She reaches down, as though to adjust one of her socks. The ghost of the feeling, maybe.

Three or four, she says. Cavities, yes. I've been. I'd been. Meaning to get those fixed. Yes. Sure.

The girl could feel them when they kissed. He winced.

The father's lips move to the captions on the TV. The girl tries to match the captions to his mouth. They don't match. Just like the captions don't match the mouths of the people on the TV. Maybe he's praying.

The grandmother licks the inside of her lip.

The girl presses her fingers together. Don't yell, she thinks. It's nice that they even let her in the house. Her parents wouldn't have done likewise. Jack didn't tell her about the visit her parents paid, but she'd found out because, as her mother said, who else can I tell? I thought your father was going to kill him, her mother said. It was like it didn't even matter that it wasn't Riley. Like he'd so expected Riley to answer the door that that's who he saw when Jack came out. I kept telling him, begging him to see that it's Jack, it's little Jack, let him go. But Jack was wearing Riley's boots. Maybe that's what confused him.

But it wasn't Riley's fault. We all saw it. We went together to see The Wandering House. Jack got scared. He fell back. He called our names.

Your father can't see it that way. He needs someone to blame.

There's the house, maybe.

I'm just explaining. And he's gone out there. It wasn't enough, either.

The phone clicks in the cradle. The mother rests her hand there a second before putting it back on her leg. Her watch has a black wristband.

The father says, So is it him or ain't it?

She looks around the room. Face after face. At the dogs on the couch.

They say it isn't, she says.

Well, what do they know about anything? the father says.

Teeth. They know about his teeth.

Riley smiles in school picture after school picture on the TV shelf. The mother has organized the shelves by son. Jack on one shelf. Riley on the other. Another of them together. Riley's smile. The gap in his teeth. Riley turning when the house exploded, the light on his face. His eyes. Big. Scared.

The police decided probably it wasn't an accident, not a coincidence that the house should explode at the exact time they approached it. A case of the wrong place, but not out of the blue. Of course, there are meth houses all over that do accidentally explode, but then there are the ones that are blown up. Because, as the police tried to explain, some guy is hyped up in that house making meth all night, for days like that because he's on the stuff, too, and he sees shapes moving in the distance, and of course he thinks he'd found some super isolated place, a place no one can ever find—or at least not before he moves again. And he has been so careful, he thinks. But then he hears voices. Voices trying not to be loud. The crunch of sticks, brush underfoot. And of course what's he going to think? He thinks the police found him. Are closing in. He imagines huge flanks of policemen, the whole country road lined for maybe miles with police cars. Because he's seen the movies. Actors in FBI costumes storming buildings via fire escapes, bursting into ranch-style homes on quiet blocks, the bad guys inside never expecting it unless it's early in the movie. So. That's what he imagines coming at him. And probably he's been imagining prison a lot because he knows it's illegal what he's doing.

So, they heard the kids coming, her father said to the policeman.

The policeman nodded. We think there was just one of them. Based on the remains we found.

But there were two, the girl thinks. The flicker of a cigarette. A woman sitting on the stairs. She saw her, just for a second. Because she'd thought, someone already found it. Someone's already there. And paused. Had she paused? Or just in her head?

And this guy just blows up the place like it's an accident? her father said. Something like a suicide?

Well, the policeman said, who knows what he was thinking? Maybe he thought he could make it, like he was setting a firework off then running away. It's crazy, really, how fast explosions like that go up.

In a flash, the girl thought.

The policeman clapped his hands.

The girl jerked, let out a sound.

Sorry, the policeman said.

And this is common? her father said.

I wouldn't go as far as to say common, but we're seeing it more, sure. You've seen it in the papers.

* * *

I think I'll go change my dress, the mother says. Maybe lie down for a little bit.

The grandmother begins to lift the lemonade pitcher with both hands, then sets it back down and wipes her hands down the thighs of her pants. Her hands are old, clearly full of bones and veins. A few lemon peels float inside the pitcher that isn't from the same set as the blue aluminum glasses. Cubes of ice appear then disappear. She fills a glass then sets it aside. Then another.

What I want to know, Riley's father is saying, is how they know what my boy's teeth look like. You tell me that.

I guess maybe they took a mold at school or something, the mother says.

Because when did we ever take him to the dentist is what I want to know, the man says. He drops the footrest against the recliner and rocks forward. Until the chair comes off the floor. Until he's balancing the whole weight of it on his slippers. She can see the metal springs under it. The backs of his feet, white with callouses. Higher and higher the chair comes off the brown carpet. She imagines him tumbling out, the chair knocking him into the coffee table, the lemonade crashing, the mother standing, the dogs going off like dumb fireworks. And if she had the woman's underwear on her head, well, that would just take the cake, wouldn't it? It might feel more real than this. More how they're feeling underneath it all.

The recliner thumps against the floor.

Usually that's how life works. Not as bad as she imagines. Until it is.

Grandma took us to the dentist once, Jack says. You remember, Gran?

Gran looks up from pouring another glass.

They gave us . . . what's the word? Not popsicles . . . Lollipops. That's it. Lollipops afterward.

Helluva thing for a dentist to give out.

They *did*, Jack says, suddenly seeming younger. Or as young as he actually is. She always forgets he's not as near to Riley and her ages because he was always with them. And he's tall for his age. Riley's short like their mother. But she remembers when Jack was five or six and Riley'd send him down to greet her on the porch while Riley got ready upstairs.

What you got there? she'd say.

You don't have to show me if you don't want, she'd say to little, shy Jack in his shirts that pulled up to show the curve of his belly.

But he would show her, slowly flying the airplane out from behind his back.

She smiled, making her eyes wide, because he'd surprised her, hadn't he? Sure he had.

Can you fly it all the way around the world? the girl said.

He shrugged.

You should try, she said.

He climbed onto the porch railing and jumped into the yard, falling to his knees.

You okay?

He stood, nodding, raising his arm so she could see the airplane was not broken.

She laughed.

He ran in large zigzags around the yard, his arm high, the styrofoam airplane with the tiny pilot on the sticker that ran along the fuselage.

When he'd reach the edge where the yard met the road, she'd call out, Are you at the end of the world? Then cup her hands around her mouth, saying, World, world, world, like an echo.

Yes! And he'd run back, detouring over oceans he swung over in the tire swing, before jumping back out and making his way back to her.

How was the world? she'd say.

He'd nod, looking at his feet. Shy again. Tucking the plane behind him.

It's a long journey. I bet you're tired.

Then Riley would come out, and the girl would stand, taking Riley's hand, Jack following after with the plane as they fell off the world onto the road.

* * *

What kind of dentist does that is what I'd like to know.

They *did* give us lollipops, Jack says, looking at her.

I believe you, the girl says.

Fucking lollipops, Jack says. Like he can tell she's thinking of him as young, much younger than he feels himself to be.

Watch your mouth, the father says. Talk like that will rot your teeth right out.

As though he forgets what he's been talking about.

Hell if I took anybody to the dentist, the grandmother says. All the glasses are full of lemonade. Only an inch left in the pitcher. The old woman rests her elbows on her knees. Don't have to go to no dentist, she says. We come from a family of strong teeth and bone. Never been to the dentist a day in my life.

Now, that's not true, Gran, the mother says.

The kind of dentist that gives out lollies is the kind of dentist that can mess up teeth molds. The father rocks hard in the chair. I wouldn't put it past him, he says.

You calling me a liar? Gran says. Look here. She's curling her lips back, until her face is mostly teeth and gums. Her gums aren't dark pink but very light. Like the inside of a box turtle's mouth. It's the first summer the girl hasn't kept a box turtle for a pet, slicing tomatoes into the box, listening for it clawing the newspaper lining the bottom as a sign it finally had its head out. Some turtles are shyer than others.

Look at them, Gran says, trying to keep her lips peeled back as she talks, turning so everyone can have a look.

The thing about it is, the mother says, it don't matter if they know Riley's teeth or not, as long as they got everybody else's teeth, they know who isn't him.

That so?

That's how I see it.

But is that so?

Did this other somebody have a gap in his teeth like Riley?

The mother's eyebrows draw together like Riley's. Should I call them back and ask? she says. Not sarcastic. Quiet.

This family, the grandmother says, has the kind of teeth and bone that if scientists find us thousands of years into the future, they'll be able to know exactly who we were.

I'll call them back, the mother says, but doesn't reach for the phone.

A woman on TV is stepping around her dishwasher, holding a yellow container of dish soap. She smiles. She had her fingernails done for the commercial.

Guess I'll never be a dish-soap model, the girl says. She laughs.

Jack looks away.

C'mon, she says. That's funny. It's okay for it to be funny.

Jack sniffs. He keeps looking down. Holding one arm over his chest.

I think I'll change my dress now, the mother says.

Maybe that dentist will let us have them, the father says.

When no one answers, the girl says, Have what?

Riley's. The mold of Riley's teeth. As long as the police have a copy, of course. Because there will be others who might be him.

Jack stands up. The ice cubes clink against the glasses. Where you going, champ? his father says.

Out.

You have company. Act right.

I'll be back, Vix, Jack says. Just need some air.

Sure, she says.

The grandmother holds out a glass. Some people don't drink lemonade in winter, she says.

The father stands.

You too? the grandmother says.

I'll be right back, he says.

Company, she says.

It's okay, the girl says.

Just a minute, he says. And she remembers that he's the grandmother's son. That he used to be a little boy, too. Long before he told Jack it was bad manners to leave a guest, he was a little boy listening to this woman tell him the same thing. And so it goes.

I was just about to leave anyway, the girl says.

The father's face falls. There's something I want to show you.

Have some lemonade then? the old woman says. I won't bite, the old woman says.

The girl never likes anyone to say that. The words themselves feel like biting words.

Really, I'm fine, she says. She knows, of course, the lemonade won't burn her hands. Of course. But deep inside her, she still fears it.

The man disappears down the hallway, then up the stairs to where all the bedrooms are. She can hear him walking around above her. The dresser drawer sliding. Then he's coming back down the stairs.

He sits down on the couch next to the grandmother. A dog

jumps off. Barks at another. He pushes the tray to the side. He holds a little blue velvet drawstring bag.

For a second, she thinks an engagement ring will slip from it. Then he'll tell her that Riley had asked his advice, had told him he was planning on asking her to marry him and what did he think, since they were only in high school, sure, but . . . And didn't she think the same thing that night? As they left the car, shutting the car doors quietly, so as not to scare off The Wandering House. Crossing the road, the bottoms of their tennis shoes against the billions of rocks sealed into the oil, sealed into a surface to walk on without it crumbling beneath you like gravel roads do. Through the weeds that scratched against their arms and the little stickers she felt clinging to her T-shirt and how irritated her mother will be when she does laundry next day. Even though Jack's with them, she thinks Riley still might pop the question. Because he's like that. Doing what you least expect. Dropping to one knee in a dark field, taking her hand. Or maybe he'll wait until they're in The Wandering House. It will be a beautiful house, made of red brick, three or four stories high, surrounded by blue violets made to seem electric under the moon, like in that dream where she's made of glass, lying beside Riley, and he's made of glass, too, and they watch each other's hearts beating and outside the beautiful blue flowers. So The Wandering House, like a dream but not a dream—and while Jack is exploring another floor, Riley will ask her. She doesn't know if she'll say yes. When she thinks of the future, he's not in it. But she can change that, surely, all she has to say is yes. And then the sky's full of light. The whole forest awash. And Riley's turning to shield his eyes, his scared eyes.

Riley's father draws the little blue velvet bag open. He reaches a finger into it. Two fingers. And takes out a little white pebble and sets it on the coffee table. It makes a little clinking.

There's a smidgen of red paint at the end of the pebble.

You see what that is? he says, gesturing for her to lean in for a closer look. He digs into the bag and takes out another.

A tooth, she says.

That's right, he says. Riley's baby teeth. I kept them all. Except the one he thinks he swallowed with his milk at school.

First grade, she says.

First or second, he says.

First, she says. In the cafeteria. Everyone thought it was so funny. He thought he might die of it, lodged in his stomach forever or something.

The father looks at her. She can feel the look on the side of her face. She can't remember which scars are on which side. The mirror reverses everything. Except time. Or maybe that, too, but it doesn't matter since no one can see it.

He looks away. That was the second or third tooth he'd lost. So, almost all of them. He sets them one by one on the coffee table. He peers down at them. She begins counting them, then stops. Riley's teeth.

You'd think, his father says, what would I want a mold of his mouth for if I have these?

She nods. Though she's not thinking that at all.

The thing of it is, he says. I can't figure . . . He touches the tip of his finger against one tooth then another then another. The motion, however light it is, spins them slightly.

The man and the girl sit there, looking.

I'm sorry it wasn't him, she says.

He nods. There's something I've been meaning to ask you. I just keep going back to it. When I replay it in my head, based on what Jack's told me and what you told me that day I talked to you on the phone.

Okay, she says. But she wants to leave. She should have left way back, instead of going to the bathroom. But she's here. She's here and Riley isn't, so she owes him. Owes everyone. Owes Riley.

Was it beautiful? he says.

What's that?

It's sort of a strange question I guess.

I guess I don't understand.

Was the explosion beautiful? I think about the light, all at once. That it must have been so bright. The sky like you never see a sky. And I think. Well, I think maybe it would be okay for Riley to be gone, to be dead, if the last thing he saw was just so beautiful that he could hardly believe it. Like maybe he saw the whole world at once in that sky. I could bear it a little easier, maybe, if that's how it ended.

He looks at her. His eyes are the same color of Riley's. The skin around them is older. The face sadder.

It was so fast, she says.

But was it beautiful?

It was bright, and Riley turned, and I saw his eyes. And then.

But the sky?

It was . . .

That's okay, he says. That's okay. He reaches out and sort of squeezes her against him. She wishes she could cry on cue.

He pulls the little bag apart and slowly draws the teeth across the table in the cup of his hand, into the blue pouch.

I don't know what I was saving them for, he says. She says— his mother says—it's bad luck keeping them like this. But he was a good boy. I remember he had this one tooth that had been loose, I can't tell you which one of these it was, they all look the same, but this one tooth that was loose for the longest time, two, maybe three weeks, a long time however long it was. Most his teeth, seems like they'd be loose a couple of days and then he'd be showing them to me, popping them into my hand, pointing out which end had been in his gum and which end had been the chewing end. The chewing end.

But this one tooth, man, for like weeks, you'd see him over

there, watching TV or at the dinner table or waiting for the bus, just working it with his tongue back and forth, or wiggling it with his fingers. For like weeks, he was at it. Get your hands out of your mouth, we'd tell him. And he would, but then he'd be at it again. Drove us all near crazy, the sound of that little tooth against his wet gum.

So finally, I say to him, That's it, we've got to get that thing out of there. So I get into my tackle-box and take out some fishing line, and he opens his mouth and lets me tie it around that tooth, and the tooth was just hanging there by a thread. I could have pulled it, but I didn't, but I could have, but I liked to be honest with the boys because my father. Anyway, so I tie the string around it, and then the other end around the front doorknob.

He pauses to look at the front door. That front door.

She looks at it.

Anyway, he knew what to do because I'd told him stories of when I was a kid, that that's how we got our teeth out. Which wasn't true, we just pulled them before our dad could get to us. He was a mean man. So Riley's tied to the doorknob, and I open the door, and tell him, Okay, you just slam it shut. And out the tooth will come. Won't hurt a bit.

Riley nods and places his hand on the doorknob, his mouth open, wider than wide. Like some trophy fish on a wall.

Go on, I tell him.

He nods, and I can tell he's picturing doing it in his mind, but he's not moving.

Go on, I tell him. You can do this.

I'm scared, he says to me, but it's hard to understand, of course because he can't shut his mouth because of the string. I try to give him pep talks. Still he can't do it. I tell him to be a man, that a man would just slam that door and be done with it. I don't mean it, of course, to hell with that. But I try it, you know, because I know I can't untie that string, the knot's too fine a knot to pull apart. Eventually I got him a chair from the kitchen to sit on because he stood there so long, through dinner and all of his mother's TV shows.

Did he ever do it?

Well, we'd all gone to sleep. By that point, I'd pulled my recliner against the door so he could fall asleep in it. Then, right in the middle of the night, bam, the door slammed shut and Riley screamed. And I run down there, and he's on his hands and knees, searching for wherever his tooth went. Guess a storm had started up, a big one, and the wind blew the door shut.

So I got down there with him with my flashlight and we looked and looked until we found it.

But we found it. We sure did.

The man stands up. For a second, she imagines him offering her the velvet bag of Riley's teeth, but he doesn't. You staying for dinner? he says.

She shakes her head.

Probably for the better. I wouldn't stay for it myself if I weren't already here.

She laughs, to turn what he said into a joke. Instead of sad.

He smiles. He puts his son's teeth in the pocket of his shirt, pats it a few times. I should go see if she needs anything, he says. He points at the ceiling, through it to the bedroom where Riley's mother makes no sound.

Maybe next time it'll be him, he says.

Probably, she says.

He eases around the coffee table, touching the recliner for balance as he passes it. He will climb up the stairs, to his bedroom, to open the top drawer of his dresser where he keeps Riley's teeth and the old coins that Riley showed her once, holding each in his hand and making her guess the date. And then she'll never see Riley's father again. Not like this.

It was a beautiful sky, she says as he reaches the staircase.

He looks back at her, confused.

The world all at once, she says.

He nods. Sort of gives her a thumbs-up. Then continues up the staircase.

She sits there a little bit longer.

ACKNOWLEDGMENTS AND THANKS

———

The following stories appeared as earlier versions with these presses or publications: "How the Sun Burns among Hills of Rock and Pebble" in the *Minnesota Review* and through The Head & The Hand Press; "The Boy Who Walks" as "Winter's Wooden Sparrows" and "The Missing Time" in *Lake Effect, a Journal of the Literary Arts*; "When the Frost Comes" through Awst Press; "This Bomb My Heart" in *War, Literature & The Arts* and through Awst Press; and "The Lightning Tree" in *Box of Delights* anthology and through Underground Voices.

The author would like to thank these people for reading drafts of one or more stories in the collection: Mark Dillon, Owen Egerton, Abby Freeland, Jack Kaulfus, Heather Keast, Rachel King, Laura Long, Tom Noyes, Marilynn Olson, Carol Pringle, Emilia Rodriguez, and Jeremy Toungate.

READING AND DISCUSSION

QUESTIONS

---

1. Several of the stories do not end with clear resolutions for the characters or for the readers. For example, "How The Sun Burns among Hills of Rock and Pebble" does not end with a revelation of the sister's murderer but with the character trying to persuade a stranger to remember her sister. What might be the benefits to ending stories in a way that may resist readers' expectations or desires?

2. Most of the characters do not have names. We often correlate our identities to our names, or other people's identities to their names. What do you think the author might be exploring about identity through not naming?

3. Swedish filmmaker Ingmar Bergman uses the same actors and actresses to play characters in many of his films, much like a theatre troupe. One effect of this repetition is that the same faces playing different characters eventually create a kind of "every woman" or "every man." This same sort of blending seems to happen in these stories since characters often don't have names,

and the settings are very similar. Did you find yourself confusing characters, or starting to think of the characters as the same, even though the events were different? Did you enjoy this blending? Why or why not?

4.   The author's style has been compared to fairy tales, perhaps for the vividness of images. What other similarities did you notice between these stories and fairy tales that you've read? In what ways do the stories not resemble fairy tales?

5.   One recurring theme seems to be the conflict between reality and desire: the life the characters are experiencing versus their imagined lives. What other books, or films, deal with similar themes? Did you think of any while you were reading?

6.   How would you describe the style of the writing?

7.   The stories are full of vivid imagery; in some ways, each story is a series of images. Which image stood out to you the most, and why do you think so? What is another pattern you noticed several of the stories sharing?

8.   Why do you think the collection begins and ends with these stories? What are the benefits or drawbacks to beginning and ending with these stories? If you had to choose a different story to begin or end the collection, which would you choose and why?

9.   In "When the Frost Comes," the girl examines the shell of a locust while her mother is inside the trailer, deceased:

> "If the locust opens its eyes inside the shell, does it know it's a body inside a shell looking out at the world? When it peels its eyes from the shell eyes and again sees the world, does it think it's the same world or a different one? Surely the world looks somewhat different, even though the world itself has not changed, like when the girl puts on her mother's glasses

to be silly. Can it know the world is the same if it now has wings? Or does having wings change the world slightly?"

What were your thoughts about this passage? What is another passage that stood out to you in this story or another story? Why?

10.   "The Boy in the Red Shirt" was inspired by the photograph of the Syrian child refugee found dead on a beach. Sometimes, people say that truth is stranger than fiction. Sometimes, people suggest that art provides catharsis for such tragedies. What was your experience with the story? What might the author be suggesting the role of storytelling is in terms of real-life tragedy?

11.   The United States has been involved in ongoing wars since 2003, but war is not always present in stories written since then, unless it's specifically a "war story." Many of the stories in this collection are aware of war. Do you think "This Bomb My Heart" is a war story? Do you think "The Boy in the Red Shirt" is a war story? Why or why not?

12.   As might be expected in stories that have characters coping with death, grief returns in the stories, often as both a beautiful and awful aspect of the human experience. What depiction of grief did you find most interesting, unexpected, or realistic?

13.   The fairgrounds, a hotel, a diner, the drive-thru of a fast-food restaurant, a church, a creek, the lobby of a superstore—all of these are places the characters find themselves while their lives are in flux. These settings might typically be considered mundane, but the author often renders them as beautiful. How do you think these settings affect the way we consider the characters and their lives and deaths?

14.   Many, if not all, of the stories are set in the rural Midwest, but many of the people's experiences are not unique to the rural Midwest. Did the stories feel familiar or unfamiliar to you, or a

mixture of both? Do you think a story that feels familiar is the same as it feeling realistic?

15.   Many of these stories have a child narrator or child protagonist. Do the children in these stories view the world and/or deal with grief differently than the adults? If so, do these differences mirror what you've observed about children and adults?

16.   Some of these stories subtly catalog the continuing move of Americans from the country to the cities, and the issues—whether farm consolidation ("This Bomb My Heart"), distances from services like schools and hospitals ("When the Frost Comes"), or isolated meth houses ("The Wandering House")—for those who remain in rural communities. Do you or any of your family members or friends experience any of the rural issues described in these stories? Do these stories offer any positives to living in a rural area? If so, what are they?

ABOUT THE AUTHOR

———

Erin Pringle grew up in a rural midwestern town called Casey, Illinois. She spent much of her childhood drawing, painting, and reading, and thanks to the people who fund scholarships and fellowships in the arts and humanities, she went on to earn degrees in English literature and creative writing at the undergraduate and graduate levels (Indiana State University, Texas State University). Her first book of stories, *The Floating Order*, was published in Scotland with Two Ravens Press (2009) and was received well. Her three chapbooks are collected in *The Whole World at Once* ("How The Sun Burns among Hills of Rock and Pebble," "The Lightning Tree," and "The Wandering House.")

She now lives in Washington State with her partner, Heather, and son, Henry. She's interested in children's literature, folklore, and visual art. And words, always words. When free time appears, she fills it by running, reading, or thinking. For updates on her writing, please visit www.erinpringle.com, follow her on Twitter (@WhatSheMight), or like her page on Facebook: https://www.facebook.com/erintpringle/.

CPSIA information can be obtained
at www.ICGtesting.com
Printed in the USA
LVOW01s2358310317
529239LV00004B/4/P